CHOSEN

Silvercrest Pack, Book 1

EVE NEWTON

Chosen

By Eve Newton

Silvercrest Pack, Book 1

Copyright © Eve Newton, 2021

Without limiting the rights under copyright reserved above, no part of this publication may be reproduced, stored in or introduced into a retrieval system, or transmitted, in any form, or by any means (electronic, mechanical, photocopying, recording, or otherwise), without the prior written permission of the copyright owner.

This is a work of fiction. Names, characters, places, and incidents either are the product of the author's imagination or are used fictitiously, and any resemblance to actual persons, living or
dead, business establishments, events, or locales is entirely coincidental.

Chapter 1

Ryker

It's late.

Way past when I should've slipped out of here.

Valerie is fast asleep, strewn over the messy bed, limbs and long dark hair taking up most of the space on the small double bed. I bend over to pull up my jeans and yank my t-shirt over my head. Shoving my feet into my boots, I zip up my fly as I head towards the door of her cabin. Dawn is coming and I need to get some sleep.

Closing the door quietly behind me, I jog down the three steps that lead up to the porch and turn right to head back to my own cabin on our Pack compound, deep in the Silvercrest Mountains.

The air that hits me is hot and sticky, which makes my need for a shower even more desperate. Summers are brutal here and we are right in the middle of a heatwave. We are desperate for rain, but there appears to be none on the horizon. Contemplating heading the mile or so to the lake to just dive in and cool off, I'm caught off guard by my name being called.

"Ryker," my mom's voice rings out in the quiet of the pre-dawn. "You need to come straight away."

I turn and frown at her, the scent of pine filling my senses from the woods on the border of the compound. Her face registers her annoyance at me sneaking out of Val's place, but there is a panic in her tone that makes me bite back the 'stay outta my business' remark that was about to burst out. What I do with my private life is no one's concern, especially hers.

"What is it?" I ask, striding towards her, running my hand over my short dark hair before I rest it on the back of my neck.

"Your father. He won't see the dawn," she says quietly and turns, expecting me to follow her.

I do.

The uneasiness settles over me like a thick blanket, stifling me. His death means only one thing for me.

It means I become Alpha of this Pack. It's not something that I was prepared for, even though it has been my path since the day I was born his first son, thirty-three years ago. It's too soon. I don't want the responsibility if I'm being honest with myself. I like my life as it is. Chosen and all that, but not expected to *do* anything about it yet. Jefferson is in his prime. *Was* in his prime until someone poisoned him with wolfsbane. We can't know for sure, but the signs are there. It surprises me that someone tried to take him out. He is a hardass. Strict, unbending, militant in his style of leadership and there are definitely members of our two-hundred strong Pack who would like to see him gone, but to do this? So far, we have no leads. Three days of constant interrogation have brought forth nothing. I'm starting to think it's an outside source. He had a couple of decades left in him to rule this Pack, it's a long time to wait for someone who wants him out of the way. There is no myth to this life. We live as long as humans do, are vulnerable to time as they are. There is no immortality here and no guarantee that you will live longer than you should. When your time is up, it's up.

Dad's is up.

"Ry!" Stevie, my younger sister out of three, exclaims when she sees me striding over. "You need to see him, say goodbye..." Her eyes are full of tears. I get it. She is his golden girl. Can do no wrong in his eyes. Whereas I am the fuck-up. The heir to the Pack and a severe disappointment to the old man.

Who gives a crap?

I sure don't. I live my life for me.

Well, I suppose I did. As soon as he fades off this earth, everything is going to change for me. I can't run from it as much as I want to. It's in my blood. If I shirked the duty of it, I would be shunned, thrown out of the Pack to live the life of a solo Wolf, which definitely isn't on my to-do list. Torn as ever between the two worlds in which I *want* to live and *have* to live, I pat her on the shoulder as I pass. I head up the steps and into my parents' cabin, just in time to hear my father cough weakly.

"Ryker," he croaks. "Come here, boy."

I grimace.

Boy.

I fucking hate that.

But I do as he says, and edge closer, pulling up a small wooden stool to the side of the bed and perching on it, taking in my father's gaunt, gray face and skeletal body.

Paling, I clear my throat. He has been ravaged by the poison. It suddenly brings a whole bunch of shit into perspective for me. Mainly, what if I'm next? Is someone targeting this Pack or just my dad?

"My end is in sight, son," he groans. "You have to pull your finger outta your ass and do what needs to be done for this Pack."

"I know," I grit out. Why bother with placatory statements telling him he'll pull through? He knows as well as I do that he is on his last few breaths.

"Do you?" he growls. "You've been living your life like a man-whore for years now, shirking your responsibility. You shoulda been shadowing me, watching me run this Pack. If you run it into the ground, I will come back and haunt your ass..."

"I got this," I snarl, knowing I shouldn't be so pissed off with him, but not being able to help it. He's a dick. Even in death.

"You better," he huffs and settles back down, closing his eyes. "I know I've been hard on you," he adds in the softest tone I've ever heard him use. "I needed to know that you are prepared for what being Alpha of this Pack means. The responsibility..." He pauses to cough some more, leaning over and spewing into a bucket on the other side of the bed. "It's not a job," he rasps flopping onto his back, his throat raw from throwing up. "It's going to be your life. I need to know you are going to step up and take my place."

"You know I will," I say, slightly humbled by the clear agony he is in.

"Find your mate, settle down, Ryker," he adds, whispering now. "Don't squander your best years away with whores and meaningless sex."

Resisting the urge to roll my eyes, I simply make a noise of agreement.

Mate.

Yeah, right.

I'd rather pass on that. Settling down is not my style.

"Goodbye, Ryker," Dad says and with a last, rattling breath, he fades away.

"Bye, Dad," I whisper, gripping his hand and feeling the sadness finally hit me.

The Alpha is gone and now it's time for me to be exactly that.

Chosen by birth.
Chosen by *blood*.
Chosen.

Chapter 2

Ryker

Staring at my dad, several minutes pass. I know I need to get up, get moving outside to let my mother know. The feeling of a dead weight around my neck is stopping me, but it's something that I need to shake off.

With a grimace, I stand up, the stool scraping on the wooden floor, loud to my ears in the silence.

I clomp heavily over to the door and drag it open, almost working on autopilot.

"Ryker," Mom says, the question in her voice.

"He's gone," I croak out. "Sorry, I should've come for you..."

She nods. "I said my goodbye before I came to get you. So did Stevie. This was time for you."

I nod back, forcing myself to swallow. My mouth has gone so dry.

"We need to make plans to announce you and send your father off as he wished," she says, her voice stronger now.

"Let me get some sleep first," I mutter. I've been up for nearly twenty-four hours. I'm beat.

Her face goes sour, but with a brisk incline of her head, she turns from me and embraces Stevie, who has started wailing. I want to comfort her, but I'm not capable right now. My other two much younger sisters, Lily and Jo, are standing silently by as if waiting for me to tell them it's all a big fat joke.

I wish it was.

With a sigh, I turn and head towards the main communal area in the middle of the compound. I need a minute before I head back home. It's too late to go to the lake now. I need to get my head down before the day hits me full on.

In the semi-darkness, I see the small glow hovering in front of Hunter. He is seated, hunched over, smoking a cigarette.

"Hey," I say in a dead tone and sit down on the big log next to him.

"Hey," he slurs and takes a drink from the bottle hanging loosely in his other hand. "Want one?" He gestures to the two beers left in the six-pack.

"Actually, yeah," I say and grab one, removing the cap carefully and twirling it in my fingers. "Dad just died," I add, before taking a big gulp. I'm not a big drinker. I know what I am. I know how dangerous I am. I'm a predator. I don't need to be adding fuel to that fire.

"Aw shit, Ry," he says, dropping the bottle that was raised to his lips. "I'm sorry, man."

I shrug. He is my best friend and enforcer of this Pack. He knows how contentious my relationship was with my dad. He knows us both well enough to know how I'm feeling right now. He knows how much I don't want to be Alpha.

"Give me this beer and I'll get my head on straight," he adds.

I turn to face him. "Yeah, what's with that?"

"Casey dumped me," he says, surprising me. They were tight as far as I knew. "Packed her bags and left me last night."

"Oh, man," I say and pat him on the shoulder. I have no idea what to say.

He shrugs, so I remove my hand. "I didn't see it coming, you know? Yesterday things were fine, we were happy and then all of a sudden, she doesn't want to live with me, doesn't even want to be with me. Says she's too young to settle down." He lets out a heavy sigh. "I guess that's what you get for falling in love with someone so much younger than you."

I bite my tongue. Casey is twenty-five, Hunter is thirty-five. Yeah, it's a big difference when it comes to thinking about your future.

"It's that fucking Bree!" he exclaims suddenly. "Ever since she got tight with Casey, she's been putting ideas into her head."

I blink. Bree is…in a word…infamous. She is known throughout the Pack as saving herself for her mating. In her twenties, she is definitely the opposite of every other female Wolf that I know. We, as a group, aren't known for our restraint in anything. Guys have tried and failed to get into her pants. Not me, though. I really can't be bothered with the chase. I like my women easy and already wanting me. It's too much effort to work for it when I can have it delivered to my door whenever I want it. I can't help the sneer that forms. "I see," I say with derision.

He snorts. "Yeah."

We finish our beers in silence.

"I need to get some sleep," I say eventually. "I'll come and find you before it's time to make the announcement. Go and get some rest yourself. Forget about that bitch. She doesn't deserve to have you pining over her."

"Yeah," he says again, softer this time.

I stand and pat him on the back, dropping the bottle into the bag for when the recycling team heads into town. I walk away, glad that I've never had to deal with the shit he's going through right now and never will. No female will ever have that hold over me. I've made sure of it up to now and will carry on doing what I'm doing. Works for me and that's all that matters.

I make it back to my cabin without encountering another Wolf. It's not surprising. Another hour and most of them will be rising, not heading to bed.

I shove open the door to my cabin and kick off my boots. I strip off my jeans and tee and with very little thought about a shower now, fall naked onto the double bed, my head hitting the pillow and forcing my eyes to close.

Sleep eludes me for a few minutes longer. As tired as I am, the day ahead is looming over me like a violent storm about to hit. When I wake up from this nap, my life is going to change and I'm not ready for it. I open my eyes and stare at the ceiling until I huff out a breath and turn onto my side, pulling the thin blanket over me and closing my eyes again.

This time the exhaustion drops over me, dragging me under its thrall until I fall asleep.

Chapter 3

Ryker

I'm jarred awake by the cabin door opening.

I groan and open my eyes. "Mom," I growl.

"Thought you might need a wake-up call," she says stiffly.

Rubbing my hand over my face, I ask, "What time is it?"

"A little after seven," she replies.

I've had about an hour and a half of sleep, and it feels like it. My eyes are gritty, my mouth is dry and tastes like shit, but I get her urgency to deal with this. To be honest, I want this over as much as she does.

I sit up, keeping the sheet over me as she stands there, wringing her hands. "You good to go?" she asks.

"Yeah," I say hoarsely. "Give me half an hour. I'll get Hunter on the way over."

She nods, the mask she is wearing slipping slightly. It hits me in the heart. "Please stop this lifestyle of yours," she whispers. "You need to focus now, Ry. Settle down..."

"Oh, don't you start as well," I complain, throwing my head back.

"Your father knew what he was talking about," she says firmly. "He used to be like you, sowing his oats..." She waves her hand around. "He thought he could do this on his own, but he was wrong, and he realized that. You have someone out there, Ryker, someone made to be with you, to help keep you strong..."

"Let me stop you right there," I say, standing up, dragging the sheet with me to wrap around my hips. "I'm not looking to make any changes and I don't want this talked about anymore. It's my life and I'll run it how I see fit."

She grimaces at me but says no more on the subject. "I'll leave you to get ready," she says instead. "I don't need to tell you how important this is."

Her code for 'don't be fucking late or I'll have your hide.'

I nod and watch her leave, closing the door behind her. With a sigh, I yank the sheet off and throw it on the bed. I'm itching to Shift, but I don't have time. It'll have to wait until after the announcement and I can run free for a while.

I head for the small shower room, sectioned off from the rest of the cabin. It houses a toilet, a sink and a small shower, all of which run from the four huge rainsaver water tanks at the back of the cabin. I step into the shower and turn it on. The water dribbles out before it spurts into my face once, then twice before it goes back to a dribble.

"Fantastic," I mutter. This summer drought has now officially become a massive problem. The shower tank is about to run dry, and I know that I can't afford to switch up any of the other plumbing to compensate. We need the rain. It usually isn't a problem, even in summer we get downpours that keep the tanks topped up, but this year has been different. The crops have suffered and now this. I manage to clean up before the tank runs out and I step out, grabbing a towel and drying off. Stepping back into the cabin, I come to a halt.

"Hey," I say, giving Hunter a surprised glance. "You okay?"

He is sitting on my couch, looking like he got kicked in the gut and then pissed on. Which, I suppose he did, metaphorically, poor bastard.

"I didn't want to go home," he says forlornly. "Mind if I shower here?"

I give him a sympathetic look. "Sorry, I've just run dry. I can offer you coffee though?"

He nods, so I go to the kitchenette in the corner of the cabin to pour us both a cup. I hand it to him before I put mine down to get dressed. I wonder briefly if it matters what I wear, but decide to fuck it and wear what I always do. Tight tee that shows off my hard body and jeans. Why change now? I just told my mother I had no desire to change my lifestyle, so why change how I dress?

"I'll come back to yours with you," I inform Hunter, picking my coffee back up and taking a hot sip. "We'll take these to go. My mom is expecting us soon."

He nods glumly and stands up.

We head to the door and step out into the bright, hot morning. "This heat sucks," he grumbles.

"Yeah," I agree, knowing that it's about to become *my* problem. I catch sight of the two laundry bags neatly placed on the porch and bend to pick them up. To save water and energy on the compound, we have a team that heads into town twice a month with all the laundry. It's a job that I would gladly see someone else do, but the two Wolves who volunteered for the job have it down like pros and run the system like clockwork. It goes out one day and arrives back, washed, dried and ironed the next. They are treasures to the Pack. I don't show that disrespect by throwing them back into my cabin but placing them carefully inside the door to deal with later.

"Let's go," I say, already knowing what will meet Hunter at his cabin, but he hasn't seemed to realize yet.

We walk in silence for a few short steps to a neighboring cabin. I wait while he opens the door, picks up his laundry bags and heads inside. I follow, prepared to take that bitch's clean clothes and burn them if he asks me to.

He doesn't. He doesn't even notice.

"I'll be five minutes," he mutters and strips off.

I turn and head out to the porch to finish my coffee. I hear the shower running and take a big gulp of the now cooling caffeine. I hate to be that dick who has to tell him that the precious double-sized rainsaver tank he has now has to go and be replaced with a single size, now that he is, well, *single*. Maybe that's tomorrow's discussion.

I lower the mug when I see Casey and Bree approach the cabin with caution.

"Ry," Casey says carefully.

"What do you want?" I ask coldly.

"I came to get the rest of my stuff," she says defensively.

"Hunter is in the shower. Get your shit and get out before he knows you've been here," I spit out.

I see her surprise and regret. We have never had an issue, were friends even, but I have my best buddy's back over hers and she knows it. She slips into the cabin, so I take the opportunity to fix Bree with a steely glare.

She holds my gaze with her bright blue eyes for all of a second before she drops it and shyly curls her long dark hair around her ear, her cheeks on fire. She is pretty-ish. I can see that with my eyes, a darker shade of gray. She is no great beauty, but I wouldn't ask her to put a bag over her head if we ever fucked. Not that we would. She is way too tightly wound up for that. I doubt any guy could pry her thighs open unless they gave her a ring first.

"You have anything to do with this?" I ask her, knowing it will fluster her up even more. I've barely ever said a word to her before. Asking her a direct question, especially now as her Alpha, which she can clearly sense, or has at the very least, heard about already, causes her to stammer and clear her throat repeatedly before she can answer me with a stilted, "Of course not."

"Hmm," I mutter, letting her know that I don't believe a word of it and taking another sip of coffee.

"I didn't," she states hotly all of a sudden, a fire lighting up under her pert ass.

"Whatever, babe," I say dismissively and turn my back on her as she blusters and huffs at me.

Casey chooses that moment to slip quietly back out of the cabin with her laundry bag. "Tell him, I'm so—."

"I think you've said enough to him," I interrupt her. "Don't go near him again."

"You're a good friend to him," she says quietly. "Take care of him."

I growl at her, getting her to move her ass off the porch. I don't bother asking where she's staying. I don't care. She has hurt the man I consider a brother, and she is dead to me now.

I stride into the cabin. "Hunter?" I call out. "We need to move."

I hear the shower switch off. "Coming," he calls back. "Cool your jets, man."

He dresses quickly and, gulping down the last of his coffee, he appears to have shaken off his maudlin mood and five beers. His professional Enforcer head is back on and with a nod, we make our way to the back of my mother's cabin, where the sight of my father's funeral pyre greets us.

Chapter 4

Ryker

I stare at the pyre and my father's body laid out on top of it. I want to look away, but I can't. Staring at it makes it more real and I need the reality check.

Hunter's hand lands on my shoulder briefly before he moves away to give his condolences to my mom.

She accepts them with grace and strength, as expected and right on cue, Stevie flings herself into his arms, weeping inconsolably. I roll my eyes as he tentatively wraps his around her. The two of them are ridiculous. She has had a crush on him for decades; he has never gone there because she is my sister and then he got with Casey. I wonder what will happen now. I mean, I wouldn't put a stop to it if they fell into a relationship. I'm not that big of a douche. But Hunter would have to be told that if he ever hurt my little sister, I would kill him. Okay, so maybe some 'douche' is needed.

I turn from them and give my mother a grimace as she holds up the burning fire torch. There is no preamble. No quietly muttered words on how brilliant he was or how much we'll all miss him. Just set him on fire and let him be at peace.

It's the Wolf way.

I take it and walk slowly to the pyre. It is already flickering to life, my mother having started it. All of us need to add to the flame and I'm next. I bend over slightly, the flames hot on my face, making me sweat even more on this stifling morning. Reaching out slowly, I hold the torch to the kindling and watch the small flames burst into bigger ones. Stevie wails and clings to Hunter, but he knows he has to push her away now. It's her time.

I hold the torch out to her. Her hand waivers as she reaches for it, but all of a sudden, when she grips it, a steely determination drops over her face. Her dark hair is drawn up in a ponytail, the ends flickering in the breeze from the fire. Her eyes, a lighter shade of gray than mine, go hard, her lips forming a grim line. She has had her meltdown and now she is stepping up for our father, our mother and sisters.

Watching with pride as she pulls herself together and adds fuel to the burning fire before she hands it to Lily to do the same, I give her a stiff smile, which she returns. I reach out and grab her hand, which she crushes in her own. We stand together in silence, watching our father's body burn.

"Congrats," she mutters to me.

"Fuck off," I mutter back. "Your timing sucks."

She snorts, but there is no amusement there. "You sound just like him."

I turn to glare at her, not happy with the comparison.

I can see a slight smirk and narrow my eyes at her. She is fucking with me. I know then that she will get through this and be okay.

She squeezes my hand and turns to be with our mother. I should go too, but I'm rooted to the spot. Only Hunter stepping up next to me gets me to move.

"It's time, boss," he says. "Everyone is waiting."

"Call me that again and I'll give you that beating that I've always threatened," I respond.

He chuckles humorlessly. "Try it, *boss*."

I snort and turn from the pyre. He is probably the only one who would give me a run for my money. I'd still beat him, especially now I'm Alpha, but he wouldn't make it easy.

"Do you feel different?" he asks quietly, curiously.

I shake my head. "Not yet. I guess I need to be acknowledged by the Pack or some shit."

"You worried you won't be?" he asks, seriously.

"Nah," I say with a shrug. "Who else would they have? You?" I punch him lightly on the shoulder.

"Hah, no thanks. I'll stick to what I'm good at," he answers exactly as I knew he would. He is damn good at his role in the Pack. There is nobody that I would trust more than I do him to have my back.

"Come," Mom says, stalking past us to the middle of the compound where everyone is gathered, staring over our heads at the enormous smoke cloud that is billowing up behind us.

The mood is somber and out of respect, all the Wolves drop to their knees when they see us coming. Stevie and my other sisters join them at the front of the crowd, with Hunter by her side.

This is between me and my mom.

She has to pass the Pack ring over to me and I have to accept it and the responsibility that comes with it.

I barely register what she says. I'm numb. I close my eyes briefly, wishing I was anywhere but here, but when I open them, I accept the silver ring shaped into a wolf's head with two glowing red eyes made from rubies. She slips it onto the middle finger of my right hand and drops to her knees.

"I accept," I say steadily. "I accept this Pack as my responsibility, and I will strive to do my very best as your Alpha. If there is anyone here who wishes to challenge me, please speak up now."

I glare out over the Pack, but not a single Wolf speaks out.

Didn't think so.

It's my birthright by generations.

You have to be a fool to throw down the gauntlet.

Hunter starts to clap slowly.

I throw him a death stare, but he just smirks up at me, as does Stevie, who joins in the clapping.

Soon the entire Pack is on their feet giving me a standing ovation.

I feel humbled and imposter syndrome hits me hard.

What if I'm not worthy of their respect, their belief?

I gulp but don't get much chance for the insecurity and doubt to settle. A warmth spreads through me that builds in its intensity until it is like lava flowing through me. I feel bigger, stronger, and faster. I want to test it out. I want to Shift and run.

Before I can stop it, the Shift takes over, forcing me to my knees with a low growl. My bones break and reform into that of the Wolf's. I grow fur, gray and white, my hands and feet turning into huge paws. My vision sharpens to the point where it almost seems out of focus and my other senses kick in. Everything is so much more. I can feel the Alpha Wolf running through my veins now. With every beat of my heart, it beats for this Pack. It's astounding and once again, I am humbled by this feeling of being part of something so special, so significant to so many others.

I leap forward, brushing past Stevie, who reaches out to stroke me quickly.

Something, *someone*, has caught my attention on the edge of the Pack. I throw my head back and howl, which causes a chain reaction of Wolves Shifting. Those around her drop to their knees, but she remains standing, rooted to the spot as I zero in on her.

Her dark hair and blue eyes are vivid with my sharp sight. I growl and spin in a circle before I take off. If I don't run now, I'm going to explode with the need for it.

I burst through the compound at speeds previously unknown and head into the woods, aiming directly for the lake where I intend to Shift, dive in headfirst and cool off the burning that is coursing through me.

Chapter 5

Ryker

Reluctantly hauling myself out of the cool water of the mountain lake, I return to Wolf form for the run home. Apart from the fact that I'm naked as the day I was born, I need more time as the true Alpha.

It's a phenomenal feeling.

So much power, so much sensation in every cell of my body. Yes, there's also the weight of the Pack on my shoulders now, but I feel that I have the strength to carry this burden now. Yesterday, I was just me. Now, I am so much more.

I pad away from the shoreline, turning back to look lingeringly over the water. My Wolf senses pick up a movement to my right and I turn my head. A few hundred feet away, I see a naked woman in the lake, the water lapping around her perfectly shaped thighs. I hadn't noticed her before, only upon returning to Wolf form, and she clearly hasn't seen me.

I edge closer, shortening the distance between us. Her back is facing me, long and lean. She is definitely a Wolf. She has a hand-sized paw print tattoo at the base of her spine, with smaller paws, walking up her back. Her dark hair is curled up on top of her head to stop it from getting wet as she bathes or cools down from the heat of the day. I start to pant as I move in even closer. I don't recognize her as someone I have been with before. I would *definitely* remember those sexy tats. I want to lick them. I want to trail my tongue all the way from her ass crack to the nape of her neck before I bite her and claim her, impaling her on my cock as I ride her from behind. I'm about to Shift back to my human form and proposition whoever this bewitching creature of the lake is, when she turns her head sharply, catching my movement.

I freeze.

Bree.

She turns quickly when she sees me, covering her tits with her hands and ducking under the deeper water to cover her bare pussy from my view.

The breeze shifts and I catch her scent straight away. If only that had been blowing downwind a few seconds ago. I'd have left well enough alone. She is the last female I want to be lusting after and with a growl of annoyance at myself for falling for her hot body and sexy as fuck tats before I saw her face, I back away, turning and darting off into the woods to cool my arousal before I do something very stupid that I will regret immediately.

As I weave through the trees, feeling the heat from the sun dappled now and again, hot on my back, I find a small clearing in the shade and turn in a circle before I flop down and rest my head on my paws, for the first time cursing my libido and insatiable desire to claim every female that I can within a hundred-mile radius.

What was I thinking?

Clearly, I wasn't.

Or I *was* but with my dick instead of my head.

Fortunately, thinking about Bree and her sanctimonious attitude puts the brakes on the burning desire a moment later.

Yeah, she is definitely a no-go.

Stuck up prude.

There is no way she would be like Valerie and let me tie her up and take out my depravities on her, and without that, there is nothing.

Not for me, anyway.

I know my darkness and I feed it. To do otherwise isn't an option, especially not now.

I huff, feeling drowsy as the last forty-eight hours catches up on me and I fall asleep in the woods, glad that I walked away.

Chapter 6

Bree

Mortified.

That is the only word I can use to describe how I feel right now.

I don't want to stand up, even though he has run off, as if he couldn't stand the sight of me.

He.

The brand-new Alpha of the Pack.

I groan out loud and cover my face with my hands.

"Bree, you idiot," I mutter to myself.

What will he think of me, standing here naked with all my bits showing? I should've gone deeper, covered up a bit more. He will think I'm some brazen hussy trying to tempt him into bed or something. I know all about Ryker Silvercrest. He needs absolutely no introduction. He is the exact opposite of the man I want to spend the rest of my life with. I push the new Alpha man-whore from my mind and think about the man that I *do* want.

Kane.

He is shy and unassuming, much like me. He is cute and has a nice body that he covers up but that's what I like. A bit of mystery. Ryker flaunts his muscles and hard body with the wolf tattoo over his heart, all over the place for everyone to see.

Ugh.

Such a turnoff.

Kane is understated. A peacekeeper of the Pack.

The Omega.

Much more my style than the *Alpha*.

But he doesn't even know I exist.

I clear my throat and stand up. I need to get out of this lake and Shift to get back home. I was desperate for a bath of some kind. My shower rainsaver tank is almost depleted, and with Casey moving in, it'll be gone before the day is out. I'm being a good host by saving the water for her, so she doesn't have to come down here today at least.

Tomorrow she will have no choice.

With a sigh, I wade a bit closer to the shoreline of the lake and then stop dead. Approaching from the right, there are three young men, Wolves from a neighboring Pack. The Ridge is the nearest one to here, so I assume they are from there.

They've spotted me.

I'm like a deer in headlights. I can't move, even though I have to.

"Well, what have we here?" one of them asks loudly, giving me a lewd look.

It gets me to back up, but I'm going in the wrong direction. I'm not the strongest swimmer. I can't go any deeper than where I can stand up or I'll start to panic. Besides, swimming into the middle of the lake is hardly the best move for getting away from them. All I'll do is trap myself further.

I shuffle to the side, away from them but they follow, entering the water and coming closer.

"Nice pair of tits," another one says. "Come over here while I suck on them. You can ride my dick at the same time." They laugh raucously and make rude gestures.

My cheeks are on fire. I start to sweat, even though I'm waist deep in the cool water.

"I want to make that fine ass mine," the third one pipes up, which makes my decision for me.

I have to get out of the lake as quickly as I can and run as fast as I can to a hiding place where I can Shift and head to the safety of home.

I am in danger. I don't need to have Wolf senses to know that.

I brace myself as they get even closer. I have to make my move. Now.

I lunge forward, rushing out of the lake as fast as I can, and coming ashore. They follow me, continuing with their disgusting comments about what they are going to do to me when they catch me. I feel sick.

I race forward into the woods, darting in between the trees, my breath coming in ragged pants. They are following me, running to keep up. I go faster. As fast as I can in my human form. The soles of my feet are torn and bruised from running over stones and twigs, but I don't care. I need to get away from them for long enough to Shift.

Rushing into a clearing, I nearly trip over the humongous Wolf sleeping next to a huge boulder. He raises his gray and white head the instant I practically step on him. I recognize him instantly.

Ryker.

"Help!" I cry out, hating the weakness, but knowing that I need it.

In the next second, he has nosed me behind the boulder

and turned to bare his teeth at the three men that have skidded into the clearing behind me.

I shiver and turn my back to the boulder, sliding down it, grazing my back until my ass hits the ground. I pull my knees up to my chest and rest my chin on them while I catch my breath. My lungs are burning with the exertion in this form. I'm not used to running for my life, but I knew that if they caught me, they would hurt me.

It slams it home to me how safe the Pack compound is. There isn't a Wolf in the whole world who would enter another Pack's living space without invitation. After this, I will never leave it again alone. I'm not even that far away, a mile at the most. But clearly the dangers are still out there for a woman, a Wolf, like me. Weak and alone, I'm a prime target for the more aggressive of the male Wolves. My breathing slows rapidly now that my Alpha is close by and protecting me. I peek out from behind the boulder to see him growling viciously and the three men backing off hurriedly with their hands up.

I draw in a deep breath and Shift, intending to get out of here while I can.

Chapter 7

Ryker

The sheer rage that is coursing through me that these three young assholes have chased a naked and vulnerable woman through the woods makes me shake and growl louder, stepping forward. A Wolf, no less. One of *my* Wolves makes it even worse. I want to rip them to shreds and eat them one by one. I bare my teeth and prepare to pounce, when they back off quickly, hands up. They start to run in the opposite direction, back towards the lake. Fully prepared to follow them, I pause briefly.

Something has struck me right in the heart. I want to whimper at the fear I feel, but it's not coming from me. I turn around to see a small black Wolf in front of me, staring at me with bright blue eyes. The feelings that have hit me are coming from her.

Bree.

Is that an Alpha thing? Can I sense all of my Wolves this way now?

I tilt my head inquisitively.

She takes a couple of hesitant steps forward until we are almost nose to nose. She darts her tongue out to lick my nose, causing a sensation that I have *never* felt before shoot through me, lighting a fire in my heart and spreading through my veins. I want to Shift so that I can grab hold of her, pull her close to me, protect her at all costs against every evil this world has to offer. I want to love her and have her love me back so fiercely, it consumes us both.

I stumble back from it, needing to create a distance but I had no need. She spins and is gone before I can blink.

I'm torn between going after the three Wolves who chased her and following her to make sure she gets home safely.

In the end, I decide the Wolves can wait. I will deal with them in the right way, even though the need to hunt and kill them is still pulling at me. Packs have rules and as Alpha of the largest and strongest Pack in the area, I need to deal with this in the right way or start a Pack war that will last until everyone falls.

I launch myself forward and follow Bree back to the compound, racing through the trees and making it back to my cabin in record time.

I Shift and climb the steps, shoving the door open and cursing the loss of my clothes and boots. Impromptu Shifting will do that. I rifle through the laundry bags for fresh clothes and pull them on quickly, hopping on one foot to get first my left spare boot on and then the right, while I make my way in the direction of Bree's cabin.

I have no idea which one is actually hers. I just know that she lives in the southwest section, so I head that way with a fast jog.

I'm startled to see her still in Wolf form only just arriving back at the compound. I managed to pass her and get dressed before she even made it back.

I slow down and watch her leap onto the porch of a nearby cabin and then dive through the open window.

It doesn't surprise me in the least that she didn't Shift before entering the cabin and that she leaves herself an opener to get in so that she doesn't have to show her naked body to the Pack. Not that she has anything to be ashamed about.

I think I start to drool a little remembering her body, her sexy tats, her pert ass and tits that I want to shove together and slip my dick in between.

Shaking my head to clear those unwanted thoughts, I pound up the cabin steps and knock lightly on the door so as not to scare her.

I wait a few seconds before she drags it open, all disheveled and cute. She is dressed in hastily pulled on grey leggings and a tight white vest which shows the curve of her tits, her pebbled nipples straining against the fabric. I tear my eyes from her chest to her face, taking in her tangled hair, loose around her shoulders.

She doesn't say a word.

She just stares at me, expecting me to say something.

"You okay?" I ask and then mentally kick myself for the dumbass question.

"Fine," she croaks out.

I nod slowly wanting to leave it at that, but I can't. "Can you tell me what happened?" I ask in the gentlest tone I can muster. Which, judging by her face, came off okay. It softens slightly as she grips the door handle tightly and leans into it.

But she still doesn't say anything.

"Look, Bree, I need to know what happened so I can go over to the Ridge and deal with this. I'm going whether you tell me or not, by the way, it would just look more official if I went with facts and not just a desire to slam my fist into their faces for no apparent reason," I say, trying to keep my tone light for her benefit.

She sighs. "They saw me in the lake and approached me making comments. I got scared and ran into the woods where I came across you," she says eventually.

I pause taking that in. "So you were naked in the lake, and they came after you?" I press.

She nods carefully.

"What did they say?" I ask, my tone going flat even to my own ears. I realize that I don't want to hear it, probably about as much as she wants to say it. The thought of her being propositioned by any male makes me feel slightly ill.

I blink rapidly and frown at her. What is she doing to me?

It has to be the Alpha thing.

That's all this is.

I'm being protective over her because she is mine. As in one of my Pack…

I clear my throat.

"Do you need to know?" she asks quietly.

"It would help to have all the facts," I reply, just as quietly.

"One of them said I had nice boobs, and that I had to go to him so he could suck them and ride his dick at the same time," she says, lifting her chin higher.

Boobs? Who uses that word?

I stifle my amusement under a blanket of indignation on her behalf at the rest of what she said.

"Did he now?" I growl.

She swallows and nods. "Another one threatened to… uhm…" Her cheeks go bright red, and she taps her ass.

I look at her fingers, my mouth filling up with saliva at the thought of taking her ass and making it mine.

"I see," I say stiffly to cover my desire along with a good old dose of 'I'm going to kill the fucker who said that'.

"They tormented me!" she says hotly, suddenly. "I felt threatened, and I ran. I'm sorry that you have to go over there and clean up this mess. In fact, just forget it. It's fine. I'm fine," she adds in a rush and tries to slam the door in my face.

I slap my hand up to it, halting its progress. She grunts as the impact jolts her arm, but she doesn't let go of the edge of the door she now has in her white knuckled grip.

"Don't you dare apologize," I warn her, almost angry with her for dismissing this.

"It's fine," she insists again, but it's weak and not at all what she's feeling. "Thank you for checking on me and for... you know..."

"Saving you?" I ask with a smirk that I just couldn't help. I could punch myself in the gut for it, but it lights up the fire in her eyes and shoves the fear aside.

"Yes, that," she grits out.

We stare into each other's eyes for a moment, time almost standing still. "I will handle this," I say eventually. "No one gets away with tormenting one of my Wolves."

She snorts derisively, pissing me off a bit as she dismisses my declaration so casually. "You've been Alpha for all of a couple of hours."

"And?" I question her. "You think that makes it any less true? You think I can't do this?"

My tone was harsher than I meant it to be. She flinches and drops her eyes. "I didn't mean that," she whispers. "I'm sorry."

Giving her a grimace, I try to straighten my face. Remembering the fear she felt, that *I* felt with her, I cut her some slack.

"I'll take Hunter with me; we'll be back later. You don't

need to be afraid anymore, but maybe don't go to the lake alone again. Take someone with you," I advise and turn on my heel to march off.

"Thank you." I barely hear her whisper of gratitude.

Needing to put some space between me and this feeling for her that is sudden and slightly overwhelming, I reply in a dismissive tone, "No need. It's my job."

I turn my back on her and walk away, making my way to Hunter's cabin. This day is going to end with retribution one way or the other.

Chapter 8

Ryker

I ignore the sigh that echoes in my ears when Bree closes the door at my retreating back. I wish I hadn't heard it, but Wolf hearing is a bitch at the best of times. Speaking of Wolves, I glance around, again wondering if I'm connected to them all in the way I felt with Bree earlier. It was a weird sensation and not one I'm looking forward to repeating if that's the case. Hopefully, it was a one off or maybe only in cases of trauma.

I find myself in front of Hunter's cabin, wondering how I even got here, I was so lost in my thoughts. He is sitting upright on the wooden bench on his porch, in the shade from this growing, unbearable heat, his head leaning back against the cabin wall. His eyes are shut and his mouth wide open as he sleeps.

"Rise and shine, Sleeping Beauty," I remark, leaning on the wooden railing, the scent of pine wafting in from the woods on the slight breeze that is a welcome relief to the heat.

"Huh? Wha?" he asks, eyes flying open and sitting forward. "I wasn't sleeping," he adds defensively.

"Yeah, okay," I snort, shaking my head. "Sorry to disturb your beauty rest but duty calls. Let's roll."

"Oh? Where to?" he asks, standing up and walking down the steps to join me.

"The Ridge," I reply darkly. "I'll fill you in on the way."

"Got it," he says and waits while I return to my cabin to grab the keys to the pickup. It's too far to walk. Their base is down the lake about three miles. To see some of their Wolves this far up the shore isn't necessarily rare, but they do usually keep to their own section, as do we. The three young Wolves who wandered this far up, probably weren't looking for trouble, but they sure as shit ended up finding it.

We climb into the old pick up and roll down the windows.

"So what's this about?" Hunter asks when we set off and bounce over the dirt track that is the shortest route to the Ridge Pack lands.

I wave to the sentry on duty at the entrance to the compound. It's precaution, nothing more, but a vital one when a few Wolf Packs live on this land.

"Three of their Wolves tormented one of ours this morning. A female. I'm not standing for it," I say shortly. I don't mention Bree's name for two reasons. One, Hunter is probably still blaming her for Casey leaving him, and two, I get the feeling she wouldn't want me to.

"Oh?" he growls darkly. "Who?"

Dammit. I shoulda known he would ask.

I shrug. "Doesn't matter," I say vaguely. "Point is...their behavior was indecent and unacceptable to one of my Pack. Either Winston sorts it out, or my fists will."

Hunter snorts. "Winston is more of a hardass than your dad was," he says. "I do not envy these dicks who fucked up."

"Me either," I say with an evil smile. As much as I want to

take this matter into my own hands, I know that going to the Ridge Pack Alpha will be so much worse for them. Winston is a major badass, but he also has a respect for the female kind that goes above and beyond. He is going to be fucking pissed when he hears what his Wolves have been up to.

We continue the drive in silence until we reach the Ridge Pack compound gates. We are stopped by the guards on duty at the gates, as expected.

I know the guy who leans down to glare into my open window. "Ryker," he growls. "What brings you here?"

"Hey, Jim," I reply. "I'm here on official Pack business to see Winston. He around?"

I already know he is around, but it's polite to ask.

Jim nods his grizzled head. "Heard about your pops," he comments. "Sorry to hear it; he was a good man."

I try not to grimace. News travels fast around these parts. "Thanks," I mutter.

"Makes you the new Alpha, don't it?" he presses, already knowing the answer to that.

"Sure does."

"Then you're welcome on Ridge Pack land as long as you ain't here to cause trouble," he says gruffly.

"No trouble," I reply blandly.

He nods and then his hand shoots into the truck, waving an empty basket in front of my face.

"I don't carry," I say, shoving the basket away in offense.

"Not you. Him," Jim says, waggling the basket at Hunter.

I cast a glance at my Enforcer. I know he carries a weapon. My dad was cool with it. Me, not so much. There's no need to add weapons when Wolves are aggressive by nature and can do enough damage with teeth and claws.

Hunter huffs out a breath and reaches around the back of his pants to pull out the Glock he is carrying. He dumps it in the basket with bad grace.

Jim waggles the basket some more. "I know that's not all you got, boy," he grits out.

"Fuck's sake," Hunter mutters under his breath and reaches down into his boot to pull out the hunting knife my dad gave him when he was promoted to Beta of the Pack. That joins the Glock, a filthy look crossing Hunter's face.

"Annnd…" Jim drawls with more waving of the basket.

"Jesus Christ, man," Hunter snaps. "Strip a man bare, why don't you."

"You ain't my type, kid, but I'm sure Phil over there wouldn't mind," Jim replies, with a nod to the male around the same age as us. Hunter reaches into his other boot for the tiny .22.

I raise an eyebrow at that. I didn't know he carried that.

"Happy?" he snarls.

"Delighted," Jim replies sarcastically, withdrawing the basket and waving us through.

"We need to talk about that," I comment as I drive us carefully through the gates and onto rival Pack land.

Hunter just shrugs and glares out of the window. He is fully aware of my feelings on this matter.

I pull up in a space near the south side of the cabins and climb out. Hunter joins me, slamming the door behind him and stretching.

Falling into step beside me, we head deeper into the compound, wary looks at our unexpected presence being shot our way.

As expected, we find Winston near the north side, chopping wood with the agility of a man half his age.

He stops when he sees us approaching.

"Ryker?" he calls out, squinting in the sun. "Is that you, boy?"

"Yeah," I say, speeding up a bit to reach him. "How's things?"

"Same. Should be asking you that," he replies.

I shrug. "You've heard."

"Sure have. Was sorry to hear about Jefferson. Do you know who did it?" he asks bluntly.

I shake my head. "Not yet."

"So you're it?" he asks, thankfully dropping the subject of my father's murder. "Is this a social call?"

"'Fraid not," I reply grimly. "Got somewhere we can talk?"

Winston nods his head slowly and drops the ax he was leaning on. He gestures with his head to follow him, which we do. It's not unusual that he hasn't acknowledged Hunter, or vice-versa. Hunter won't speak unless he is spoken to by the Alpha Wolf first and it's unlikely that Winston will start up a conversation with him. Hunter's presence here is to have *my* back, not meddle in Pack affairs.

Winston leads us into his cabin a short distance away. "What's up?" he asks, closing the door.

The cool blast of air that hits me fires up my envy. Air conditioning. Lucky bastard. He indicates we should sit, but I remain standing as the severity of the situation dictates. It instantly sets his Wolf on edge.

"Three of your Wolves harassed one of mine this morning. A female, to be precise, while she was bathing in the lake," I state, getting straight to the point.

Winston narrows his eyes at me. "Oh?" he growls. "And you know this how?"

"I was in the woods when she rushed in naked with them following, intent on raping her, it would seem from the comments that were made," I growl, my skin crawling with the thought of those creeps with their hands all over Bree's exquisite body.

"I see," Winston says, his eyes cold.

There is no way he can deny it, now that he knows I was there. Or half there. Sure, I didn't witness anything apart from Bree's fear and naked dash into the woods with them on her tail. But I believe what she said. She isn't the type to make shit up to save face or get others into trouble. Don't ask me how I know, I just do. Her fear was real. I felt it and that's all I need to be convinced.

"I don't suppose you have names?" he asks.

I shake my head. "Never seen them before. Youths, three of them," I press to ensure they all get what's coming to them. "Two with dark hair and one lighter. I'm guessing they hang around together to be up our end of the lake as they were."

"Hmm," he says, his eyes hooding as he thinks about that.

I think he knows who the culprits are, but he's playing it close to his vest.

"Can you give me anything else?"

"To be crude about it, one of them asked to suck on her tits while she rode his dick, and another insinuated he would ass-rape her. Is that enough for you to deal with this, or do I need to take this matter into my own hands?" I've had enough now. The *Wolf* inside me has had enough. I want action and he knows it by my aggressive step forward, fists clenched.

"I will handle them," Winston says. "You don't need to worry about that. Thank you for coming to me and *not* taking this matter into your own hands..." The warning hangs there like a noxious gas. His Wolves might be in the wrong here, but he would still defend them if I crossed a line. It makes me glad that I did this the right way, as much as it kills me and goes against my nature. Doesn't mean that if the opportunity should arise where I see them again, I will just let this go. But they have that saying that revenge is best served cold. For now, Winston can deal with his Wolves, and I will wait until I can teach these assholes a lesson in messing with one of mine.

I nod grimly. "I expect to be informed when retribution has been exacted. My Wolf was terrified earlier and won't feel safe going anywhere on her own for a while. Not. Acceptable." If he thought he could give me words and not action because I'm new to this and have no clue what I'm doing, he is dead wrong.

"You'll be informed," Winston says tightly and opens the door to his cabin to let us know we are dismissed, effective immediately. We need to leave and get off his land in record time now.

Fine by me.

Without another word, Hunter and I make tracks back to the pickup and set off, only stopping to collect Hunter's hardware before we drive in complete silence back to Silvercrest lands.

Chapter 9

Bree

Sitting on the bed, my hands are shaking as I pull on my usual blue jeans and baggy white tee. I felt indecent opening the door to the new Alpha in hastily pulled on tight clothes, that I know gave him more than enough to look at.

I cringe with embarrassment when I remember that he has seen *all* of me, even if it was only for a few seconds.

The door to my cabin opens and I jump up, fists clenched, ready to do something...I'm not even sure what, to the intruder, but it's just Casey.

"Hey," she says, stopping short when she sees me ready to pounce. "Everything okay?"

I relax but nod stiffly. I don't want to tell her what happened. I don't want to tell anyone. If Ryker decides to make this public knowledge, I'll kill him with my bare hands. I should've said to him to keep it between us, but he makes me so nervous. Those gray eyes have an intensity to them that unnerves me to the point where I want the ground to open up and swallow me, just so I can get away from them. I don't think there is any attraction there, thankfully. He is just doing, as he said so caustically, *his job*, when he came to check on me. It's nothing to do with *me*, but rather he needs to assert his authority as the new Alpha.

I turn my back on Casey as she gives me a curious look.

"Are you sure? You look like you've seen a ghost."

"Don't think ghosts exist," I point out, sitting again to pull on my sneakers.

"I bet ghosts say the same thing about Wolf Shifters," she counters, making me smile.

"Yeah, you're probably right," I agree and stand up.

"Can I ask you something?" she ventures, twirling her blonde ponytail around her finger.

"Of course," I reply.

"When the new Alpha was announced, why didn't you Shift? I mean, the need to was overwhelming for me. I figured it was the same for everyone." Her green eyes are questioning me almost to the point where I feel uncomfortable.

I shrug. I can't answer that. I mean, I *can* but I feel silly. He zeroed in on me and I was so intimidated, I froze. I don't know why I caught his attention out of so many Wolves surrounding him. Maybe *because* I didn't Shift? I don't know. Was it expected? I'm only twenty-three. I wasn't even born the last time a new Alpha took over the Pack. I don't know what protocol is, no one has ever told me. My parents left the Pack a few years ago, leaving me as soon as I turned eighteen. They'd had enough of the life and wanted to try their hand at passing for humans. They didn't even ask me if that's what I wanted as well. They just told me their plans and left.

I can't say that I would've gone with them, I like it here, safe and familiar, but it would've been nice to have been asked – by my own parents, no less. As a result, for the last five years, I've had to make my own way. I think I'm doing okay. I don't *need* anyone to look after me, but I like having Casey here, just in case.

"I think he has the hots for you," Casey jibes, interrupting my thoughts.

My cheeks go bright red, and I splutter.

She laughs at me. "And you have the hots for him! Oh, Bree, don't go there, girl. He's a man-whore."

"Oh, you don't need to tell me that," I spit out, probably with more harshness than I meant. The very idea of being with him makes my skin crawl. Everyone knows he's been hooking up with Valerie and that Wolf makes my eyes water with all the male Wolves that enter and exit her cabin. "I have absolutely no interest in the new Alpha that way," I reiterate strongly.

She raises her eyebrow at me, almost as if she knows I'm lying.

Well, *lying* isn't quite right. I wouldn't go near Ryker with a barge pole, but there was that 'something' between us in the clearing. I don't know what it was, nor do I want to explore it, but all I wanted was for him to take me in his arms and protect me. I wanted him to love me so that I could love him back.

It was weird and gross.

I definitely do not want that with him. It was probably just that he rescued me, and I felt grateful or something. In order to push Ryker from my mind, I concentrate on Kane. I can't help the small smile that crosses my face at the thought of his cute face and calm, responsible attitude. I turn from Casey, so she won't see my doe-eyed gaze. She will mistake it for being over Ryker.

"Did you see Kane outside?" I ask her casually.

"Think he's clearing the weeds over on the north side of the section," she answers absently, thankfully dropping the subject and concentrating on rifling through her laundry bag. "Dammit," she mutters.

"What?" I ask, happy to divert the attention away from me.

"My pink top...it's not in here."

I frown. "That's not like Sasha and Gail, they're usually meticulous. You sure it went in there?"

Casey nods, a worried expression dropping over her features. "Hunter must have it," she mutters. "I don't want to go back over there, would you?" she pleads suddenly.

"Err," I stammer, really not wanting to get in the middle of that mess.

"Please," she cajoles. "I will take your next week of cabin cleaning duty."

I pause. That's a mighty fine offer. It's my chore this coming week to do the south-west section cabins and I hate it in summer. Cleaning and the heat are not a great combination. "What are you supposed to be doing this week?" I ask, knowing that I can't hand off my chore to her if she already has enough on her plate. It's not fair to the rest of the Wolves if she ends up not doing *my* chore properly.

"Gardening with Kane," she says, her eyes suddenly lighting up.

I dislike that immensely. I've been hoping that our chores would match up for weeks now. Even though gardening in the outside heat will be so much worse than cleaning indoors, I blurt out. "Can we swap?"

Her eyes land on me with interest. "But what about my top?" she asks.

I don't give a crap about her top. "Fine, I'll go to Hunter's, but will you swap chores with me this week?" I snap.

"Wow," she comments, holding her hands up. "Go for it. Spending the day outdoors doing heavy work was not on my list of things to enjoy. But you'll go for my top? Today?"

I nod with a grimace, knowing I've shorted myself out of an exchange here. But to spend time with Kane will be worth it.

"I'll think of something else to swap for the top," I say, suddenly feeling the need to assert myself. I have no idea where it came from. It's not in my nature. I'm usually a pushover. I know it, everyone knows it.

Casey's surprised expression confirms that she wasn't expecting that. "Sure," she says cautiously. "Let me know."

I nod and then head outside to Pete, who deals with the schedules on this side of the compound to make sure I get that swap duty sorted.

Chapter 10

Ryker

I pull up and leave the engine idling. Staring straight ahead, I say, "About earlier..."

Hunter huffs at me. "You know that I'm not some gun-toting moron who thinks my dick is bigger because I carry a weapon," he interrupts. "I have a job to do around here. A job your father gave me and trusted me with. I enforce Pack law, but I also have a duty to protect everyone inside this compound. I would rather have the piece and not use it, then need it and not have it. You get me?"

I turn to face him.

He is deadly serious.

"I get you," I say carefully. "But why the hidden twenty-two?"

His eyes meet mine steadily, a sadness dropping into his gaze. "I was going to teach Casey how to use it in case she ever needed to protect herself. That's obviously no longer an issue now that she's dumped me," he adds bitterly.

I can see he is absolutely gutted by his break-up and once

again feel glad that I won't ever have to go through shit like that.

"Fair enough," I mutter, leaving it for now. He looks like he's gone ten rounds and lost. I don't want to add to that right now.

Turning off the engine, I withdraw the key and open the door.

"Who was it?" he asks, stopping me momentarily.

While I debate whether or not to tell him, he continues, "If a member of this Pack was harassed, I need to know about it. I'm not asking to be a gossipy little bitch. I'm asking so that I can do my job properly and keep an eye out for her."

He's right.

With a grimace, I sit back in my seat and say, "It was Bree."

I wait for it.

It comes as expected.

"Oh," he says with a sneer.

"Look, I knew you'd be like that, which is why I didn't want to say so in the first place," I snap at him.

He frowns at me. "You're being really defensive. You got the hots for her, or something?"

I growl loudly. "I do not," I spit out. "She is part of *my* Pack, of course I'm going to look out for her."

He nods slowly. "Yeah, she's not exactly your type."

"What's that supposed to mean?" I ask, knowing I'm being shitty but not being able to help it. I know she isn't my type, but to have it insinuated that I want her has made the hackles rise.

Hunter snorts. "I know all about you and Val. And as your best friend, I feel inclined to inform you that you aren't the only Wolf she's hooking up with. You're using protection, right? Because that bitch is nasty."

I grimace at him. "Of course I am, you dick. You think I

want her declaring one day that she's pregnant, and it's mine? Besides, I know who she is. She is a cum dumpster, and that's fine with me. Protected from her bodily fluids all the way."

Hunter's disgusted expression makes me smirk at him. "She is such a whore," he remarks. "Don't let her drag you down to her level."

"Already there," I state in a tone I know sounds dead to my own ears. "Can we drop the subject of who I bang now, please? It's kinda none of your business."

He holds his hands up and shoves open the car door. "Bang who you want, just don't get into shit because of it," he says and stalks off, leaving me scowling after him.

All this talk of sex has made my dick go a bit hard. I wonder briefly if Valerie is up for a round of 'service the new Alpha'.

That is until Bree catches my eye, and my dick deflates slightly.

Her eyes meet mine and she stops with caution oozing out of her.

I give her a swift nod.

She licks her lips and returns it, turning her back to me and scampering away.

I watch her go with a sigh.

What is she doing to me?

I know it's something, I just can't figure out what it is.

Wearily, I trudge back to my cabin and kicking off my boots, I fall face first onto my bed, fully clothed and I'm asleep within seconds.

Chapter 11

Ryker

She is pressed face down and naked into my bed, my body covering hers. I slide my hand into her dark hair, pushing it out of the way so I kiss the nape of her neck, that sexy little tattoo of a paw print. She gasps with desire. I trail my mouth down her back, following the path of paw prints back down to the base of her spine where I lick the larger tat, making her shiver.

"Ryker," she moans, parting her legs to allow me access to that prized place that she has saved just for me.

"Bree," I murmur, gripping my cock and positioning it at her entrance more than ready to fuck her this way.

I press against her.

She cries out my name, "Ryker."

It makes my dick go even stiffer.

"Bree," I mumble. "Bree."

I moan, knowing that I'm awake now and that it was just a dream. My dick is aching, busting against my pants desperate for a release. I contemplate taking care of it myself for a moment but where's the fun in that?

"What the fuck are you doing to me?" I mutter, rolling onto my back and rubbing my face with my hands.

I'm starting to get an idea.

I need to speak to my mom about this. Something she said is echoing in my head and it's needling at me: *You have someone out there, Ryker, someone made to be with you, to help keep you strong...*

Made to be with me. I need to know what she meant.

Climbing off the bed, I realize that dusk is coming. I've been asleep for hours. My stomach growls with hunger, but I ignore it in favor of trying to figure out what the hell is going on in my head and my heart right now.

Pulling my boots on, I march out of my cabin and directly to my parent's cabin. Well, my *mom's* now. I bite the inside of my lip, figuring she must feel really alone right now. I should try to come over more often, make the time, find excuses.

This one is a good start.

I knock lightly and she calls out for me to come in. She is sitting in her favorite chair by the window, knitting. She'd have seen me coming.

"Don't think you need to check on me," she says by way of a greeting.

I grin at her. "Busted," I say but then shake my head. "I'm not. At least not today. I need to know something."

She peers at me and my now serious expression. She puts her knitting down and leans forward. "What is it?"

I slump into the other chair opposite hers, the one that my dad sat in to read while she knitted. It hits me in the heart suddenly. I never thought before about my parents having a 'relationship'. I mean obviously I knew they were in one, but the details, the small things escaped my notice until now.

My mouth goes dry.

My palms sweat a little in contrast.

"What you said this morning..." *Christ, was it only this morning?* "...what did you mean by it?"

"Which bit?" she asks.

"About there being somebody made to be with me."

"Oh, that," she says with a smile and sits back. "You feel it?"

"I don't know," I reply warily. "What am I supposed to be feeling?"

She chuckles. "Like you've been hit in the head with a sledgehammer. That's how your dad described it."

"Explain it," I demand quietly, leaning my elbows on my knees.

"As Alpha you have a mate out there who is destined to be with you, Ry. A Fated Mate. Someone you have seen every day but won't have had any idea until this morning," she says.

"Destined? Fate?" I ask with more than a little skepticism.

"I understand your reluctance to believe. We never talked about it. Your father didn't want to. He didn't want you lying in wait, wondering who it could be. But it's the truth. One of the female's out there was born to be with you. Do you know who yet? Has she made herself known?" she asks curiously, picking up her knitting again.

I gulp.

"I'm not sure," I croak out, feeling like I've been hit with something hot, right in the gut. Bree? Is that what this is? I shake my head to clear it of that unwanted thought. No. Not her. Anyone but her. She is the exact opposite of what I want in a woman. How would we work? Simple answer is, we wouldn't. There is no way she would find me acceptable as her mate in the same way. We are incompatible.

No, whatever is going on with her is a blip. This Fated Wolf is someone else. Question is, who?

I sigh and stand up. "What happens if I don't want this?" I ask, walking slowly to the door, my back turned towards her.

"You can't fight Fate, Ry," she replies.

Fucking great.

I half turn towards her. "You sure about that?"

"Fucking sure," she replies, eyes on her knitting.

I gape at her. I never heard her swear so blatantly before. I snort with amusement. "Bye, Mom," I say quietly.

"Don't fight it, Ry," she calls after me as I leave the cabin with a lot on my mind.

Almost instantly, I'm assaulted by Casey racing up to me a panicked look on her face. "Ryker! Come quick!"

"What is it?" I ask, immediately going into Alpha mode. I didn't even know it was a mode to go into before now.

She doesn't answer, she just gestures for me to follow her. I hurry after her to the main communal area, where a small black Wolf is growling and snarling at anyone who comes within ten feet of her.

"Bree?" I ask in surprise. I turn to Casey, gripping her arm. "What happened?"

"The twins made some comments about her, and she freaked out," Casey says, her eyes wide. "She bit me!" She holds her bleeding hand up.

"What comments?" I growl, dismissing her pain.

"Nothing they haven't said before," she says. "Just how tightly wound she is and how it would take the jaws of life to pry her thighs apart...the usual..." She shrugs as if that excuses it.

My vision goes red for a moment as the anger settles over me. I turn slowly towards the hovering twins. They are only about seventeen, eighteen, and stupid in their attitude towards women and life in general. I stride over and grip them both on the sides of their necks, shoving their heads together to bang off one another.

"Don't be dicks all your life," I growl at them. "Think that words hurt. I know your mama raised you better than that, you little idiots." I let them go, dazed and rubbing their melons, dismissing them as I turn towards Bree. She is still fairly rabid, but when I approach her slowly, she calms slightly.

That alone is enough to know that everything I have been feeling for her is real. Her wild blue eyes take me in warily, but she stops backing off.

"Bree," I say quietly. "You're safe here. You don't need to be scared. I'm here."

"What the fuck?"

I hear Casey's surprised exclamation but ignore it.

Bree shakes her head and spins around, bolting off into the growing night towards the woods. I groan. Silly little Wolf.

I stalk away from the crowd of onlookers, pulling my t-shirt over my head and kicking my boots off. I undo my jeans and yank them off, not bothered in the slightest about my nudity.

"Where are you going?" Casey calls out.

"To get her back!" I growl, starting to move so I can Shift mid-run. It'll save time because Bree shooting off on her own in the state she is in, into the dark woods, is about the stupidest thing I have ever come across.

In Wolf form a few seconds later, my nose hits the ground and picks up her scent immediately. Yet another sign that something bigger is going on. I know her Wolf scent already.

I shove the knowledge and my mother's words aside, intent on finding the runaway Wolf as quickly as possible. I end up tracking her to the clearing where we were earlier. She is cowering against the boulder, whimpering.

I slow down but keep approaching her. She is like a scared rabbit trapped under the paw of a hungry Wolf.

On a whim, I Shift back to my human form, slowly so as not to startle her. Her eyes bore into mine, but she doesn't move. So I walk forward.

"Come to me," I murmur to her, holding out my hand and dropping to my knees a few feet from her.

It takes her a minute, but she edges forward until I can reach out and stroke her behind her ears. She makes a cute keening sound as if she is enjoying the touch.

"Shift for me," I whisper, needing to hold her close.

I slowly pull my hand back. Her curious gaze intensifies, but she does as I ask, Shifting slowly, which is the sexiest thing I have ever seen in my life. My cock bounces to attention, my heart pounds in my chest. When she is fully human again, I shuffle forward on my knees. Her eyes go wide, dropping immediately to my cock, jutting out in arousal. I wonder briefly if she has ever seen an erect cock before. She must've. Wolves Shift all the time in front of each other, appearing naked all over the compound. It's not an unusual sight. But in this case, with me so close to her, turned on *by* her, it's a different experience for her.

"I won't hurt you," I murmur, stopping in front of her, so close I can see the pulse beating in her neck. She lowers her eyes, but she still doesn't move away from me. With a steady hand, I reach out and cup the back of her neck, sliding my hand under her luscious hair, feeling it tickle the back of my hand.

The air suddenly goes heavy. I can barely take my next breath. The cloistered, humidity that is common at this time of night in midsummer builds in its intensity. Her breathing goes heavier as her lungs struggle to find the air they need.

"Look at me," I whisper.

She raises her eyes to mine, her hand resting lightly on my upper arm, covering the tribal tattoo that I have there. I'm desperate to look at her body, her perfect tits, her shaven pussy that no man has ever tainted before. But I keep my eyes on hers. With my other hand, I tilt her chin up gently, leaning forward so that I can press my lips to hers. She moans softly as they connect with a heat that catches me off guard.

I'm not a kisser.

Yeah, I've kissed women before, early on, but since I discovered that I prefer my sex on the darker side, I've never laid my lips on another woman's since. That has to be ten years, easy.

This is natural. I'm drawn to her in this way. Instead of slamming her to the ground and claiming her, I want to be gentle with her. Show her that she doesn't have anything to be afraid of with me. I want to wait until she is ready to take the next step instead of demanding it.

It drives it home once again how different she is to the women I hook up with. They *want* to be dominated, they want to feel the pain, the humiliation, the rough fucking that I give them.

It makes me pause, but for all of a moment.

There isn't a Pack of Wolves the world over strong enough to drag me away from her now.

But I don't press her.

I dart my tongue out to lightly lick her tightly closed lips. She drops her head back further when I move my mouth over her jaw and down the side of her neck, needing to feel her pulse against my lips.

"Wait," she says breathlessly, placing her tiny hand on the wolf etched into my chest.

It's like an electric shock, like lightning has struck me.

I groan with restraint, but I don't move away.

"No!" she says and shoves on me with all the strength she has, which is nothing compared to mine. I don't move an inch, which causes her to jolt her head back, her eyes wide open and full of fear again.

"Bree," I whisper, but she ducks around me and runs off back in the direction of the compound.

I sigh and squeeze the bridge of my nose as I let her go. Following her will accomplish nothing, and I don't chase.

Incompatible.

There's no getting away from it.

She might be my Fated Mate, but we don't belong together.

That much is very clear.

Trouble is, she has affected me. Badly. My cock is demanding attention and my own hand isn't going to cut it.

I Shift quickly and race back to the compound, heading straight for Valerie's. I don't give a rat's ass if she is in there with someone else. She is going to let me use her, and that's all there is to it.

Shifting on her doorstep, I don't even have to knock.

She opens the door with an inviting smile, beckoning me inside. I follow, slamming the door behind me.

Chapter 12

Ryker

"You got a drink?" I growl, my voice hoarse with thirst.

"What's your poison?" she asks.

"Strongest stuff you've got." Fuck thirst, I need to go numb. I need this feeling deep inside me for Bree to go numb and then go away.

Val raises her eyebrow at me, knowing I don't drink heavily but pours out a glass of bourbon and hands it to me.

I down it in one gulp, resisting the urge to cough at the burn of it sliding roughly down my throat. I hold the glass out.

She pours more, eyes on mine.

I swallow that one just as quickly as the first and hold my hand out unsteadily for another.

Val smirks at me and takes the glass, handing me the bottle instead.

"On your knees," I mutter, placing the bottle to my lips. I

can't erase the trace of Bree's mouth against mine. This isn't working.

Val drops in front of me, and I finish off the bottle, knowing that I will pay for it in spades later, but I don't care. I just need to forget about Bree.

※

The next thing I know, the sun is streaming in through the windows, rousing me from a deep sleep.

My head is banging, and my tongue is stuck to the roof of my mouth.

"Mornin', Sunshine," Val chirps at me, thrusting a cup of hot coffee under my nose.

I sit up, still naked but covered by my own sheet. I glance around. I'm back in my own cabin. How did I get here? I don't remember a single thing after I took the bottle of bourbon from Val.

I frown at her. Did we fuck? I don't remember it if we did. I know I wanted it. I went to her to fuck away the desire that Bree riled up in me. She was on her knees in front of me and then...

I groan, my eyes fixed on her laughing ones as I fall back to the bed, forgetting about the coffee and spilling it all over the sheets.

"Shit," I exclaim and steady the cup, placing it heavily on the nightstand. "Not a fucking word of this to anyone," I snarl at Val, standing up and wrapping the coffee-stained sheet around me to preserve whatever dignity I have left.

She holds her hands up. "It happens," she says.

"I was tired..." I start lamely, but she shakes her head.

"You don't need to make excuses, stud. I'm not insecure enough to think it was me. It was definitely *you*," she jibes.

"Get out," I spit out, irrationally pissed at her. My dick not functioning last night when I really needed it to, is definitely nothing to do with her, or me. It's that fucking tiny black Wolf that plagues my every thought.

Val laughs. "I won't say a word, if you promise we'll try again later. I want to fuck the Alpha of this Pack."

"Don't forget who you're talking to," I say darkly. "No one fucks *me*."

She shrugs. "Whatever. Be at my cabin tonight or I go and tell everyone that the new Alpha can't get it up." She laughs again, waiting for my answer and I wish she was a guy so I could flatten her nose. As it is, that's not me. I might use females to satisfy the Wolf's dark appetite deep inside me, but I would never raise a hand to one. It's why this whole Bree thing has gotten to me. Well, that and the annoyingly obvious fact that she is tied to my future in a way that makes me shudder. How do I get away from that? Is there some sort of formal rejection or do I just keep my distance and find someone else? I wish I knew the answer, but I'm fucked if I know.

I stride forward and grab her by the arm. She squeals as I squeeze much harder than she expected. Dragging her to the door, I open it and shove her out roughly. I can see the desire in her eyes, hear her soft pant at the way I'm treating her.

"I said, get out," I snarl, clenching my fists.

Her usually brazen attitude deflates a little, and she nods quickly, turning on the porch to head down the steps. She felt the Alpha come out. So did I. She isn't dumb enough to fuck with that. Just as I'm about to shut the door, I freeze. I hadn't seen her before because Val was blocking the doorway but now that she's moved, all I can see is Bree standing stock still a few feet from the cabin, staring at me with an expression that I can't quite place. Disgust? Disappointment? Desire? Definitely not the last one.

I grimace at her and step back to slam the door as hard as I can without breaking it. She doesn't get to come here and judge me, the prissy little bitch. She can take her displeasure at seeing me with Val elsewhere. This Wolf isn't interested.

Liar.

"Fuck off," I mutter and turn as there is a knock at the door to yank it open, ready to give Bree a piece of my mind, but instead I come face to face with Hunter.

"Whoa," he says, taking in my thunderous expression and hungover state. "You stink like a bar floor after St. Paddy's Day," he adds, waving his hand about.

"Get lost," I growl and turn from him to grab a glass of water from the tap. My stomach rolls in protest as I gulp it down. I haven't eaten in a day or more. No wonder I passed out with my dick as soft as a piece of overcooked spaghetti. It makes me feel a bit better.

"Shift and go for a run," Hunter advises. "It's the best cure for a hangover and then when you get back, I need your head in the game."

I pull my face at the thought of Shifting. It makes me feel nauseous.

"Power through and trust me," Hunter says, taking in my hesitation.

"I need a shower," I mutter but then realize I have no water to take one. "Fuck," I complain. "Lake it is. What's up?" I add.

"We need to sit down and go over this investigation. We are getting nowhere. Fast."

"Shit," I mutter. Yeah, that needs my full attention. "Give me an hour," I state and head for the door, dropping the sheet on the bed as I pass. "Have food ready. I'm starving."

"Yes, boss," he says with a smirk and steps out of the way of the door. "Do it quickly. Prolonging the Shift will make you feel like shit."

"I already do," I tell him, but take his advice on board. This is the first and last time I ever drink enough to get drunk. It's just not fucking worth it. Even to try to forget.

Chapter 13

Bree

I don't even know what to feel about what I saw earlier. Sick mostly. Even though I knew he was hooking up with her, to see it wasn't something that I thought would hit me so hard. Maybe because of the 'moment' or whatever it was we shared in the clearing, I expected more from him.

Should have known better.

It's *Ryker*.

I'd gone there this morning to try to clear the air, to see what last night meant, but clearly it meant nothing. He tried to take advantage of me and when I shut it down, he went back to his whore.

Big, fat, *old* whore. I can't help the venom in my thoughts, but I don't know why I'm letting this bother me so much.

I sigh and dig in a little deeper with my trowel, angrily flicking the dirt up along with a weed, covering myself and Kane in soil.

"Hey," he grunts, brushing it off himself. "Not so rough."

"Sorry," I mutter, taking in his cute face covered in dirt as I brush my hair over my shoulder. I really should've tied it up. The heat is already bearing down, making me sweat.

He makes a non-committal noise and stands up to move away from me. I guess my sour mood is affecting him as well. I watch as he picks up a shovel and leans it against his leg while he strips off his shirt and wraps it around his waist.

I lick my lips, my breath coming in short pants. He has a really nice body and for my sins, I want it pressed up against me. It has more of an effect on me than Ryker's completely naked body did. Suddenly, all I can see in my mind's eye is Ryker's enormous cock. It's huge. I've seen dicks before, it's hard not to around here, but fully erect ones pointed in my direction was a new experience. I bite the inside of my lip and lower my eyes back to the ground. I have to stop thinking about Ryker and his dick.

"You're a really good gardener," I blurt out to Kane before he sticks the shovel in the ground on the other side of the patch of land we are clearing. I curse myself for my idiotic remark, my cheeks burning.

He frowns at me. "Thanks," he mutters and carries on digging.

I sigh again and go back to my task. He is difficult to talk to, or maybe it's just me. Maybe he just doesn't want to talk to *me*. The insecurity that falls over me, makes my hands shake. It doesn't surprise me. The only time a man wants to talk to me is to either mock me for being a virgin and saving myself for my mate or to mumble responses to my inane babble.

Except Ryker. He hears you.

That thought came out of nowhere and I shove it aside with another forceful dig into the ground.

I lick my lips again, trying to erase the feel of his mouth on mine. It did things to me that are wrong. All wrong. I look up and fixate on Kane's lips. They are full and pursed as he concentrates on his task. I want to stand up, march over to him, grab him and plant a kiss on him that he will never forget.

But I don't.

I can't move. I'm frozen in place with only my thoughts, not actions.

I'm pathetic.

I wipe the sweat out of my eyes with my arm and with a grim determination, I try again. "It's really therapeutic, gardening. Don't you think?"

He shoves his foot on the shovel and pauses to look up at me, his hazel eyes showing some signs of curiosity. "I do," he says. "Is that why you switched with Casey? Because you actually enjoy this, or did you just want to get out of cleaning duty?"

I blink at the harsh tone that he directed at me. I open my mouth, but nothing comes out.

He huffs at me and goes back to shoveling. He thinks I'm a shirker. I'm humiliated beyond belief. My hands are shaking even more now.

I need to say something, convince him that I'm not afraid of hard work but my throat has closed up and my breathing has gone ragged.

"I en-enjoy it," I stammer quietly, but I don't think it was loud enough for him to hear me, based on the fact that he completely ignores me.

This is a disaster.

I stifle a small groan and focus solely on digging up the weeds, flinging them far more roughly into the growing pile than I should be.

"Be sure to stay hydrated," he says after a few minutes, not even looking at me as he says it. "Working out here, we take regular breaks. Why don't you take yours now?" It's an order not a question.

He is trying to get me out of the way. *His* way. That much is clear.

"Sure," I mutter and stand up. I am hot, sweaty and thirsty. A quick drink and maybe a wash in the sink wouldn't go amiss.

I make my way back to my cabin, pushing the door open and stepping into the cooler indoors, actually feeling the slight breeze that is blowing the pretty voile gently in the windows.

I grimace at the pig sty that confronts me. Casey is such a messy person. It really irritates me in my hot and pissed off mood.

Casting a glance at the sink, I march with a grim determination to the bathroom, kicking off my shoes and stripping off my white tee and jeans in the process. If she can't even give me the courtesy of tidying up after herself, I'm not going to save the last of the shower water for her, even if it does make me a shitty host.

I step inside the small cubicle and turn on the tap, setting it to a lovely cool that makes me moan with delight as it hits my hot skin.

Closing my eyes, I stand there for a few seconds before I pick up the soap and give myself a quick wash, conscious of the sputtering which signifies the water is draining. We need rain. Desperately.

As I glide the soap in between my legs, I gasp, once again picturing Ryker's hard body next to mine. I let out a soft whimper and replace the soap on the dish. I slide my hands down my body until I find the spot that needs attention. I rub my clit gently, all the while seeing Ryker's intense gray eyes focused on mine, his expression full of desire, his lips on mine. I come quickly, my body shuddering under the trickle of cool water, my muffled moan loud in my own ears.

"Damn you," I mutter, removing my hand at the same time that the water runs out. "Damn you!" I say more forcefully. "Get out of my head!"

In a temper now at my own actions, regardless of whether I needed it or not, I turn off the shower and grab a towel roughly when I step out. I dry myself off harshly, rubbing my skin until it's raw. For a moment before the climax hit me, I wanted Ryker's hands on me. That is *not* okay. I can touch myself, there is no shame or harm in that. But wanting someone else to do it, especially the depraved new Alpha of our Pack definitely falls into the 'all wrong' camp.

It makes it even worse that I'm thinking of Ryker at the same time that I am trying to start something, anything, even just a conversation, with Kane.

"What have you done to me?" I ask quietly as I get dressed again, this time tying my hair up into a tight bun and grabbing a bottle of water on my way out. "Whatever it is, you need to leave me the hell alone."

I haven't convinced myself in the slightest.

Chapter 14

Ryker

Hunter was right. This was the perfect cure to my hangover. In human form, I swim with strong even strokes back from the middle of the huge lake. I've probably been gone way over an hour by now and I need to get back, even though I want to stay out here for the rest of the day. The day before yesterday, I could have. Today, not so much.

The responsibility, the change to my life weighs down on me, slowing me down as I reach the shallower water.

A group of female Wolves are gathered near the shore but not even the sight of one of them stripping naked to splash into the water draws my attention away from what I need to do. I'm totally losing it. Bree has made me lose myself in her and now I'm a useless male with a dick that won't work unless I'm thinking about *her*.

I shove her image aside, not needing to see it right now. I wade out of the lake, knowing that I've caught the attention of the females, but I ignore them and Shift, padding off back to the compound with a heavy heart.

When I arrive back at Hunter's cabin, I lope inside and Shift again. He is waiting for me with clothes and food.

"You are a prince among Wolves," I growl hungrily as I forego the clothing to pick up a huge sandwich and bite into it.

He chuckles. "Figured you'd be starving."

"Famished," I mutter with my mouth full. A couple of more bites and the first sandwich has disappeared, but it has barely touched my hunger. I give Hunter the courtesy of getting dressed now before I sit down on any of his furniture.

I slump into a chair at the small dining table that is filled with food and files. "What have you got for me?" I ask, picking up another sandwich.

Hunter sighs. "Not a whole hell of a lot," he replies and then spends the next three sandwiches explaining to me how far he *hasn't* got in the investigation of my father's murder.

An hour later, after I've sated my hunger and thirst, if not my need for a hard and fast fuck, I replace the last file, chucking it grimly onto the table.

"So, we're screwed, is that what you're telling me?" I ask.

He shrugs. "Not exactly. We've cleared everyone in the compound, which is *good news*, by the way, it just seems to point to an outside job."

"You think another Alpha did this to try to take over the Pack," I state, having come to the same conclusion.

"Yep," he says.

I frown at the thought of it. It's so insidious. I think I'd rather someone killed my father just because he was an asshole. "Winston?" I ask slowly.

Hunter shakes his head. "Nah, he's too old to be taking on

a whole new Pack and fighting you for the privilege. Besides, he and your dad had a mutual respect I believe was genuine."

"His son then?" But even as I say it, I don't believe it. Tyler is…weak. I truly believe that Winston will live forever just so that his Pack doesn't fall into his son's hands. "Nah," I say at Hunter's shaking head. "I don't think so either. So that leaves the Silver Peak Pack. They are the next closest, fifteen miles or so around the lake. Their Alpha is still fairly young, in his early fifties and has been in charge for only about ten years."

"I think it might be Jackson," Hunter agrees, sitting back and stretching his legs out. "His Pack is small, and he has big ambitions."

I chew the inside of my lip while I mull that over. "So that means if he *did* kill my dad somehow, he is also after me."

"Probably," Hunter says, matter-of-factly. "Why do you think I made all of this food with stuff I got from Eddie in the next section over?"

I raise an eyebrow and snort with amusement. "Fucking idiot," I mutter. "I won't change how I live."

"You sound too much like Jefferson when you say things like that," he says, face creased with a fierce frown. "Don't be a dick, Ry. Take this seriously."

I sigh. "I am," I say, rubbing my face with my hand. "Okay, two things to figure out. If this is true and how did he do it?"

"Jefferson went there a few months ago. Jackson gave him a bottle of Scotch…maybe he only just opened it."

"Jesus," I mutter.

"We can't go there and ask him outright. It would start something that I don't think you are ready for," Hunter says seriously. "We need a sneaky tactic…"

"How about the Recruit?" I ask, interrupting him. "We are due out in a few months before fall ends. I know my dad used to moan that Jackson always wanted to buddy up on our

Pack name for better pickings. If we go over there and offer to buddy up this year, we can scope out his place and attitude. Maybe if he thinks he will get better quality Wolves interested in his Pack because of us, he might think twice about killing off another Alpha. *If* he did it, of course," I add as an afterthought. He is already guilty in my mind. It all seems to slot into place.

"It's a good idea. Especially if *you* go on the Recruit as normal. At least for a few days. Show your face. They know who you are out there, it's more likely to bring out those interested in joining a Pack this year. We are as desperate for new blood as we are for rain right now. The baby boom eighteen years ago has suddenly landed at your doorstep, you need to get those Wolves thinking about mating."

"Tell me something I don't know," I mutter, thinking once again about Bree. She is consuming my thoughts, which is pretty much ruining my day. Actually, this entire conversation is ruining my day. I don't want to leave even for a few days. I sure as shit don't want to bring back a male that Bree takes a liking to and decides to mate with.

"You have to go, Ry," Hunter states, seeing my reluctance. "I get that you don't want to leave so soon after becoming Alpha, but Jackson's motives aside, we need the Recruit to be successful this year. Last year was dismal to say the least."

I don't disagree.

"Fine, a few days but no more. You have to stay here though this time, so find me someone who will have my back to come with."

"You know I will," he says. "Now, we will go to Silver Peak tomorrow, so go about your day, but don't eat or drink anything that I didn't make for you."

I give him a sour look. "You sure know how to ruin a man's day with all your doom and gloom."

Hunter chuckles.

"How're you doing?" I ask him then.

He sighs. "I'm okay. I guess the signs were there for a while, I just didn't want to see them."

"You going to go after my sister?" I ask the question I've been dying to know the answer to for the last day.

Hunter's cheeks go red, and he coughs and splutters. "Too fucking soon, asshole," he chokes out, but I can see right through him. Yes, he will go there when he thinks an appropriate amount of time has passed. Makes me wonder how serious he was about Casey to begin with. If he was holding a candle for Stevie all these years, then it's better that they split now rather than when it was too late.

"You can, you know," I comment idly. "I won't stop you."

"Fuck's sake," he mumbles and stands up. "Get out," he adds and marches over to the door to open it for me to see myself out.

"Fine. A guy can take a hint," I say, also standing up and heading for the door. "I'm just saying…"

"Go!" he roars at me, still not looking me in the eye.

I smirk at him and slap him on the back as I head out onto the porch and down the steps. He slams the door behind me, and I let out a loud laugh, knowing I've riled him up good and proper.

Almost straight away, a large male Wolf approaches me. "Ryker," he says, getting straight to the point. "Just got back from town. They say a storm is rolling in from the north."

"Thank fuck," I reply to his enthusiastic nod. "We need to make sure that everyone knows and catches what they can if we do get some rain."

"On it," he states and lumbers off.

I stare up at the clear blue sky, not a cloud in sight. It's a long shot, but this dry spell has to end sometime. Why not today?

I head off to my mom's place first to make sure she is

prepared and then onto Stevie's and my other sisters before I make it back to my place several hours later. The entire compound is on edge, waiting for the rain, hoping and praying that it falls, even just a few drops.

I sit down on my porch steps, taking a breather after the heavy work of opening up all the tanks to catch as much water as we can. It's not like there's much left to evaporate quicker, so this is the most effective way to be prepared at the hint of rain.

I glance up again and offer up a silent plea that on my second day as Alpha of this Pack, something will actually go right.

Chapter 15

Bree

Shoving a few loose tendrils of hair out of my eyes, I curse this day. Stuck up a ladder, struggling with the lid on these blasted rain tanks is not how I wanted to spend today. Although gardening with Kane wasn't exactly going according to plan either. I was almost grateful when the rain alert resounded through the Pack.

"Dammit," I mutter, when the wrench slips off the bolt for the hundredth time.

"Need some help?"

The deep, unexpected voice down below startles me. "Ah!" I cry out and to my horror, my foot slips, plummeting me to the ground.

I brace myself for impact, but instead fall into a pair of muscular arms.

"Saved again," Ryker comments, not letting me go, but instead tightening his hold on me.

"Get off me," I growl, struggling in his arms.

He chuckles and lets me go, propping me up on my feet.

"What do you want?" I ask, irritated with the humidity, on edge by his presence and anxious about the storm. If it doesn't hit today, we are sunk. There won't be another storm forecast for a while in my limited experience.

I avoid his eyes. I can't look directly at him, or things start to happen to me that I don't like. I stop thinking and that is not good around him. He will hurt me, that much is obvious.

He reaches out to take the wrench from me. "I'm here to help, Bree," he says with a slight reprimand. "Take it."

"I can do it myself," I insist. I don't need an alpha male to sort my DIY out. And I especially do not need *the* Alpha male to do it.

"You seemed to be struggling," he says, looking up at the tanks. "And we need those lids off."

I huff at him. He's an ass. "Fine. Have at it. I'm only struggling because your dad tightened them up last time."

The brief glance I give him lets me know I've caught him off-guard with that statement. The realization dawns on his face in the next second though.

"My dad looked out for you," he says quietly. "Why won't you let me do the same?"

I clench my jaw and look away. I was always grateful for Jefferson's visits after my parents left. He *did* look out for me, especially in the beginning. He stopped coming around as much when I got older, but I know it wasn't because he couldn't be bothered with me anymore. He was letting me stand on my own two feet.

"I don't need anyone to look out for me," I say, just this side of coldly. It's mean of me, but I need him to back up. He is too close; he is taking over the way my body reacts and the way my brain thinks.

"Well, I'm here now," he says matter-of-factly, striding

past me and up the ladder with all the grace of the Alpha Wolf he is.

Putting my hands on my hips, I glare up at him. He already has the top off the first tank and jumps down the ladder, from the top, clearly showing off. I roll my eyes at him as he grins at me.

"Next!" he says and grips the ladder, lifting it easily and moving it to the next tank.

Just as he is about to shimmy up, Kane rounds the corner saying, "Casey asked me to come by and help you with the tanks..." He stops and looks up at the Alpha, halfway up the ladder. "Oh, you don't need me."

My heart literally stops beating in my chest. "Wait!" I call out as he turns. "Ryker was just leaving. He has to go and check on Violet, don't you, Ryker?" I grit out, giving him a death stare, not to mention a perfectly valid excuse to leave. Vi lost her mate only a few months ago. There is no way the seventy-year-old female Wolf is going up a ladder to loosen lids and not a single male Wolf on this compound would let her. I just hope he hasn't already been there.

Ryker's intense gaze boring down on me, unnerves me. "Actually, I was with Vi before I came here," he states, the ice tinging his tone. "You think I'd put your needs over hers?"

Ouch.

Okay, that hurt. I knew he would hurt me, but I didn't think it would be today with words. I lower my eyes, knowing that I've crossed a line, but I need him to leave so that I can spend some more time with Kane. He has fallen into my lap and I'm not sending him away so that Ryker can dominate this situation.

"Yeah, okay," Kane mutters, clearly this is the last place he wants to be, and I don't blame him. The atmosphere is seriously uncomfortable.

"Here," Ryker says and throws the wrench to Kane. "I do have somewhere else I need to be."

Kane catches it easily as Ryker leaps down from the ladder. I swallow loudly and step back as Ryker presses past me. He doesn't say another word as Kane goes up the ladder, but when he reaches the corner of the cabin, he turns back around. I clench my fists, ready for his parting shot, but it isn't me he speaks to.

"Kane," he says, looking up at the Omega Wolf. "The Recruit is being brought forward this year. I need you on the road with me."

My eyes shoot to Kane.

He stops what he is doing for a moment but then resumes loosening the bolts. "Oh? Why is that then? My skills are put to much better use here when the Recruits make it to base."

"I know that and usually I wouldn't disagree, but this year we need a successful Recruit. I think your skills will be better at the forefront this year."

Kane mulls it over as my mouth goes dry. He can't refuse our Alpha. He is going to agree and leave for several months. I want to interrupt and say that he can't go, but who am I to get in the middle of this?

Simply no one.

I am no one special and my opinion is about as low on the chain as it can get.

"Sure," Kane says, after a beat. "If you think that's where I'm best suited..."

"I do," Ryker states. "This year."

The last two words were said directly to me.

My tongue is stuck to the roof of my mouth. I dip my head to get away from his thunderous expression. He is fully aware of what he is doing and that is getting Kane away from me.

But why?

Why does he have this need to have me to himself? We are about as incompatible as they come. I should be flattered that the new Alpha has taken a liking to me, but all it does is make me uncomfortable and wish the ground would open up and swallow me whole.

"Let me know the details," Kane says, dropping off the ladder with a sexy agility that takes my breath away. Ryker did it to show off, whereas Kane put no thought into it.

"Will do," Ryker says and saunters off, disappearing around the side of the cabin and lifting some of the tension in the air.

"Thanks," I mutter as Kane moves the ladder to start on the freshwater tank that connects to the drinking water tap.

"Filter need changing while I'm up here?" Kane asks absently.

"No, Jefferson did it a few weeks ago," I reply.

He nods and then carries on with his work in silence.

I grimace at him and then where Ryker disappeared.

I stand awkwardly around while Kane finishes up and then waves to me as he too leaves me alone after passing me the wrench.

"Thanks," I call out again, feeling like a fool. What am I doing? I don't even know anymore.

"Have you been for my top yet?" Casey asks, striding over.

I frown at her. "No. Last night was...stressful and I've been busy today, in case you hadn't noticed."

"Yeah, real busy," she says with a smirk. "I sent Kane here to you as the swap for my top. So will you go and get it please?"

The sweetness in her tone only just covers up her irritation.

My frown increases. She isn't a very nice person at all. Was she always like this and I didn't see it, or did she just use me to get away from Hunter and have somewhere to stay?

"I'll go now," I mutter but only because I want this non-issue to be put to bed. It's a top, for goodness's sake. Why is she being such a bitch about it?

"Great," she says brightly. "Hunter is helping out over in the south sector so you can slip in, grab it and get out before he comes back."

"You want me to break in?" I ask incredulously.

"It's hardly breaking in," she scoffs. "The door is always open."

Well, that makes it better then.

I push past her to throw the wrench in the toolbox and close it up. I bend to pick it up and head around to the side to place it back into the outdoor cabinet.

"Fine," I mutter and stalk off, not caring that I'm being rude, and still reeling from Ryker's overbearing attitude. Casey's demand for her top is ridiculous. It's a *fucking* top. But I said I would get it, so I will and then I will hand it to her and ask her to pack it, along with the rest of her shit, up and get out of my cabin.

Maybe.

Chapter 16

Bree

I hastily mount the steps to Hunter's cabin. It belatedly occurs to me why Casey didn't come herself if she knew he wasn't here? What is she up to? It gives me a massive case of the pause. But then I grit my teeth and reach for the door handle. If I go back there without it, I will never hear the end of it.

The handle turns and I call out quietly, "Hunter?"

Nothing.

I look over my shoulder, feeling like I'm being watched and slip in quickly. I don't even know where I'm supposed to be looking but decide the dresser is the most obvious place. I open the drawers one by one, rifling through the neatly folded clothes until I find the pink top at the bottom of Hunter's underwear drawer. I pull it out gingerly, not wanting to disturb his boxers any more than I have to. He is meticulously tidy, just like me. He will notice if anything is disturbed. Makes me wonder how he ever coped with Casey's pigsty mess.

I grip the top in my hand and shove the drawer closed. Making my way back to the door, I listen for signs of someone on the other side, but all is quiet, so I open the door and peer out.

Seeing the coast is clear, at a rapid rate, I leave the cabin, shutting the door quietly and racing down the steps and back to my cabin, not stopping until I burst in the front door, panting with fear that someone is going to come and accuse me of burglary.

"Did you get it?" Casey asks as soon as she sees me.

"Here," I snap at her and fling the top to her. "Don't ask me to do that again."

Casey giggles and flings it back to me.

I wasn't prepared, so I don't catch it. It lands on my head, so I yank it off in fury.

"It's for you," she says and sits on the sofa, propping her legs up on the coffee table.

"What?" I spit out. "I don't want it."

"Maybe you don't *want* it, but you need it, hunny," she says, her tone going sympathetic. "Your crush on Kane is cute, but you have to up the game play. You are not the only Wolf in this pack with eyes on the adorable Omega, and let me tell you, Bree, you need all the help you can get."

"What is that supposed to mean?" I ask, my cheeks flaming with annoyance at hearing that other females have their eye on Kane.

She stands up again and strides over to me, taking the pink top and holding it up. "You've got to show your assets off. These other females know how to play the game, they're flashing their tits at him every chance they get. You are all covered up like some kind of nun. Wear this next time you go gardening with him and guaranteed he will look twice. You've got an okay body under those baggy clothes, a nice rack and those sexy tats which are wasted. Use them to get what you want."

I blink at her, completely dumbfounded. *Use my body to get Kane to notice me? What the actual hell?*

She waggles the top in front of me, drawing my eyes to the sexy piece of pink fabric. It has thin straps and a really low-cut neckline, a few buttons hold the scraps together and it is totally *not* me, at all.

"Pass," I say and push past her. "Look, I don't really know what all of this was about, but I just committed theft to get that for you. Hunter had it in his drawers. He obviously wanted to keep it."

"Yeah, he probably did. He bought it for me. He loved seeing me in this," she says, glancing at it and then flinging it on my bed dismissively.

"And when he sees *me* wearing it?" I ask, because how can I not think he will go ballistic when he does. He already doesn't like me. I know he blames me for Casey leaving him, the last thing I want to do is prod the hurting Wolf. A *Beta* no less.

She shrugs. "I'll take the fall," she remarks. "Just wear the damn thing. Trust me, it will work." She waggles her own assets at me with a cheeky grin. "Now, are you going to be okay on your own if this storm hits?" she asks, a smidgen of concern dropping into her tone.

"Of course," I scoff. "I'm not a child."

"I know you aren't," she chides me just as if I were. "It's just I'm leaving so I want to make sure you'll be okay."

"Leaving?" I ask suspiciously. "To where?"

She glances over her shoulder conspiratorially. "Can't say," she whispers.

"And if something happens to you? How am I supposed to know where to find you?" I ask, losing some of my anger at her.

"I'll be fine," she says, waving her hand at me, "But if you must know, I'm going to the lake to meet someone."

My eyebrows shoot up. "In this weather?" I ask, already hearing the wind whipping around the cabin. Rain is definitely coming, and it will not go easy on us. Not that we want it to. We need everything it can give us.

She shrugs. "He wants to meet today. I'm not standing him up."

"And who is 'he'?" I press, getting worried.

She mulls it over for all of a few seconds, but she is obviously desperate to spill the beans.

"Tyler," she eventually whispers, leaning forward.

I frown at her. Tyler? I don't know a Tyler.

"Which sector does he live in?" I ask.

She rolls her eyes at me. "Tyler from the Ridge Pack. You know, the soon-to-be-Alpha." Her eyes are sparkling but it is clear that it isn't about the male but the title that has lit the fire in her.

I take that in for a few seconds, my frown deepening. "How long has this been going on?"

She shrugs, looking a little shifty. I know instantly that she has been hooking up with Tyler while she was living with Hunter. My stomach rolls and I feel a little bit sick. This female is awful, just awful.

"A few months," she mutters. "But that's why I had to leave Hunter. I didn't love him anymore, but Tyler..." She gazes off dreamily no doubt thinking about becoming Queen Wolf of the Ridge Pack in the future. I wouldn't hold my breath if I was her. I've heard that Winston is as tough as old boots and would rather hand his Pack over to *anyone* except his son.

Casey shakes her head to clear it. "So, I'll see you later, okay? And remember, this is between us girls." The warning in her voice is hard to miss.

"Whatever," I mutter, not really interested in her sordid games. I just feel bad for Hunter.

She waves at me and takes off, leaving me alone to contemplate all that she said about Kane. I'm not happy that he has other admirers, but it doesn't surprise me. Of course his quite calm, peacekeeping ways and sexy, *understated* attitude would've caught the attention of some of the female Wolves ready to think about mating.

I huff and turn to look at myself in the mirror.

Whipping off my baggy tee, I stare at my old graying bra covering my 'nice rack' and cringe. I desperately need new underwear but I'm too embarrassed to add it to the list and I won't go into town on my own, if I even had a way to get there. I glance at Casey's pile of clothes, but she is quite a bit bigger in that area than me, so I ignore the bra, as usual, and grab the top off the bed. I slip it on over my head. It's slightly baggy again because I'm smaller than Casey, but I can't deny that it looks sexy. I preen for a few seconds before I shake my head at myself. I could *never* walk out of this cabin in this top. It shows off the swell of my breasts and turning around to glance back over my shoulder, it shows off most of my tattoos as well. Casting a little look at the door, I creep towards it. The rain has started, which means most of the Wolves will be indoors now. What would it hurt to run outside in this outfit and run back in? No one has to see me, but I'll know that I did it.

I bite the inside of my lip and open the door. I race out into the pouring rain, a laugh escaping my lips as I get drenched almost immediately. I keep running until I'm in the middle of the communal area and then I just stand there, letting the rain fall down on me, the top clinging to my curves, feeling...free.

Chapter 17

Ryker

Throwing the last of the fire logs into a neat pile, I drag the waterproof covering over them. The shed has walls and a roof, but no door and only big open spaces for windows. I can't risk the logs getting wet in the rain that has started to pour from the sky. I pause, feeling my heart speed up.

With a frown, I straighten up and glance behind me. Something has caught my Wolf senses and I see what it is almost immediately.

Or rather *who*.

Bree.

She is dancing in the rain, wet through in a sexy pink top that is clinging to her gorgeous body, showing me the swell of her tits and her nipples puckered up as if inviting me to bite them.

I emit a low growl, fighting off the urge to Shift that struck me out of nowhere. I want to march out there and drag her inside, covering her up so that no other male can see what I'm seeing right now.

I can't believe that I ever thought she was just okay looking. She is a fucking goddess and soaking wet, laughing in delight as she spins around in the rain, her arms wide open, she is absolute perfection.

"Dammit," I groan as my dick stands to attention. It presses against my combat pants needing a release. It has been too long. I'm used to sex every night, but without her, it's impossible.

Never taking my eyes from her, I slowly reach up and unzip my pants. Pulling my painfully erect cock out, I start to stroke myself, watching her from a distance with her, completely unaware of my presence. How come I could sense her, but she couldn't sense me? Is it because I have realized who she is to me, and she is fighting it?

Knowing how potentially creepy this would appear to anyone who knew about it, I tug on my cock, my eyes on those pebbled nipples as she spins, imagining all the things I would do to her if she would only let me. The mere thought of breaking her virginity, claiming her as mine and only mine stiffens my dick even more.

I want her.

I need her.

I cannot stop until I have her.

She belongs with me. Fate has stated that and I'm not going to fight it no matter how incompatible we seem. I have to believe destiny wouldn't throw us together if it wasn't for a damn good reason.

She is mine.

"Mine," I growl softly, jerking off with more speed now, needing my release. "All mine."

My breathing is ragged, my heartbeat is thundering in my

ears as my fist gives me what I need to sate the danger that lurks beneath the surface.

"Fuck," I rasp as Bree stops twirling and just stands there, a beautiful, serene smile on her face.

She runs her hands into her hair with an embarrassed giggle and it's my complete undoing. I tug one last time and then with a low groan, I come against the inside of the shed, splashing my cum on the wooden wall wishing it was her face, her tits, her pussy.

That thought of coming all over her, marking her in such an intimate way consumes my thoughts. I have to accomplish this and soon before she and Kane fall into a relationship with each other. He isn't interested now, I could see that earlier, but she definitely is and what man in their right mind would refuse her?

Only a fool.

Bree darts off with a shriek of delight as the rain comes down even harder, flashes of lightning splitting the sky.

I stash my dick back in my pants and sigh. I have to make her see *me*. Somehow, I have to get her to look past the dickhead that I know I present to the world so that she can see what lies underneath.

I turn away and tie off the covering to ensure that the wood stays dry in this downpour and then race back to my cabin, arriving wet through to Hunter waiting on my porch with a suspicious looking bag.

"What's that?" I ask, eyeing it up.

"Inside," he says and indicates with his head that we should go in.

I shove open the door and kick off my wet boots. Grabbing a small towel, I dry my face and then fling it on the counter.

Hunter shuts the door and places the bag gently on the

table. "That," he points to it, "is the bottle of Scotch from your parent's place."

My eyes narrow at it. "And?" I ask the dreaded question. We had discussed him going for it. Before we can accuse anyone of anything, we need proof.

"It's half empty. As you know your mom doesn't drink so she's safe. I'm headed into town now. I know a guy, who knows a guy. He can test it for wolfsbane and then we will know if it was that or not."

I nod grimly. "Be back by tomorrow. I want to go over there and look that fucker in the eye before we make a deal with the devil."

Hunter nods and holds up the cooler bag. "Only eat and drink from this until I get back," he instructs.

"Yes, Mom," I drawl but give him a grateful smile for having my back.

He snorts and then fucks off, leaving me alone to contemplate the day's events. It occurs to me as I strip off my wet clothes that I can take a shower. I know enough about rainfall to know that there is definitely enough for a hot shower already with no sign of it stopping anytime soon.

It's a relief that hits me hard. I fully appreciate the weight that my dad carried every second of every day now. It makes me see him a bit differently.

"Shame you had to die, you old bastard for me to understand why you were such a dick to me," I mutter. Fact remains that he *was* a dick, but he was trying to toughen me up. I won't be as hard on my kid.

My kid.

Will I even have one?

With a sigh that my future now looms in front of me with a big ticking clock on it, I duck into the shower and hear the generator fire up as I turn the water on and all the way to scorching hot.

Chapter 18

Ryker

Later that night, I'm reading and trying to take my mind off tomorrow. Facing my father's potential murderer has unnerved me now that the prospect is looming.

A knock at the door brings a welcome relief from my own thoughts. I climb off the bed and pad barefoot over to the door, pulling it open.

I sigh instantly.

Val is kneeling in front of me wearing hardly anything, a spiked collar with a leash attached to it, around her neck.

A few days ago this would have made my dick stand up but now, all it does it annoy me.

"Get up," I growl at her.

She shakes her head.

"That's an order," I say quietly, knowing that she can't refuse. The depraved part of her that drew me towards her in the first place won't allow it.

"I want to play," she pouts as she reluctantly gets to her feet, her huge tits falling out of her skimpy vest top.

I barely glance at them and focus on her eyes instead. She is more than a bit drunk and while that didn't bother me before because it brought out her wild side, now it just turns me off completely.

"Not interested," I say shortly. "Go home."

"Is this about the other night?" she asks earnestly. "I can get you up, Ry, just give me a chance."

Gritting my teeth, my hand clenched on the door frame, I glare down at her, trying to exude every ounce of Alpha Wolf into my attitude that I can.

It works.

She drops her eyes instantly and backs away.

"Don't come to my cabin again," I spit out. "If I need a cum dumpster, I'll come and find you," I add nastily and slam the door. I don't know why I'm so angry. Probably because she has offered me the one thing that I want, but I don't want it with *her*. No, I want to attach that leash to Bree and pull on it tightly while I fuck her.

Actually, I realize with a start, that I *don't* want that. I don't want to hurt or humiliate her in any way.

"Jesus," I mutter, shaking my head at myself. I've either gone soft or the Fated Mate sledgehammer has damaged my brain.

Either way, when there is another knock on the door, I yank it open with a look of fury on my face, until I see it's my mom.

Her disgusted expression tells me all I need to know about how much she saw a few moments ago.

"Have you lost your mind?" she asks, pushing past me and dumping a bag on the table.

"No, in fact, I seem to have found it," I retort, folding my arms over my chest.

She narrows her eyes at me. "You know your mate?"

I nod carefully, wondering how much to tell her.

"Please don't tell me it's that filthy whore out there," she says dryly.

"Ugh," I mutter and shake my head.

She brightens up considerably. "Let me guess then…Bree Henderson. Am I right? Tell me I am right. I know I am, so you might as well just admit it…" Her excitement over this is obvious and a little bit annoying.

"What makes you think it's Bree?" I ask instead.

"She's perfect for you," Mom replies simply.

I snort in disagreement. "She is completely imperfect for me. We are not compatible on any level."

"Only because you choose to live your life as if you don't have any responsibility to others. That's all changed now, Ryker. This will make you grow up and face facts."

"And what fact is that?" I rumble, getting pissed off.

"That you are Alpha now. This Pack belongs to you, and you need your mate to help you control the darkness that I know lurks inside you." She places her hand lightly on my chest, over my heart. "Your father had it until the day he died, but he didn't let it rule him, because he had me."

I don't even want to ask, let alone think about what that means. She removes her hand. "Bree is a good girl. Stronger than everyone thinks. Tell me she is your mate."

I let out a sigh. "She is. But she wants nothing to do with me."

"Do you blame the poor girl?" Mom asks incredulously. "She looks at you and sees you messing around with Val, who, by the way, messes around with anything with a dick dangling between their legs. She sees a man who doesn't have respect for women because of the way you treat them."

"I *do* have respect for women!" I bark out, pissed off that she thinks otherwise.

"I know you do, Ry. You have a good heart and a moral compass, but you let your dick rule and that has to change. You have to show Bree that there is more to you."

Seriously wish she'd stop talking about dicks.

I glare at her. "It's all very well saying that, but the damage is done. She is falling for Kane and maybe I should let her," I say, flinging my arms up into the air in surrender. "He is the type of man she deserves. Not me."

"*You* are Alpha of this Pack, Ryker," she says determinedly. "Don't let your insecurities talk you out of being the very best man, best *Wolf*, you can be. For Bree, the Pack and for yourself."

I turn away from her in exasperation. She isn't telling me anything I don't already know. I just don't know where to start with Bree. I've tried to be her hero, to save her, to protect her, *defend* her, but it's gotten me precisely nowhere except watching her from a distance with my dick in my hand.

There's that fucking dick thing again.

Mom is right. It rules my head. It has to stop. That isn't the way to Bree, but neither is anything else I've done. I just don't know.

"I hear you," I mutter as she's waiting for an answer. "But tonight, I need to focus on this meeting tomorrow."

She nods briskly when I turn back around. "You and Hunter really think it was Jackson?" she asks quietly.

"I don't know. I hope not, but who else and why? I need to look him in his eyes and see if he is a murderer," I snarl.

"Be careful," she says, opening her arms to give me a hug.

I return it, needing some comfort of the mom-kind. "I will," I promise and let her go. "We'll stop by when we get back."

She nods. "I have knitting club tomorrow afternoon."

I blink at her. "What does that have to do with anything?"

She gives me a sly look and shrugs vaguely. "Just some of us gals gathering to knit and talk about stuff."

"Okaay," I draw out, wondering why the fuck she's telling me this.

"Bree will be there," she adds, finally getting to her point.

"Do not mention me," I warn my mother. "Stay out of it."

"Hmm, but if your name comes up, I'm not going to ignore it," she says breezily, spinning on her heel and heading out of the door with a backward wave.

"Mom!" I call after her. "Mom!"

I stride quickly over to peer out into the dark rainy night. "Mom? Fuck! Don't you dare mention me!" I yell.

I hear her laughter come back through the air and grit my teeth. I'm done for. I should never have told her it was Bree.

I can see this is going to go from bad to worse with her nose stuck in the middle. I slam the door shut and walk back to the bed, sitting down and picking my book back up. But no amount of reading is going to distract me from everything that is going to happen tomorrow. I just hope not all of it ends up being a shitshow.

Chapter 19

Ryker

The following morning, I'm up bright and early, waiting for Hunter while I sip a hot cup of coffee. It's still pouring down outside, which is excellent news. We will be able to replace the lids on the rainsaver tanks later on, which will be a weight off my mind.

Frowning as my eyes catch the bag left on the table last night by my mom, I amble over and pick it up. I open it and peer inside.

Knitting stuff.

Remembering what she said about Bree, I bite the inside of my lip and have a bit of a root through. It's full of cute little baby clothes in a variety of pastel colors. This will be for the drive next week. Mom and her group knit all year round to sell the goods to the local craft market in town.

I drop it lightly back on the table. I don't have time to go over and deliver it to her, but she knows she can come and get it whenever she remembers she left it.

The door being pushed open makes me look up.

"Hey," Hunter says. "You ready?"

"Are you?" I ask, taking in his slightly disheveled appearance.

"Nothing a cup of coffee won't fix," he says, eyeing up my mug.

I hand it to him. He looks like he needs it more than I do. "Trouble?" I ask with a frown.

"Nah, just a busy night," he says before taking a big gulp of coffee.

"Did you get the results?" I ask hopefully.

He shakes his head as he swallows. "Too soon, but the plan hasn't changed. We go there and feel him out."

I nod. I agree. This needs dealing with for my own mind.

I scoop up the keys to the pickup and as we head out, Hunter says, "Jake'll be back at the weekend."

I brighten up at that news. It's been way too long since I saw my brother-in-arms. Second Beta of the Pack, he is a hotshot lawyer in the big city and one of the Pack's biggest donors. "Oh, good," I say.

"Also, Philippa will be returning indefinitely," he adds. "She needs to talk to you."

"About what?"

He rolls his eyes at me. "The books, obviously. She bases her series on this Pack. With your dad gone and you in charge, she needs to know, you know, stuff for her books." He shrugs.

"Oh," I say with a grimace. While I greatly appreciate Philippa's contribution to our society, as in she donates three quarters of her earnings to the Pack funds, I'm uncomfortable with being the Wolf she bases her character on.

"Needs must and all that," Hunter says, matter-of-factly.

"Mm," I mutter and climb into the pickup, shaking off the excess water from my arms. I look up at the sky. It is dark and still pouring down.

Hunter joins me, draining the last of his coffee and stashing the mug under the seat for the bumpy ride over to the Silver Peak Pack.

"More news," Hunter pipes up after we set off. "Winston has dealt with the Wolves who harassed Bree," he says.

"Oh?" I growl, gripping the steering wheel tighter as the fury surges through me at the reminder.

"Yeah, he kicked their asses, and by that, I mean literally. Two of them won't be rising and shining for a few days."

"Good," I snarl. "They got off lightly compared to if I'd gotten my teeth into them."

Hunter turns to stare at me.

I avoid his intense gaze.

"You seriously have the hots for her, don't you?" he says.

Clenching my jaw, I make a non-committal noise.

"I have never seen you so up in arms about, well, anything," Hunter continues incredulously. "You want to hit that up!"

I take offense on Bree's behalf at Hunter's crude comment. "It's not like that," I mutter.

"What?" Hunter says, putting his hand behind his ear as if he didn't hear me.

He did.

He's a dick.

"I said, it's not like that," I growl louder because he won't drop this now.

"Oh? Then what is it like?" he asks.

I throw him a death stare, one that should have him quaking in his boots, but he just laughs at me. "Oh!" he exclaims. "Like that is it."

"Shut the fuck up," I snarl at him.

"She's a conquest," he continues. "A virgin Wolf to add to your bedpost notches, yeah?"

I slam on the brakes, jerking us both forward and turn to

him. "Watch your fucking mouth before I smash it up and you can't speak for a week," I threaten, clenching my fist in his face.

He raises an eyebrow at me. "It was a joke, Ry. Jesus, what's got into you?"

He appears to be genuine, but I'm so riled up by that tiny black Wolf, I can't think straight.

I sit back in my seat and unclench. "She's my Fated Mate. Long Alpha story, but yeah, there you go. Okay? Happy now?" I huff out a breath and grip the steering wheel, slamming my foot back on the gas, which causes us to lurch forward straight into a pothole the size of this vehicle.

"Christ!" Hunter yells out, gripping the dash to steady himself. "Want me to drive?"

I ignore him and grimly slow down so that we can take this mountain road a little bit easier.

"Fated Mate, huh?" he asks after a minute or two has passed. "That's some declaration. How do you know?"

"I just know. So does my mother, apparently."

"Well, Maria is known for her foresight," Hunter comments idly.

"Mumbo jumbo," I mutter. "Point is, now that I'm Alpha, I have a Fated Mate and those stupid bitches have decided to pair me up with the one Wolf that is the opposite of what I want."

"How do you know that?" he asks a few seconds later.

"Know what?" I snap at him.

"That you don't want what she offers."

"She offers nothing, that's the point, fucker."

"So, you're basing this on the fact that she is a sweet girl who has decided to save herself instead of putting it out there for all and sundry to take for a test drive first? You are such a dick, Ry. Seriously."

I shoot him an incredulous look. "Are you joking? You

can't stand her and now you're defending her? Against *me*? Way to have my back, *brother*."

"I never said I couldn't stand her," Hunter points out, stabbing the dash. "I thought she might have had something to do with Casey leaving, but that was a knee jerk reaction. She is way too nice and mild to convince someone to be so hurtful."

"Great, well you go and mate with her then," I grumble, but the thought of Hunter and Bree's bodies twined around each other does a thing to me that makes me kind of murderous and I growl at him, gripping his shirt with one hand, while I keep the other on the wheel.

"Even look at her and I'll bite your head off," I threaten.

Hunter just laughs, so I let him go. He is impossible to intimidate. He's a fucking fucker.

"You've got it so bad. I love it, Ry. Honestly, this will be good for you. Give you a chance to prove yourself worthy."

"Too bad she wants nothing to do with me," I mutter.

"She will if you let your guard down with her. Show her the real you," Hunter says confidently.

"Problem is, I don't know how to do that," I murmur.

"If she is truly your one, you'll figure it out," he says and then we fall into a silence that lasts until we hit the road to the Silver Peak Pack but are forced to pull over as the road narrows too much to get a vehicle through.

I peer out of the windshield at the rain. "Guess we arrive wet and pissed off," I remark.

"Don't do anything rash, Ryker," Hunter says before I shove the car door open. "We need to figure this out the right way."

"I know," I mutter, knowing that if I even get a whiff of murdering bastard from Jackson, I'll probably kill him where he stands.

If he is responsible for this, he is the one that has thrown my life into chaos before I was ready for it.

It's a double whammy and whoever did this, will pay in pain and blood.

I guarantee it.

Chapter 20

Ryker

We trudge through the mud, getting soaked to the skin to make it to the compound. I take a moment to appreciate their setup here. It's pretty impenetrable except from the way we've come in on foot.

Stopped at the gates, Hunter obliges the request to hand over his weapons, but keeps hold of the .22 in his right boot. Not as grizzled and jaded as Jim, the young Wolf on duty doesn't question him, so we head in armed and more than a little anxious. The hostility is noticeable, but no one bothers us.

Yet.

"Ryker," Jackson says, striding towards us.

I take in his graying brown hair and blue eyes, searching them but coming up with nothing so far that would suggest he is a piece of filth murderer.

"Jackson," I say and take the hand he offers, squeezing it harder than is socially acceptable.

He raises any eyebrow but then smiles and retracts his hand, shaking it out. "Some grip you've got there," he jokes.

I grimace at him but then at Hunter's throat clearing, I turn it into a smile. "You got somewhere we can talk? We are piss wet through here," I say.

"'Course," he says and leads us away. "Needed though, no?"

"Definitely," I agree, deciding small talk will do for now. "I was bathing in the lake yesterday."

Jackson snorts. "Two weeks ago here."

The obvious passive aggressive tone makes me clench my teeth. He is referring to our bigger tanks, which signifies the bigger wealth of the Pack.

He leads us silently into a big mess hall and indicates we should sit. "So, what brings you here?" he asks, his eyes landing briefly on Hunter as he sits next to me but doesn't acknowledge him with words.

"Well, you must've heard about my dad," I dive straight in and pause.

Jackson nods, adopting a sorrowful expression that I narrow my eyes at. "It was a shock. Thought that old bastard would live forever," he remarks. "I was sorry to hear it, son. But I hear you've stepped up good."

I nod, recognizing the compliment.

"But you didn't just come here to tell me news I already knew, so what's up?" Jackson asks directly, sitting back and folding his hand over his stomach, seemingly relaxed, but I can see that he is ready to pounce if he gets a whiff of danger from us.

"I've come with a proposition," I say, staring into his eyes. So far, I don't see any sign of deception, guilt, fear of being called out or fear of me. That speaks volumes.

"Oh?" he asks when I stop to search his eyes some more.

"Yeah, the Recruit," I say. "I know you asked my dad in

the past to buddy-up on the Recruit, but he always refused. I'm here to open that up, see if you wanted to join us this year?"

Surprise registers on his face. Of all the things he must've thought from the time his guys radioed him that we were on our way up to now, that wasn't one of them.

He sits forward, dropping his hands on the table in front of him. "Oh?" he asks, clearly stumped.

I nod. "Yeah. Last year was dismal for all of us. We stand a better chance if we go out together."

"I don't disagree," he says slowly. "Your dad was always so precious about it though. Why the change?"

"I'm not my dad," I grit out, earning his respect thrown my way.

"No, you're not. You have a good head on your shoulders, Ryker. Thank you for the offer. I would be honored to join you on the Recruit this year."

His sincerity is genuine. I can see it; I can sense it. There is absolutely nothing there with regard to him murdering my dad.

I nod. "We're going early. End of summer. You'll be ready?"

Jackson nods eagerly. "We'll be ready."

"Good," I say and stand up, Hunter following my lead. "I'll send word with a few days' notice. That cool?"

Jackson nods. "Thanks, Ryker. You have no idea how much it means that you came with this offer," he says quietly.

I suddenly feel bad for doubting him.

"Not a problem," I grit out and turn, catching Hunter's eyes. He is feeling the same way.

We head out of the mess hall silently and back down the road to the pickup, via the guards to get Hunter's weapons.

When we climb in, Hunter sighs. "Not him."

"Nope," I agree.

"Dammit," he mutters.

I turn the key in the ignition and turn the pickup around.

"Fuck!" I roar suddenly, punching the steering wheel and busting my knuckles wide open. "Fuck!"

"We'll figure it out, Ry," Hunter says quietly, knowing we have hit a huge dead end.

"Yeah," I mutter with a sigh and set off.

The only Wolf I want to be with right now, doesn't want me within ten feet of her. It worsens my feeling of desolation.

I fall into a dark mood that Hunter is all too aware of and stays out of my way, not saying another word until we arrive back home.

"Don't do anything stupid," he says quietly before he climbs out of the pickup.

I ignore him, feeling myself sink even further under the blanket of darkness.

Chapter 21

Bree

I haven't been looking forward to this week's knitting club visit for two reasons. One, I have no idea what to say to Maria about the loss of her husband. It's now been several days without me saying anything at all because I'm so awkward about it, and secondly there's the whole Ryker situation. Whatever that actually is. I have no idea, but he's seen me naked, twice. I've seen him naked and there was the whole kiss and touching thing in the shower and now I have to face his *mom*.

Awkward doesn't even cover it.

I suck in a breath and knock lightly on the door to Maria's cabin.

She opens it with a bright smile, which I wasn't expecting, and beckons me inside. "Bree, honey. Come in."

I clear my throat. "Maria, I'm so sorry about Jefferson," I mutter, eyes on the floor.

I feel her hand land on my shoulder and look up. "Thank you, love," she whispers, but there is a finality that makes it impossible to continue the conversation, to my relief. Giving her a shaky smile, I take a step inside, clutching my knitting bag.

"Are you doing okay?" she asks with concern.

"Me?" I choke out, surprised. "Y-yes, I'm fine."

She nods sagely as if she knows something I don't. "I know Jefferson looked out for you. If you ever need anything, anything at all, you can come to me. No questions asked."

A small frown drops over my face, but I quickly turn it into a smile. "Thanks," I say, even though her words have shaken me a little bit, like she's expecting some odd request to tumble from my lips.

"Do you need anything, Bree?" she asks bluntly.

I think of my tatty underwear but shake my head, my cheeks going slightly pink.

Maria narrows her eyes at me. "What is it?"

"It's nothing," I insist, shaking my head. "I'm fine." I walk past her and drop my knitting bag on the table, wishing everyone else would hurry up and arrive.

"Okay, if you're sure…" she says, leaving it hanging there in case I wish to change my answer.

Suddenly, the thought of Ryker seeing my old saggy panties and gray bras makes me cringe so badly, I blurt out, "I need new underwear!" The blush that hits my cheeks is furiously hot and I shake my head, floundering like a goldfish out of water. "It's no big deal…" I stammer. "I'll figure it out."

"What do you mean figure it out?" Maria asks kindly. "If you need new clothes, Bree, you are entitled to order some. The budget is there for a reason."

"I know," I wail, turning my back on her. "I'm just…It's embarrassing, that's all…" I feel like such a fool.

"Oh, honey, I hear you. Do you want me to order them for you? Have them delivered here?"

I gulp back the tears that are threatening to pop and turn back to face her. "You'd do that?"

She beams at me. "For you? Anything. Now, tell me your sizes and what you want." She scoops up a notepad and pen.

Feeling so completely grateful, I mumble out my sizes and order of plain white cotton matching sets. Several, so that I can throw all of mine out, or burn them even.

"Done," she says. "I'll let you know when they arrive."

"Thank you," I murmur. "I'm sorry for putting this on you. I've just never been able to get past someone knowing what's under my clothes…"

Except Ryker. He's seen everything you have to offer, girl.

I shove that annoying, persistent thought away.

"Now, let's see what you've been up to this week," Maria says with a nod and thankfully, we get down to knitting talk as the others arrive. I find it strange that she knew something was bugging me and even though it is something so small and fairly insignificant, I feel like a weight has been lifted off my shoulders, now that she has taken on the responsibility for me. I don't even care how that makes me sound.

Sometime later, Maria smiles and stands up, walking over to the door to open it before anyone has knocked. I peer up curiously, wondering how she knew, but that falls into the 'duh' camp when I see it's Ryker.

I duck my head back down, pulling my baby blanket up higher in the hopes that it will provide me with some cover.

No such luck.

I can feel his eyes on me. It forces me to look up. It's magnetic. My eyes are drawn to his in an inexplicable way that takes my breath away.

He is not happy.

Thankfully, that has nothing to do with me.

He tears his gaze from mine and grimly whispers something to his mother.

She tenses up but then shakes her head and whispers something back.

He huffs out a breath, looking away and nodding.

"Oh!" Maria exclaims suddenly, drawing all attention to her, as if we weren't all sneakily spying on her conversation, anyway. "I left one of my bags at yours last night, Ry. Bree, be a dear and go back with Ryker to bring it back to me?" She turns to give me an expectant look, giving me absolutely *no* choice but to stammer a response.

"Uhm, s-sure," I mutter, putting my knitting down carefully and standing up.

"That's fine, Mom," Ryker interjects before I can take a step. "I'll get it."

"No, Bree can go with you," Maria insists brightly, giving me a smile and sidling over to back that up with a small shove. "She was just saying she could do with stretching her legs."

Was I?

I glare at her, wondering what she is doing, not enjoying the spotlight on me at all. A few of the older women are smirking behind their knitting and it becomes obvious that she is trying to set me up with Ryker for some inexplicable reason. She must know we don't fit.

"Fine," I say grimly, because if I know one thing about Maria, is that she does not let things go. It's easier to give in than to fight.

"Whatever," Ryker mutters under his breath, clearly not happy to be lumbered with me, but knowing his mother's persistence.

He turns on his heel and heads back out into the rain, not waiting for me to catch up. Feeling like an idiot, I jog to catch up and fall into step beside him, which doesn't last long as his stride is twice the length of mine, so I end up jogging next to him.

"Fuck's sake," I mutter and slow down. I rarely revert to cursing but this man is infuriating!

"Sorry," he mumbles and slows his pace. "Not used to walking next to short shits."

"Hey!" I growl, clenching my fists. I can't help my five feet, two inches of height.

I see him give me a sidelong smirk, which makes me grit my teeth.

We carry on in silence, me wishing I was anywhere except here when we finally make it to his cabin. He goes up the steps ahead of me and reaches for the door handle.

He stops dead.

I bump into his back, feeling the heat radiating off him even though he is, we both are, wet through with the rain.

"Wait," he whispers and shoves the door open.

Curiously, I peer around him and see that his cabin has been turned upside down. "Oh my," I mutter.

"Stay back," he growls, throwing his arm up to stop me from ducking inside. Not like I was going to. I don't run into danger. I run *from* it and I'm not ashamed to admit it. I'm about to do exactly that, when a low growl freezes me to the spot.

The next few seconds go by as if in slow motion. A huge gray Wolf launches itself at Ryker from inside the cabin. He puts his arm up to defend himself, receiving a very nasty bite in the process. I stumble backwards, unable to move much more than that until I'm knocked off my feet by the Wolf lunging past me, sending me sprawling onto my ass on Ryker's front porch as he spins in fury, fists clenched but his face softens as soon as he sees me on the ground.

"Go!" I urge him, looking after the Wolf.

He glances briefly where the Wolf has now disappeared

into the darkened day and then back at me. He holds his hand out to help me up. "Are you okay?" he asks.

"I'm fine!" I snap. "Go and get them!" I gesture madly after the intruder Wolf.

He hesitates but doesn't move. "They're long gone," he mutters. "Are you sure you're not hurt?"

I glare at him. What is he doing? Why is he standing here worrying about me when his cabin has been tossed by a stranger and he could be tracking them down as we speak?

"I said, I'm fine," I grit out, dusting my hands off on my bruised ass. Yeah, okay, my pride has taken a bit of a hit but otherwise I'm of sound body.

He grimaces at me and grabs my elbow, leading me inside the cabin and out of the chill that being soaking wet has brought. He gently hands me a towel, all the while scoping out the place.

I dry off my hair, knowing I should leave but I can't. I'm rooted to the spot when his eyes land on me again.

"You could have been hurt," he muses.

"But I wasn't. You were though. You need to Shift to sort that," I point out.

He glances at his bleeding arm. "It's fine," he says dismissively. "I'll walk you back to my mom's and then come back to walk you back to your cabin later."

"No, I'm fine," I say again.

"Bree," he growls. "You could've been hurt. I'm not taking a chance with you."

I frown at him. "What does that even mean?" I ask quietly.

He growls softly and turns from me, running his hand through his wet hair. Keeping his back turned, he says, "You aren't ready to hear it."

"Hear what?" I ask, getting annoyed.

"Just trust me, Bree. As much as I want to get into this

with you right now, you need to get back to my mom's where you'll be safe."

"I'm safe here," I say stubbornly.

That gets him to spin back to me and stride over, lightly taking my arm and shaking me. "No, you are not. We startled that Wolf, but they could just as easily have gone for you. I would never forgive myself if anything happened to you because of me."

"Why?" I whisper, staring up into his gray eyes and suddenly wanting him to kiss me so badly, I'm aching for it.

He must see it.

He has to.

Will he act on it?

He doesn't.

His face closes off.

"I wish you were ready to hear it, but you aren't," he states almost coldly. He lets me go and leans over to pick a bag up from the floor. "Here. I'll walk you back to my mom's."

"No!" I screech at him unexpectedly, startling both him and myself. "I want you to tell me right now Ryker, what is going on? Why do you have this sudden interest in me when a few days ago you barely even glanced in my direction? You make these comments to me, you act like you care about my well-being, *kiss* me, and then you go off and hook up with your little Wolf slut right after that..." My breath is coming out in small pants, I'm so worked up. He has worked me up into a ball of confusion and irritation at his attitude.

"I didn't hook up with anyone after that kiss," he says so softly, I barely hear him. "I couldn't..."

He trails off and shakes his head, rubbing his face with his hands. "I can't do this right now, Bree."

"Fine, then we don't do it all," I spit out, furious that he is giving me the brush off after I've asked him to fill me in on what is going on with him. I hate games and he is playing me for an absolute fool right now.

I shove past him, stalking off into the rain, clutching the bag close to me, realizing that this can't get wet. Cursing Ryker, I wrap the towel I seem to still be clutching around it and race towards Maria's, the feeling like I'm being watched unnerving me, but not enough that I turn back with my tail between my legs to ask Ryker to walk me over. I'm a grown Wolf. I don't need a chaperone, especially one with such intense gray eyes, brooding manner and more complications than you can shake a stick at.

I leap up the steps to Maria's porch and push the door open, wet, pissed off and I don't care who knows about it.

Chapter 22

Ryker

For the second time in a few short minutes, I'm left to watch as a Wolf I really need to chase gets away. Every cell in my body is screaming at me to race after Bree, grab her and kiss like she has never been kissed before, but I don't.

I can't.

She has absolutely no idea that this bond between us exists. It is obvious that she is in the dark about what this heat between us is. I want to tell her, but all I will end up doing is scaring her off if I throw around words like Fate and destiny. She needs more time to come to terms with the connection that we have. More time to get to know *me* and not just the idea she has of me. Okay, which is pretty damn bad. I get that. I have a lot of work to do before she is even close to being ready to accept me. I slam the door shut and hiss as the pain echoes through my arm from the bite. I probably should Shift and get rid of that, a perk of being injured in human form is that a Shift will usually sort it out. I can kill two birds with one stone. I need to catch the scent of the Wolf that was in my cabin as well, and I can only do that as a Wolf. I strip off, throwing my clothes on the messy bed and relish the pain as my bones snap and reform into my Wolf shape.

Sniffing around, I know that I don't recognize the scent, so definitely not one of mine. It fucks me off on a level that I can't even comprehend that an intruder made it onto our land and into my cabin and no one even knew about it. Someone is going to get their hides torn strips off of and real soon.

I let out a low rumble as the door opens and Hunter rushes in, clearly having been on the receiving end of the news somehow.

Probably Bree and her fiery temper. Who knew she was such a firecracker? It turns me on in ways that make my mouth water. I want that temper directed at me more often so that I can see the fire in her eyes. I want to feel her nails raking over my skin when she slaps me with all the strength she has. I want her to fight me, bite me, claw at me...

Oh, I'm so fucked up.

"Ry!" Hunter yells when he sees me. "What the actual fuck happened?" He looks around, taking in the mess.

Needing to be in human form when I speak to him, I Shift back and chuck my clothes back on grimly before I face him. "Place was tossed. Don't recognize the scent. A stranger was here and could've hurt Bree."

I can't get past that. If she'd even a scratch on her, I would have committed Wolf murder on the spot.

"Yeah, I heard," he replies. "How did they get in?"

"Good fucking question," I growl. "I know we leave our woods side fairly open for access to the lake, so that's most likely where they came in. But they knew. They headed back that way."

"You didn't follow?" he asks with a confused frown.

"What's the point? The rain will have washed away their scent before I could track them and besides, I needed to make sure Bree was okay."

"Oh, she's okay all right. Spitting feathers over at Maria's right now. What did you say to her?" Hunter asks with a laugh.

"Fuck. Off," I spit out.

"Well, that will piss a woman off..." he jokes lamely but then holds his hands up when I take a step towards him.

"I was worried about her," I grit out. "She got all pissy about it. Fuck knows why? I mean, I wanted to make sure she wasn't hurt. I don't get why she was so mad with me."

"You chose not going after the Wolf to stay with her," Hunter says quietly. "Wow. You've been hit hard, haven't you?"

I want to rip his head off with my teeth, but he is serious, and he isn't wrong.

"She probably thought you were taking pity on her, or thought she needed defending. Some girls can get annoyed by that. Clearly, Bree is one of them, although it does kind of go against the image she presents..." He trails off, deep in thought.

"Don't think about her," I snarl. "Get your dirty thoughts away from her."

He snickers at me. "Oh, Ry. You need to sort this out. If she ends up rejecting you, the consequences will be far-reaching."

"Yeah? And what do *you* know about that?" I ask nastily.

He sighs. "I'll tell you a story, one that I'm only telling you because you need to hear it."

I sit heavily on the bed as he paces, wondering what the hell is going to say. I've known Hunter for over twenty years. I thought I knew everything about him. He definitely has a secret that he hasn't shared though, and I'm intrigued as to why.

"When your dad found me, he promised my parents before they died, he would never reveal my origins," Hunter says quietly. "They didn't want our Pack to find me. Well, the Pack we left. Ran from. My dad was Alpha and my mom his Fated Mate. I know all about how this shit works, Ryker. My mom told me one day when we were on the run, to make sure I was ready in case I ever became Alpha to another Pack. The bond is strong, Ryker. I don't need to tell you that. But what you do need to hear is that the rejection can be fatal. If Bree chooses not to accept you, or you her, it will eat at you, claw at your insides until you are nothing but dead in your heart. Sure, you could live and go on to be okay, and be with someone else, but you will never be happy. The Fates will ensure you live a life of misery and pain. Bree, on the other hand, isn't as strong as you are. She will suffer and unless you tell her what is going on, real soon, she might make the wrong choice. I've seen how she looks at Kane, all starry eyed and shit. You need to nip that in the bud and tell her how you feel. Tell her about the bond."

"And if I do that, what's stopping her from just accepting me because she wants to save her own skin?" I ask, stunned about Hunter's revelation. I had no idea he was in line to be an Alpha. I need to know more, like why isn't he? Why did his family run?

"Doesn't work that way," he says. "The Fates demand it be real."

"Jesus," I mutter, rubbing my hand over my face. "You're not leaving me much choice, are you?"

"Not if you care about her as much as you are acting like you do," he says.

"Why did your family run?" I ask bluntly.

He sighs and bends down to turn a chair right way up so

he can sit down. "My dad was challenged, and he lost. We would all have been killed if we'd stayed. He barely made it as it was..."

"Oh," I say and leave it at that. It is clearly painful for him. "I wish you'd told me before," I add on impulse. "That must've been tough."

He shrugs. "Is what it is. The Pack hunted us down, killed my folks but not before they reached out to your dad to save me. The rest you know."

"Fuck, Hunter," I mutter. "I'm sorry, man."

"No need. Ancient history. I've only told you so that you know that I know what I'm talking about. Go to her. It's the only way."

I nod slowly. Hesitantly.

He sighs and stands up again. "I'll find out who was in here and why, but it's not a leap to assume it has to do with your dad."

"Nope, no leap there," I agree.

"What do you think they were looking for?" he asks, going business-like again.

"Beats the shit out of me," I mutter. "Can't think of anything."

"Well, think some more. They risked coming here for a reason."

"Yeah."

He nods and leaves me alone to tidy up this mess and to try to think of why someone would toss the place. I give up after a few minutes. Everything Hunter said is weighing heavily on my mind. Will my need to not hurt Bree, end up hurting her even more? I don't think I have a choice but to sit her down and tell her who she is to me. I slide down the wall by the door and drop my head in my hands. This day has been the worst and I just need to forget. It's then that I look up and see the half empty bottle of Jack that I'd stashed under the sink. The last time that was out was the last time Jake was here, and we'd had a poker night. I crawl over and pick it up. Ripping the lid off, I press it to my lips and sink into the warm smoky taste of it sliding down my throat. I gulp a few times, feeling the effects hit my head hard, but I keep on going. The darkness falls over me, tempting me, teasing me with all the things I could go and do right now to make myself feel better.

Only thoughts of Bree's blue eyes, alight with the fire of her temper, stops me.

Chapter 23

Bree

Scampering across the compound in the dark has made me realize that I wish Ryker was here next to me. Not just for safety, but because I *want* him next to me. I can't stop thinking about him and even though he infuriates me, there is something between us. He says I'm not ready to hear it. Maybe I'm not, but I want to. I need...

"Ryker?" I ask, seeing a shadow on my porch swing seat, my heart thumping in my chest.

"Yeah," he says gruffly. "Sorry, didn't mean to scare you."

"You didn't," I lie, scooting up the steps and shoving my front door open but then remembering Ryker's tossed place and stopping dead.

"It's okay, you're safe," he says from directly behind me. I hadn't even heard him rise and move across the porch.

He stinks of booze which sets my alarm bells ringing. I rush forward, taking his word for it but seeing my place neat and everything in its place, apart from Casey's mess over by the couch.

"You camped out on my porch?" I ask quietly. I can't help but feel special in that moment. Then I remember he is drowning in a bottle of bourbon that he still has clutched in his hand.

"'Course," he drawls. "You wouldn't let me escort you, so here I am." He opens his arms widely as he spins around on the porch.

"You can come in," I say as he wobbles slightly. "You don't need to hover on the doorstep like an uninvited vampire."

He snorts with mirth. "Uninvited vampire," he chokes out. "They are a myth."

"Maybe there is a vampire out there saying the same thing about Wolf Shifters," I say lightly, remembering what Casey said to me about ghosts.

His eyes land on mine, suddenly focused as he takes a step over the threshold. "You're sure you want me in here?" he asks huskily.

No.

"Yes," I say steadily. "You need a cup of coffee and I have a fresh pot ready."

"You shouldn't drink that stuff this late at night," he chides me.

"It's not that late and I find it comforting to come home to the smell of fresh coffee, is that okay with you?" I ask, a bit of bite in my tone.

He chuckles. "You do what you need to do, Bree," he says and takes a long gulp of his bourbon.

I press my lips together and throw my knitting bag lightly on the bed. I fold my arms defensively. He is mocking me, and I don't like it. I thought he was above that, but it seems he is like every Wolf on this compound after all. The fact that it upsets me is telling. I don't care what other people think about me and my choices. Right now, though, with him? Yeah, I care what he thinks.

He gestures to the pot. "Go on then, don't let me stop you."

"You're an ass," I grit out and march to the kitchenette.

"Your ass is really sexy," he slurs. "And those tattoos…" he groans, making me freeze.

I blink, licking my lips before I turn around. "What about them?" I ask boldly, ignoring the ass comment. I'm not ashamed of them, even though I never show them to anyone. They are mine and mine alone until I find a mate to share them with. Is that going to be Ryker? Not a chance in hell. He will use me, discard me and hurt me beyond anything I have ever felt except for my parents abandoning me.

He shocks me by dropping to his knees, his head hanging slightly, the bottle of bourbon, loose in his hand.

"I have never seen anything so fucking sexy on a woman before and I've seen plenty of women naked," he says slurring again.

I grimace at him. I don't need, nor want, to know about the women he has seen naked and done other things with that make me both uncomfortable and wildly jealous.

"Nothing to say?" he asks when I remain silent.

"I don't know what you want me to say, Ryker?" I say, trying to stay calm. He is unnerving me. I don't *think* he would hurt me physically at least, but I don't know him really.

"I want you to say that you will let me see them again, touch them, lick them…" he growls low and dangerously, but not in the scary sense. His tone is full of passion and desire.

I just stare at him, frozen to the spot.

"I want you to say that you will drop your walls and let me get to know you," he continues in a whisper. "I have these feelings for you, Bree. They are driving me wild. *You* are driving me wild. I need you. I can't explain it…"

"Uhm," I stammer, stunned by his words. I want to run at the same time I want to stay and hear more. I have never had anyone declare that they 'need' me. It hits a button inside me that I didn't even know existed until that moment.

"Shush," he mutters. "Let me finish."

I blink and remain motionless.

"I want to be with you, Bree. I know you have your doubts about me, and you are right to. I haven't behaved very well, and I have flaunted that all over the Pack. I've changed. Can you see it?" His eyes snap to mine suddenly, making me jump. "Can you?"

"I-I don't know, Ryker," I say carefully.

"No, you won't. All you see is a man-whore living a carefree life. You haven't seen me be the man, the *Wolf*, I know I can be, that I am trying every second of every day to be now. I am *Alpha*. That means something, you know?"

There is a plea in his voice, as if he is asking me to agree.

I nod slowly. "I know," I whisper.

"Can you ever be with me?" he asks.

"Ryker, this is very sudden. You've gone from not saying a single word to me to telling me you want to be with me. It's confusing and I don't know what to think. Not to mention you are drunk," I point out.

"I know it's sudden. It is to me too..." he trails off, his gaze on mine, dropping once again. "But don't you feel it, Bree?"

There is that plea again.

It spurs me on to tell the truth, even though I want to hide from it. "Yes," I whisper. "I feel it. I don't understand it..."

He shakes his head vehemently. "Don't question it," he mutters.

My stomach clenches into a tight ball. I need to back out of this conversation before he lures me into saying something that I know I will regret later.

"You are drunk," I say again. "I can't take anything you say seriously."

All the fight seems to go out of him then, not that there was much to begin with. I have never seen him look so defeated, so lost. He sits back on his heels and drops the empty bottle to the floor. "I mean every word I'm saying to you, Bree. I want to be with you. I will still feel this way tomorrow when I wake up with a raging hangover, and when I sober up completely tomorrow afternoon, I will still feel this way."

"I've heard a Shift will get rid of a hangover," I mutter absently.

He shakes his head. "I'll suffer for it. Suffer for you," he says dramatically.

I can't help the smile and snicker that comes out. "Really?" I drawl, relaxing slightly.

"Yes," he says intently. "I will do anything if you would just give me a chance to prove my worth to you."

"How about you just go to sleep for now and we'll see in the morning," I say eventually, with a sigh. I can't take him seriously, no matter what his words are. I would be a fool to believe a single word that is coming out of his mouth right now.

"My cabin is still tossed," he mutters.

"You can stay here," I say, feeling sorry for him, but also knowing deep down that I want him to stay.

His eyes shoot to mine hopefully, but I shake my head in exasperation and point to the couch. His face falls, but it's more comedic than serious. "Fair enough," he mutters and walks on his knees to the sofa.

I rush over and gather up all of Casey's crap, dumping it on top of her bags in the corner. "I'll get you fresh sheets," I murmur as he climbs onto the couch and promptly passes out.

I sigh. He is about as non-threatening as you can get right now and watching him sleep is proving to be fascinating. He doesn't look at all peaceful. Maybe it's the booze, but maybe there is a darkness inside him that needs some light.

"Can I be that light? Do I even want to be?" I mumble, reaching over to run my hand over his short hair. I yank my hand back when he lets out a soft, happy sigh, his face relaxing instantly. As soon as I'm not touching him anymore, he goes back to being tormented in his slumber.

"Weird," I mutter and then move away before I do what my body is crying out for me to do and that is crawl on top of him and hold him, have him wrap his arms around me, keeping me safe.

I pull the blankets from the back of the couch that Casey was using and dump them on top of her clothes. Retrieving another blanket out of the cupboard, I throw it gently over him and stopping at my bed to gather up my pjs, I head into the bathroom. I can't risk taking a shower, being naked in here, while he is out there, only a few feet away, so I quickly clean up and get changed.

A few minutes later, I crawl into bed, wondering where Casey is and if she will bother to show up tonight. It's tough if she does. Her bed is taken. She'll have to sleep on the floor.

I sigh and turn onto my side, fighting the urge to go to Ryker. I don't know what it is, but it is like I'm being pushed towards him. I've never felt anything like it before and puts what I feel for Kane to shame.

Even though it is still early, I close my eyes and hope that sleep comes soon, so that I can forget about Ryker and his words for a little while.

Chapter 24

Ryker

The light is bright against my closed eyes. I groan and chance to crack them open. Fucking bourbon. I really need to stop drowning myself in a bottle. It's not helpful in the least.

Remembering the drinking, I freeze and clutch at the blanket that is covering my still clothed body. I even have my boots on. I raise my head and take in a cabin that isn't my own and for a second, I panic that it is Valerie's but then last night comes flooding back to me in a nauseous wave.

This is Bree's cabin.

"Morning," she says.

I curse under my breath and prop myself up on my elbows to peer over the back of the couch. She is sitting at her small round kitchen table, knitting, a huge cup of steaming coffee in front of her.

"Uhh, hey," I mutter, feeling like such an idiot. Big, bad Alpha Wolf? Yeah, not so much right now as I take in her amused gaze.

"How do you feel?" she asks.

"Like shit on a stick," I reply, my mouth so dry, I wouldn't be surprised if dust came out on my next breath.

"And?" she asks, eyes on her knitting.

And?

I hesitate. What is she expecting me to say?

Suddenly, I remember everything I told her...and everything I *didn't*.

"I still feel the same way, Bree," I rasp. "Nothing has changed."

"You're still drunk," she accuses me.

"No," I say, shaking my head and then wishing that I hadn't when I go dizzy. "Hungover? Yes, definitely," I add with a snort.

Her eyes find mine, the amusement dancing in them hitting me in the heart and giving me a feeling of warmth deep inside.

"But I still want to be with you, Bree. Everything I said last night stands," I say quietly.

She nods slowly. "I'll come and find you this afternoon," she says, standing up. "I have to find Kane. The rain has let up and duty calls."

I nod back, letting her go. She has a confidence about her this morning that surprises and delights me.

"You okay to let yourself out?" she asks as she passes by the couch.

The Alpha in me wants to sneer at her comment and inform her that I'm not a child but a grownass Wolf but the *man*? Yeah, he wants to say no and beg her to stay with me and take care of me.

Fuck's sake.

I'm whipped.

The tiny black Wolf has whipped me.

"I'm fine," I croak out and watch as she nods and leaves,

fortunately not taking the huge coffee with her. I'm guessing it's for me. I flop over the back of the sofa and stumble to the table, picking up the mug and taking a big, satisfying gulp. I need a shower and a Shift…

No, not a Shift. I said I would suffer for her, and I will. She needs to see that I did so she will believe what I told her last night.

I bite my lip, knowing it wasn't the whole truth. I didn't tell her about the Alpha bond. I wanted to; it was there ready to come out, but something stopped me. Her hesitancy stopped me. I couldn't tell her it is Fate that we belong together. She would doubt that my feelings are real, and I can't have that. No matter what happens next, I can't tell her. Not yet. I need her to admit her feelings for me first. I need her to admit to herself what she feels for me is real and deep.

Then I will tell her we are Fated.

Coming to some sort of uneasy peace with my decision, I finish the coffee and then head back to my cabin, needing to tidy the place up, see if anything was stolen, find Hunter to see if he found anything out about the intruder, and then make my way around the compound to make sure everything is in order after the two-day downpour.

It's muggy and overcast when I head outside, but not raining. We had enough to see us through until the season's change, which is a weight off my shoulders. Too bad it has been replaced with strange Wolves prowling my land and targeting me. It is nearly enough to make me reconsider pursuing Bree. It would rip my heart out if anything happened to her because of me. I don't want to put her in danger, but the other side of me says she will be safer with me than away from me.

In the end, after spending an hour righting my cabin, I decide that not even this threat is enough to force me to pull away from Bree. Not now. Not when I am so close. If she was going to reject me, she would've just gone and done it last night. Her waiting until this afternoon to ask me again if I mean it, is a stall tactic to test me.

I appreciate the way she thinks, and I look forward to passing her test to see what she will do next.

※

Several hours later, after fighting through the worst of my hangover, I think all the sweating and heavy work has cured me. I take a long gulp of water, leaning on the shovel that I was using to clear the smaller dirt pathways around the compound of more mud than I have seen in a while. I wipe my forehead on the sleeve of my unbuttoned shirt, grimacing and then deciding to just take it off.

I sense Bree before I see her. She is approaching me from behind, from the direction of the gardens she was clearing with Kane. Yes, I snuck up to make sure she was okay, and that Kane was keeping his mitts off her. Luckily, he was ignoring her, or I would have had to smash his face into a pulp.

I turn with a smile before she reaches me. "Hey," I say.

"Can't sneak up on you so it seems," she says, returning my smile with her own bright one.

"Alpha Wolf," I remind her, feeling the stab of guilt at the not entire truth, but pushing it aside.

She nods and looks to the side. "So, how're you feeling?" she asks tentatively.

"Back to normal," I say steadily. "All clear-headed."

She bites the inside of her lip. "If you feel differently, I understand," she blurts out. "I mean, you were very drunk last night and this morning you were in my cabin and probably didn't want to make me uncomfortable. I don't hold you to it, Ryker. You don't have to…"

"Whoa," I say, with a small laugh, holding my hand up. "Don't convince yourself that you know what I'm going to say before I've said it," I chide her gently.

"Sorry," she mumbles, her cheeks going red. "I just mean that I get it if you were just saying all of that last night to try and get into my pants. You wouldn't be the first..."

"Is that what you think?" I bark out, not angry at her exactly but at the fuckers she is referring to and apparently dumping me in with them.

She shrugs.

"Bree," I say, more gently, knowing that I frightened her with my tone. She withdrew into herself, her confidence from this morning has vanished and I don't want that. I don't want her to feel that she needs to be wary of me at all. "I will tell you right now that I still feel the same, but if you want to ask me, do it to appease your own mind."

"Do you still feel the same?" she asks instantly, her eyes swimming with worry.

"Yes," I say, letting the shovel drop to the ground so I can take a step closer to her. I drop my shirt as well, not really giving a crap that it lands in a pile of mud. I reach out and tilt her chin up so she can meet my eyes. "I want to be with you, Bree. You have taken over my every thought. I can't stop thinking about you. You are consuming my every thought, every breath I take, every beat of my heart. I need you in my life, but the question is, Bree...what do you feel?"

Her tongue darts out to lick her lips. Her blue eyes are riveted to mine. "I want to trust you," she whispers. "I don't know why, because we are so different, but I feel something for you that has snuck up on me and taken over. I close my eyes and I see you. I lie in bed at night and want you next to me. It's sudden and exciting but it's also frightening. I have never had a real relationship before. I don't know if what I'm feeling is real or lust or something else. I'm ten years younger than you, and I feel it. I feel insignificant and unworldly and too innocent for you to take seriously. I am incapable of giving you what you want because I don't know how to trust someone enough to be physical with them. But despite all that, if you mean what you say, I want to trust you."

I search her eyes. She hasn't said that she wants to be with me. Not exactly. She just wants to trust that I want to be with her.

"I don't need you to be physical with me to give me what I want," I point out, understanding why she would think that but still taking a bit of offense all the same. I'm not some creature with a constant hard-on. Okay, maybe sometimes, but I'm capable of thinking with my head as well.

"Don't you?" she cries, suddenly going skittish and pulling away from me. "Your last girlfriend is a big ho, we all know it...that's not me and if you're expecting that from me, then I can't do this."

"Firstly," I say, trying to remain calm at the accusations she is hurling at me. "Valerie was never my girlfriend. Secondly, have I ever made you feel like all I want from you is sex?"

Her cheeks flame at the word. It's cute and only makes me fall even harder for her.

"Have I?" I press, needing her to admit it so she can convince herself.

She shakes her head slowly. "No," she mutters.

"There you go then," I say gently and take her chin in my hand again. "For the first time in my life, Bree, I'm thinking about the bigger picture. I want to be with you and if that means that I wait for you to be ready to trust me completely with your heart and your body, then I'll wait."

"You will?" she croaks out, surprised.

"Yes," I say with a small smile.

"I mean, really, truly you'll wait? For *me*? You won't go looking elsewhere..."

"Bree, if you say to me now that you are going to give us a shot, I promise you that I will wait for you, and I won't go looking elsewhere for sex." I enjoy saying that word in front of her and watching her blush. It's fucking adorable. "If you say you will be with me, then I am completely yours as you will be mine."

Her lips part.

She stares up into my eyes, taking a tiny step closer to me.

I know what she wants, and I want to give it to her. For the first time in a really long time, I want to kiss her full lips and feel her tongue twist around mine. I want, no, I *need*, the intimacy of a perfect kiss with her.

I lower my mouth to hers and whisper, "Well, Bree. The ball is in your court."

"Kiss me," she demands, her small hands running up my bare chest, setting my skin on fire from her light touch. "I want this. Kiss me," she says again, more forcefully.

Moving my hand to the back of her neck, I grip her tightly and crash my lips against hers, driving my tongue into her mouth so that I can taste her.

She moans softly, spurring me on, pressing her body close to mine. She has to feel my erection, but she doesn't shy away from it, showing me she is putting her faith in me not to pressure her.

Her tongue duels with mine, she devours my mouth, and I let her take all the control. She needs it more than I do. She needs to feel secure and in charge.

Fine by me.

I have been a master of controlling my sexual encounters for the last decade or more. She brings out a completely different side to me.

It's startling but beautiful at the same time.

Breathlessly, she pulls away, a soft smile playing on her lips. "I'll see you later," she murmurs. "I need to get back to Kane."

"I don't like how that sounds," I growl but giving her a wink, so she knows I'm not being entirely jealous and possessive.

She giggles, enjoying it, apparently. "Can I come by later?" she asks shyly.

"You don't even have to ask," I say. "I'll make dinner."

What?

Her surprised look must reflect my own. "Okaaaay," she drawls. "I look forward to it." She turns on her heel and stalks off. She turns back suddenly, "Oh and by 'physical' I mean intercourse," she says, her cheeks on fire but her eyes boring into mine. "I'm open to other stuff."

"Fuck me," I groan making her laugh at me. "I'm your slave for life, Bree Henderson," I call after her which I can see delights her. It fucking delights me too. I go back to shoveling, rampant thoughts of jerking off over her hot body and covering her with my cum, getting me through the next few hours of grueling, tedious work.

Chapter 25

Bree

Smiling all the way back to my cabin to shower and change out of the wet, muddy clothes stuck to my skin, I'm disappointed to find Casey waiting for me on the porch, arms crossed, a sly look on her face.

"Kissing the new Alpha...niiiiice. Moved in with lightning speed, didn't you, Bree. Is that what you've been waiting for all this time? Ryker to become Alpha so you could ride your way straight to the top out of the gate?"

I grit my teeth at her insinuation and the spark of anger lights up into something so much more. "Fuck you, Casey," I spit out. "Keep your mouth shut about shit you know nothing about."

I shove past her as she gapes and splutters at me.

"And while you're here, you can get your stuff and get out of my cabin," I add before I practically kick the door open.

"You're throwing me out?" Casey asks, storming into the cabin behind me. "Where will I go?"

"I don't care," I inform her. "You are not a friend to me,

Casey. You never were. I don't need you in my life and I certainly don't need you in my home."

"Wow, big talk coming from the timid little Wolf. Alpha must be rubbing off on you," she sneers.

"Did it ever occur to you that I don't like being treated like shit?" I ask her, rounding on her, fired up. "I might avoid conflict where I can, but I've had enough of you, Casey. You used me to get away from Hunter and then you leave my house in a mess and fuck off for two days without a word. You are a bitch, Casey. Plain and simple. I want you to get your stuff and get out."

"And you are a two-faced little slut," Casey hisses at me. "You don't have it in you to keep an Alpha satisfied. You are nothing but a notch on his bedpost and he will move on from you the second he gets bored with white cotton underwear and missionary style."

I clench my fists, biting my tongue nearly in half. She is poking at every insecurity that I have, and it is killing me to know that she knows it. Everybody will think the same. I will be a laughingstock and I'll only have myself to blame.

Her mocking features bring tears to my eyes. She has me beat, and she knows it.

"Bree asked you to leave," a deep voice says from the still open doorway. "Pack your stuff and get out."

I cringe recognizing it instantly. I don't even have to look over to know that Hunter has turned up and heard everything she said to me.

Casey turns to him, shock registering on her face. "You're taking her side?" she asks incredulously.

"Damn straight," he says, entering the cabin, his huge frame looming in the doorway.

I gulp. I'm frozen to the spot. I'm utterly humiliated that he heard Casey's insults and want the ground to swallow me whole.

"Well, fuck this," Casey mutters. "I'm not staying where I'm not wanted."

Hunter folds his arms across his chest and waits as Casey starts to pack up her stuff, throwing it into her bags.

"I'm surprised you fell for her act," she spits out at Hunter. "Sweet and innocent doesn't usually turn you on, lover."

Hunter's jaw clenches but he doesn't respond to her taunts.

She shakes her head. "Who knew you'd have all these males drooling all over you," she scoffs at me. "I guess virgin Wolf is in this season."

"Fuck off, Casey," Hunter drawls. "I wish I'd known what a bitch you were years ago. Could've saved myself a whole helluva lot of time."

"You can call me a bitch all you like, but I know you are still in love with Stevie. You have been this entire time, making a fool of me," she shrieks at him, picking up one of the small vases and throwing it at him.

"Hey!" I snap, but Hunter catches it and replaces it on the end table.

"No you made a fool of you all by yourself," he replies. "Go now. In fact, leave Pack lands. I know all about you and Tyler. Go and ask to live with him for a while. I'm sure he will come to his senses soon enough and throw you out as well."

"You're banishing me?" she croaks out, paling. "You don't have that right. Only the Alpha can..."

"I can act on the Alpha's behalf when the Pack's best interests are at stake. You are a rotten Wolf in this Pack, and you are no longer welcome here."

I'm rooted to the spot. I have never witnessed a banishment before. It is the worst punishment a Pack Wolf can receive, short of death. I daren't breathe, never mind move, even though my hands are cramping from being clenched into fists all this time.

"You will regret this," Casey hisses at him eventually. "You all will."

With as much dignity as she can, she picks up her bags and leaves my cabin, taking the tension with her.

Hunter closes the door behind her as I breathe out slowly.

"I'm sorry that you got pulled into her nastiness," Hunter says. "What she said about Ryker..."

He doesn't get to finish because, to my absolute horror, the tears that were pricking my eyes fall and I start to ugly cry, snorting and sniffling like a complete idiot, my face crumpled up against the pain Casey inflicted on me.

"Uhm," Hunter stammers.

I wave him away. "You-you don't have to stay," I get out in between gulps and snorts.

"Ryker cares about you," he says earnestly. "Don't listen to a word she said. Don't doubt your connection to him."

"It's not me I'm doubting," I croak, brushing my tears away. "This is all so sudden, and I still don't understand it..."

I watch as Hunter's face falls into confusion before it hardens slightly, and he grimaces. "He cares about you, more so than I have ever seen. Don't doubt him," he says.

Feeling cold and confused and hurt, out of nowhere I launch myself at him, needing some comfort, just a tiny bit so I have the courage to pull myself together. "I hope you're right," I sniffle against his shirt.

"Hey," he says gently, wrapping his arms around me lightly. "Trust what you feel from him, okay?"

I nod and then pull away, wiping my nose on my sleeve. "I'm sorry for all of this, Hunter. You didn't need to swoop in and rescue me."

"That wasn't just for you," he says with a small smile.

I try to return it, but I don't think I succeed very well. "Thanks anyway."

"If you ever need anything, I'm here. You know, if Ryker isn't," he adds with a smirk.

"Is it so unfathomable that he could want me?" I ask, suddenly and then shake my head. "No, don't answer that," I mumble and turn away.

"Not at all," Hunter replies lightly. "You are perfect for each other."

Surprised, I turn back to him, but he is gone, slipping quietly out and leaving me alone to contemplate everything that transpired in the last few minutes.

Chapter 26

Ryker

Just as I'm finishing up the last of the pathways, I see Hunter striding towards me, his face grim. Well, grimmer than usual.

"What is it?" I ask before he gets within sniffing distance of me.

The second he does, I recognize her scent instantly, all over him. A red haze drops over my eyes and I let go of the shovel. I face off with him and he pauses, understanding falling over his face, knowing the Wolf has come out.

"Ryker," he says, holding his hands up. "It's not what you think."

"I can smell her all over you, you bastard!" I roar and launch myself at him, bunching my fist up to smash him in the face first and the guts second.

Doubled over, he lets out a grunt, "Oof, Ry, wait…"

"Fuck you!" I seethe at him, kicking his feet out from under him. "She is *mine*. You know that but still you go to her and try it on?" I bend down to clench his shirt in my fist covered with his blood from his busted nose.

"Ryker, let me explain," he rasps. "It was Casey, she was being a complete bitch to her. I defended her, and she broke down. She needed comfort, that's all it was. I would never... you know that, man..."

He has his hands held up in surrender, knowing that if I choose to, I can continue this tussle and he wouldn't fight me back. He can't. He would be putting his life in jeopardy not only because I would beat him into the ground, but as Alpha of this Pack, the rest would defend me no matter who challenged me.

"She needed comfort?" I ask, trying to calm the fuck down before I kill my best friend with my bare hands and teeth.

Hunter nods carefully, and I let him go. He sits up, wary of the predator that is still so close to the surface, simmering under my skin. He knows I want to Shift and rip his throat out for touching Bree, for being close enough to have her mark her scent all over him.

"Casey really laid into her when Bree threw her out. It was brutal. I happened to be passing, I heard everything. I wasn't about to let her stand there and be spoken to like that. Not when she's a part of this Pack, not to mention your girl."

"Bree threw her out?" I ask, sitting back and frowning fiercely.

Hunter nods again. "You'd have been proud of her," he says quietly.

I sigh and rub my hand over my face. "It should have been *me* there to defend her, not you."

"I know that. But it is what it is. Which, by the way, is a bit of a hiccup."

"What do you mean? Is Bree okay?" I demand, standing up again.

"She's fine, her feelings are hurt, but she's fine. Casey, on the other hand...I banished her. I'm not sorry and I'd do it again," he says, also standing up and giving me a fierce look as if I'm going to twist his nuts over it. Not fucking likely. She got off easy. If I *had* been the one there, I would have probably killed her. And I don't mean that as something you 'just say'.

I nod, trusting and accepting that my Beta did what he had to do to protect this Pack in my absence. "Fine," I say but giving him a sour look, anyway. "She will need replacing. As much as she turned out to be a big bitch, we needed her."

"Yeah, I know," he grumbles. "She was close to coming into her heat and ready to mate. Maybe that's what made her break it off with me. She was always a wild card and didn't want to be tied too far down. But that just proves she isn't a good fit for this Pack," he adds with a growl.

"Okay, okay. You don't need to keep trying to convince me. You did the right thing. I just wish you hadn't rubbed your okay-looking body against *my* female," I say with narrowed eyes. "Your dick had better not have stood to attention when she got close to you."

He snorts. "Sorry, buddy. She doesn't affect me that way. She's more like a little sister."

"Good," I growl. "Keep it that way."

He nods and then looks away before he sighs. "You didn't tell her about the Alpha bond, did you?"

I clench my jaw. "No," I grit out. "I wanted to, but I was drunk last night, and it didn't come out and then today she was so willing to give me a chance, I couldn't ruin it. I couldn't risk her turning from me."

"You need to tell her," Hunter insists. "She deserves to know."

"I will when the time is right. When she is secure and

happy with us. She is still skittish, and I'm still worried she will run."

He sighs. "Ry, this will not end well if you keep it from her."

"Just a little while longer," I snap, knowing that I also need to tell my mother to keep her mouth shut about it. "I've got this, okay?"

"Sure," he says, but it's nowhere near convincing.

However, it doesn't change my mind.

"I'll catch up with you later. I've got shit to deal with," I mutter and turn from him, bending to scoop up my filthy shirt and head towards my mom's cabin. I'm sure she'll be thrilled to know that Bree and I are together, but I also know that she will give me grief just like Hunter did.

Doesn't matter. I'm doing what I know is right for right now. Bree will run if she learns how much responsibility falls onto her and onto this relationship and I don't blame her. I wanted to run but the force of nature that is the Fates has made it impossible.

She has made it impossible.

I need her to feel that being away from me is just as impossible. Only then will I tell her the whole truth.

Chapter 27

Bree

My hands are shaking as I approach Ryker's cabin later that day. I'm still shook up over what happened to Casey and what she said to me, but I'm also nervous about this 'date'. What is he going to expect from me? I was bold and trying to be cheeky when I said about being open to other stuff. His face lit up like the blazing summer sun and while I meant it, I'm not sure I'm ready to dive straight in *tonight*.

I pause at the bottom of the steps and look up at the door as it opens.

"You were watching for me?" I ask with a small smile.

"Something like that," he says mysteriously, which piques my interest but not enough for me to pursue it. Especially when he smiles and holds his hand out for me.

I smile back and mount the steps, reaching for his hand when I get close enough. I gasp at the sparks that fly from that small touch. I gaze into his eyes curiously, but he says nothing, so I don't know if it was just me that felt it or if he did too. I don't want to make a fool of myself, so I say nothing.

"I'm starving," I say instead as I smell something cooking.

"Good," he says, "me too."

He leads me inside and I have a look around. The place is neat and tidy again. It's bigger than mine, naturally, and completely clean. I can't help the sense of relief that descends on me that he isn't a slob. I've never been in here before except for the other day when I saw the cabin had been turned upside down.

"Any news on the intruder?" I ask suddenly.

He shakes his head, but I get the feeling he is hiding something from me. "No, but you don't need to be worried about that. I will keep you safe."

I lick my lips at his possessive tone.

"In fact," he continues, turning his back to me. "I want you to move…"

"Excuse me?" I blurt out, rudely interrupting him. "You're asking me to move in here? With you?" No, just no! What is he thinking?

He turns back to me with a smirk. "Err, no," he says. "Not right away, anyway. If you had let me finish, I was going to say, I want you to move closer to me, into this sector. I need to know where you are and that you are safe."

Not right away?

Know where I am?

"I see," I say. "Well, I'm happy where I am and there are no free cabins on this side," I say stiffly.

"Not yet, but I'm Alpha. If I tell someone to move, they move," he says in a tone etched with a darkness that makes me shiver.

Alpha.

I'd almost forgotten that part. What the hell am I doing here? I don't belong here. I'm a nobody. I'm still a few years away from going into my heat and able to reproduce. There are other females in this Pack that are more worthy of the Alpha's attention than me.

I lick my lips again. They're going to be cracked by the end of this night. "That's not necessary..."

In a flash, he is in front of me, taking my hands gently. "I heard about what Casey said to you. I should've been there to protect you from her," he says earnestly.

"I don't need protecting from a silly bitch with a big mouth," I point out, the fire his words have lit under me igniting. I'm not some weakling that needs a male to rescue me. But he seems to think that. Is that why he wants me? Because all of a sudden he has this hero complex after he saved me from those idiots at the lake? I try to drag my hands back, but he tightens his hold on me.

"I know you don't," he says stiffly, "but Hunter was there, and you went to him for comfort. That should have been me, Bree."

I raise an eyebrow at him, again with the possessiveness. So that's what this is all about.

Hunter.

"I don't care about Hunter," I point out lightly.

Ryker's eyes narrow. "Does that mean you care about me?"

"Not what I said," I say with, what I hope is, a sassy smile. I'm trying to diffuse the tension that has ratcheted up a few notches because it's making me uncomfortable. I've never had a male go all growly over me before. It will take some getting used to. I'm figuring out that Ryker, for all his whoring ways, is a male that once he has found the right female, will move heaven and earth to protect her. I'm flattered in a way that it's me, but I still don't get it.

He purses his sexy lips, which drives me slightly crazy. On impulse, I quickly raise up onto my tiptoes and plant a soft kiss on those lips, which catches him off-guard. But only for a second.

He exhales slightly, his grip tightening on my hands as he pulls me closer, letting go to wrap one arm around me as the other goes into my loose hair. With a soft growl, he deepens the kiss, swishing his tongue against mine, probing my mouth, exploring every inch of it in a kiss that makes my knees go weak.

Literally.

They buckle.

His arm tightens around me, holding me up but not stopping the kiss for even a second.

I'm breathless, my heart is pounding, my blood is roaring through my veins. This feels so right. I feel whole in his embrace, and I want more. My traitorous body needs more. I press my breasts against him without thinking.

He groans quietly and stops the kiss, pushing me away slightly. "No," he rasps. "Don't do that."

"Do what?" I ask with a frown, my cheeks flaming with the rejection.

"Don't do something that you haven't thought through properly. Don't feel you *need* to give me something that you aren't ready for. I said I would wait, and I will."

My heart swells with a feeling that overwhelms me.

"Okay," I say quietly, not feeling the need to explain or blurt out something stupid to cover up. He gets it.

He gets *me*.

"Food?" I ask, moving away from him before I do something I will probably regret. My body is still on fire for him. I want to leap on his hot body, wrap my legs around him and explore what this sudden explosion of emotion is.

He chuckles. "Yes, food. You like grilled cheese?"

I turn back to him, mouth agape. "Grilled cheese?" I ask

in disbelief. I was under the assumption I was being fed real food. I've gone hungry all afternoon in anticipation.

He shrugs with an embarrassed expression. "It's all Hunter brought round for me on short notice. He has me under strict instruction not to eat or drink anything unless he hand delivers it," he explains.

"Oh," I say, blinking rapidly. It doesn't take a genius to figure out why. He is more worried about this intruder than he is letting on. I decide not to make a big deal out of it. "Well, I *love* grilled cheese," I declare. "It's my favorite."

He laughs gently, seemingly relieved I didn't push the issue. "Liar, but I'll take it as intended. Dinner is served."

He whisks out a chair for me at the round table and I sit with a grin, my stomach rumbling, glad that this has turned a bit of a corner from awkward to easy.

Chapter 28

Ryker

I watch Bree eat with a gusto that makes me smile.
 I try to hide it behind my hand, but she sees it and asks, "What?"
"Nothing," I say, shaking my head. "Just enjoying you."
"Oh," she says, her cheeks going pink. "Don't stare at me."
"I enjoy staring at you. You are so beautiful," I murmur, reaching out to twist my hand into her hair.
She gasps, tilting her head back, looking for a kiss. I don't disappoint her. Leaning over, I press my lips to hers, making sure to keep my body a safe distance away. It took everything I had to pull away from her earlier. I didn't think I would be able to. But the last thing I want to do is hurt her in any way.
After tasting her sweetness for a moment, I grip her chin and pull back. "Are you still hungry?"
She shakes her head.
"Shall we go to the couch?" I ask.
She nods, rendered speechless, it seems.

I help her up and lead her over. We sit and she clears her throat.

"Can I ask if you've found anything out about the intruder?" she asks carefully.

"Hunter is on it. He has doubled security around the compound. Are you worried?" I ask.

She shrugs. "Not really, I guess."

I can see she is putting on a braver face than how she really feels. I reach out to cup the back of her neck. The need to keep touching her is overwhelming. "Move closer to me," I murmur.

She shakes her head. "I like where I am, Ryker," she says. "I don't want to be a burden."

"You are definitely not that," I tell her.

She smiles shyly.

I bite the inside of my lip. I'm not used to this. Conversation has never really been my strong suit, preferring to get right down to business with a woman.

"What is it?" she asks, interrupting my thoughts.

"Hmm? Oh, nothing," I reply, not wanting to scare her off.

"No, it's something," she presses. "Tell me. You can tell me anything."

I smile. "You are too sweet, Bree."

She scrunches up her face, "Ugh. Sweet."

I chuckle. "But you are. I'm not used to it, that's all. But that's on me, not you."

"What do you mean?" she asks warily.

"Nothing," I mutter.

"No," she says sharply. "What did you mean?"

"Bree, it's nothing," I insist, wanting to get away from this conversation.

"Look," she says with a huff and stands up. "Just because

I've never had a relationship before or kissed a man before you earlier, doesn't mean you get to treat me any differently."

As her words sink in, I leap off the couch as well and move away from her. "You've never kissed anyone before me?" I croak out.

Jesus. I start to sweat. She is far more innocent than even I could have imagined. What am I doing here? This makes no sense.

"No," she says defiantly. "What of it?" She folds her arms over her chest.

"Why didn't you tell me?" I implore her, sitting heavily on the bed and then wishing I had gone nowhere near it.

"Why should I? Are you going to tell me how many women *you've* kissed before me?" she challenges me.

I snort, knowing that number I can count on one hand, her included. "You don't get it, Bree. You aren't ready for this. If you were any other woman, we wouldn't be eating and talking. I would have you handcuffed to my bed with my dick in your ass. Do you understand that? Do you understand who I am? Do you get that I don't understand how to be with you yet and you just keep making it more difficult."

Shit.

Her face goes thunderous.

I knew it was the wrong thing to say as soon as it came out of my mouth.

"Oh? Do I?" she hisses. "Maybe it's time for me to leave."

"No!" I say, standing up quickly. "Please don't leave. That was an idiotic thing to say and I'm sorry. I'm being a complete ass. I was just surprised, that's all. Virgin is one thing, never having been kissed is something else. If I'd known, I would've treated you differently instead of engaging in our first kiss like a half-naked, sweaty, muddy dickhead."

"Maybe I don't want to be treated differently," she says

hotly. "I wanted that kiss as much as you did, and it was..." She trails off, clamping her lips shut.

"It was what?" I ask quietly.

"Everything I'd ever dreamed of," she mumbles, looking away.

I move towards her silently, but she puts her hands up to stop me. "I'm not as innocent a little wallflower as you think I am," she blurts out. "Did you know that I stood in the shower the other day and brought myself to an orgasm thinking about you? Did you?"

Her words hit me in the heart and the dick at the same time. I groan and drop to my knees in front of her, grabbing her hips and pressing my forehead against her stomach.

"Oh, Bree, you bring me to my knees," I murmur.

She huffs but it only takes her a second to run her hands over my head before she tilts my chin up to look at her. Her bright blue eyes are full of mischief, even though they are tinged with a wariness that I actually do understand. She is worried about what I will think about her, but all I can think is that she is a goddess.

My goddess.

"Tell me more," I murmur.

"How about you tell me if you have ever done the same," she says quietly.

I grab her hands and stand up. "Oh, I've done that and more," I say darkly. "Are you sure you want to hear it?"

"I want to know everything, Ryker. This is what I'm trying to say, badly, I know. No secrets, no protecting me from the truth. If we are going to make this work, I need you to be fully honest with me."

I gulp, knowing the huge secret that I'm keeping from her, that I've roped Hunter and my mother into keeping from her as well. But staring into her eyes now, I know I can't lose her. I can't give her an excuse to run.

"The other day, I saw you twirling around in the rain," I whisper. "You were in a sexy pink top, that showed off your curves to perfection. Your nipples were straining against the material, and I wanted to bite them," I add with a low growl.

She licks her lips, nerves hitting her.

"I watched you be free, and all I wanted was to take you to my bed and ravage you. My dick was so hard at the thought. I needed a release. I watched you and jerked off in the woodshed, coming all over the wall and wishing it was your face, your tits, your body. Does that scare you, Bree?" I ask her.

"It's a little bit creepy," she says after a pause. "But also kind of flattering."

I snort. "Flattering?" I ask. "Bree, you have whipped my dick into only working around you. You…" I sigh and rub my hand over my face.

"You want more from me," she says astutely.

"Only when you are ready," I insist, even though I'm practically drooling on my shoes at the thought of her touching herself, bringing herself to a climax while she thinks of me.

"I can give you more," she says. "I said it outside, and I meant it. I want you to be satisfied with me, Ryker."

"Oh, Bree," I say sadly, brushing her loose hair over her ear. "You don't need to say that."

"I want to," she says. "I want you to know that this isn't just about me."

"You are perfection," I murmur, drawing her to me again so I can kiss her, press my lips to hers and taste her. "You tell me what you want, and I will listen."

"Right now, I just want to get to know you and kiss you a few more times before I go home," she says with a small smile. "Is that enough for you?"

"Yes," I say honestly. "Yes, it's enough for me." I know that it is for now. She will come to me when she is ready, and

I don't think she will leave me waiting very long after she just admitted to what she's done. If she could let me touch her that way, coax an orgasm out of her that will make her so wet before I plunge my tongue into her and make her come again. If she will touch me, jerk me off until I spray my seed all over her, then I can do without full on sex. For now.

Chapter 29

Bree

Several days after my first date with Ryker, things have gone quiet in the compound. It's late afternoon and where there would normally be hustle and bustle, it's dead. All except for Ryker prowling the grounds in Wolf form, along with Hunter and the doubled-up guards.

An official warning was sent out after, where Ryker told me in confidence, the bottle of his dad's Scotch came back negative for wolfsbane. I don't really know what that means for him, or us, or the rest of the Wolves. We are all on edge, wondering if the murderer is one of us. It was easier to think it was someone from outside. No one else knows about the intruder Wolf except me, so I'm sure whoever it was came from outside. So are Ryker and Hunter. But they don't want to cause a panic, so it remains quiet for now. I sit on my porch and watch two of the guards patrol past my cabin for what must be the hundredth time.

Ryker has *definitely* told them to pay more attention to me, which both annoys me and makes me feel special at the same time. It's always the same with him. His possessiveness is endearing and frustrating. His admission of secretly watching me and jerking off the other day was definitely shocking and falls into creepy stalking if I didn't know better. But is what I did any worse? I used his image to bring my own climax forth.

No, his is worse. Way worse.

I brighten up when I see Maria approaching my cabin.

"Hi, honey," she says, climbing the steps. "You okay?"

I nod and stand up. "Are you? Is Ryker watching you as much as he is me?" I roll my eyes as she snorts.

"Oh, I told him to get lost days ago," she says, waving her hand about. "Got something for you." She shows me the package under her arm.

I know straight away that is my new underwear, so I usher her inside and close the door. She places it on the table.

"There's a little something extra in there. From me," she says.

I blink and undo the wrapping on the package to see my requested white cotton sets and a pretty dark pink package nestled underneath.

"What is it?" I ask, shoving the underwear out of the way.

"Open it and see," she says with a smirk.

I suddenly get an attack of nerves. What has she done?

Licking my lips, as my mouth has gone completely dry, I pluck the tissue paper away and peer at the contents, a blush rising up from the tip of my toes to the top of my head.

"Uhm," I stammer, staring at the scrap of black lace, prettily arranged in the tissue paper.

"Go on, look at it," Maria urges me.

With shaking hands, I pick it up by the thin straps and hold it up in front of me, dying slightly from embarrassment when my eyes take in sexy lingerie that will barely cover up any of my bits. It's completely see through.

"Put that on and you will feel your power," Maria whispers to me, leaning in closely.

"Power?" I ask in confusion.

"Your womanly power," she explains.

"Err…" I stutter and quickly drop it gently, wrapping it back up. Is she seriously suggesting I wear this in front of her son? Is she mad? Is this a nightmare that I will wake up from? I sure hope so.

"Thanks," I mutter, remembering my manners. "It's pretty."

"It's *sexy*," she amends and then turns to the door. "I'll see you tomorrow for knitting club," she adds with a smile. "I'm so glad Ryker saw sense and snatched you up. You are a good girl, Bree. Good for him. But do me a favor, would you?"

"Anything," I say quietly.

"Tell him how you feel tonight, please. I mean *really* feel, deep in your heart. He needs to hear it," she implores me.

"I—I…" I trail off. I don't know if I can tell him because it's so confusing.

"He needs to know," Maria says firmly. She then opens the door and disappears, leaving me wondering what all of this is about.

I purse my lips at the dark pink package and on impulse, pull the item out of the wrapping again and hold it up.

"What the hell. It's just me here," I mutter and strip off quickly, slipping it on and turning to the full-length mirror in the corner to glare at myself. That glare soon turns to one of surprise. I thought I would look ridiculous trussed up in this scant strip of fabric, but I *do* look sexy in it. Like a Wolf ready to pounce her mate. It's sheer with darker flower shapes over my nipples, not that it hides them, but it's something. The rest of it, not so much. If I wore this for Ryker, he would be able to see all of me.

It occurs to me that he already has.

Twice.

Would it really be so bad to give him something like this to look at next time?

A soft knock at the door makes me jump a mile and dive for my baggy t-shirt to throw back over my head, and yanking my jeans on, I hop to the door, calling, "One minute." Barefoot, I open the door to see Hunter on the porch with Wolf Ryker next to him.

I can't resist the urge to reach out and stroke him on his massive grey and white head. He is enormous, especially next to my little Wolf. He makes a noise that sounds a bit like a purr deep in his throat.

Hunter chuckles and says, "He is escorting you back to his cabin. I'll stay here to make sure it's safe for you to come home later."

"Ugh," I exclaim in frustration. "That's really not necessary."

Ryker snaps at my fingers in annoyance at the same time that Hunter says, "Try arguing with him if you will. I'm just doing what I'm told." He sits on the small chair on the porch and pulls out his book.

"Hunter, no," I say, shaking my head. "I get that you have to do what he tells you, but this is silly. At least sit inside and make yourself at home."

Hunter smiles and stands up. "Much obliged," he says and enters the cabin when I make way for him, glaring at Ryker. I get that bland Wolf expression back and sigh.

"Let me get my shoes on," I tell him.

He waits patiently outside, not entering as I haven't invited him in. He has a respect that borders on slightly obsessive at times. It's surprisingly opposite to what you expect from him. There again, his parents are good people. Or *were*, as the case may be.

"I won't be too late," I tell Hunter.

He waves me off, engrossed in his book and I only hesitate for a second about leaving him in my cabin. I doubt very much he would root through my belongings, but I take the cotton underwear package off the table anyway and stuff it under my bed.

Ryker pads along next to me as we walk towards his cabin. There is obviously no conversation, but it's not awkward. He makes me feel oddly comfortable.

We reach his cabin in a few minutes and I shove the door open for him. He bounds inside and I follow, closing the door behind me.

I watch as he Shifts to his hot, naked human form, keeping his back to me, once again out of respect for me.

"Thanks for not making a big deal out of Hunter waiting at your cabin," he says, reaching over onto the bed for a laid out white t-shirt.

He snatches it up but freezes when I blurt out, "Don't."

Keeping his back turned, I see the muscles bunch up.

"Don't get dressed," I murmur, making a decision and removing my own t-shirt slowly and unbuttoning my jeans.

"Why not?" he asks huskily.

I slide my jeans down and kick off my shoes before I remove them.

"I want to see you. I want to touch you," I reply. "Turn around."

"Bree," he says, inhaling deeply. "Are you ready for this?"

"I'm not saying we are going to have sex, Ryker," I point out. "I just want to see you; I want you to see *me*."

He spins round, his eyes going as wide and round as saucers when he sees the sexy lingerie barely covering my body.

Womanly power, was it?

Definitely getting a heavy dose of that right about now.

"Jesus fuck," he mutters and drops his t-shirt on the floor.

Chapter 30

Ryker

My mouth waters at the sight of her. My Wolf roars to the surface, begging for release. My heart pounds in my chest; my blood rushing through my veins.

"Bree," I breathe. "Do you have any idea what you're doing to me?"

Her eyes drop for a few seconds, a smile playing at her lips. "I have a rough idea," she says, meeting mine again.

"Fuck," I mutter. "You are a goddess."

She lowers her eyes, her hair curtaining her face at the praise. She doesn't believe it, but I will make her see herself as I see her.

"Come here," I murmur.

She tilts her head up again, eyes narrowed.

I see her thoughts on her face. She believes I've ordered her to come to me. That's not the case. I'm rooted to the spot. I can't move for the desire coursing through me.

"Touch me, Ryker," she whispers. "I need to feel your hands on me."

If anything was going to get me to move, that was it. I close the distance between us quickly. I see the triumph in her eyes and let her have it. I don't care that I'm her Alpha. She can have all the power as far as I'm concerned. I relinquish it for the first time in my life. Her breath hitches when I pause just in front of her. She raises her gaze to mine, surprising me with the desire I see burning in those blue depths. With a steady hand I reach out for her, tracing my fingers lightly up her arm. She shivers and then gasps when my hand settles loosely around her throat. She doesn't struggle. She gives me a level gaze.

"Tell me what I can do to you, Bree," I murmur. "I need to know how far I can go with you tonight."

I hold my breath as I wait for her answer. If she says, just a kiss, it will rip my guts out, but something tells me she won't. She didn't come here with this sexy underwear on just for me to kiss her. But the question is how far she will let me go.

"I'm not ready for sex," she mutters. "But I want to know what it feels like when *you* bring me to a climax."

I let out a soft groan, my dick twitching at the thought of it.

Gripping her upper arm tightly, I let go of her throat and spin her around quickly, shoving her hair over her shoulder. With no hesitation, I press my lips to the nape of her neck and flicking my tongue out, I lick the paw print tattoo inked into her smooth skin.

She inhales deeply, turning her head slightly to the side so that I can see her profile. She is absolutely beautiful.

Hooking my fingers into the thin straps of this scrap of lingerie, I fight the urge to rip them roughly, snapping them against her skin, but instead, slip them over her shoulders.

She trembles but doesn't resist. I trace my lips over her shoulder, my hands cupping her tits, which are the perfect size for my hands. Kneading them gently, I take her peaked nipples between my fingers and roll them around softly, making her moan. I find that I don't have to shove back any aggression that I would normally feel in this situation. I don't want to bite her, restrain her, and take her. I want her to enjoy every second of what I'm about to do to her and leave her panting for more. Letting go of her, I move back slightly. She exhales and turns around, confusion on her face.

"Touch me, Bree," I murmur. "Feel every inch of my body. Get to know it as well as you know your own because it is yours, flesh, heart and soul."

"Ryker," she murmurs and steps into my personal space, her tits jiggling with the movement.

I am riveted.

Her small hand shakily reaches out, her fingertips resting lightly on the Wolf over my heart. She traces it carefully before she places her lips on it and to my delighted surprise, licks it lightly.

I start to pant.

When her other hand slowly makes its way down my abs and eventually clasps around my cock, I nearly come all over her hand.

"Fuck, Bree," I mumble, closing my eyes. "You don't know what you do to me."

She strokes me gently, almost as if she is afraid of hurting me. I cover her hand with my own, opening my eyes to gaze into hers.

"Harder," I mutter and show her what she can do to me.

I'm glad that she doesn't get embarrassed by my instruction as that wasn't my intention. I just want her to know that she doesn't have to be soft with me.

She tightens her fist around my length and jerks me off

slowly, enticingly before she speeds up. I want nothing more than for her to drop to her knees and take me in her mouth, but I doubt she is ready for that. So instead, I switch the focus back to her. I remove her hand and scoop her up in my arms, carrying her to the bed and laying her down. A wariness falls over her face, but I smile at her.

"I want to show you how I can make you feel, Bree," I whisper. "You're going to want the sheets to hold onto."

It lightens the mood, and she giggles, wiggling down to make herself more comfortable. "That's big talk, Mr. Alpha," she murmurs.

"Wait," I reply with a smirk and climb on the bed as well. I pull the lingerie off her body and drop it lightly on the floor. Her hands twitch as if she wants to cover herself, but I don't let her. I part her legs and run my fingers up the inside of her thighs. She shivers and tenses up when I brush over her pussy. She is bare and has the prettiest pussy I've ever seen. The fact that it is completely untouched by a male nearly makes me drool all over her.

I don't tell her to relax. It will come across as patronizing and I don't want her to feel inferior in any way. I want her to feel like the goddess that she is.

I do, however, murmur, "If you want me to stop, just say and I will."

Relief and gratitude flood her features and she nods but doesn't say anything when I circle her clit with my thumb. She closes her eyes and inhales sharply.

I go slowly at first so that she can get used to the sensation of someone else touching her. When it becomes clear that she is enjoying it, I speed up a bit. She is slippery and wet and as much as I want to drive four fingers up her pussy, I don't. No invasion. That's her rule and I will stick to it.

"Ryker!" she pants, letting me know she is close to letting go. "Yes! Yes!"

I don't let up when I feel her tense, hear her gasp as the climax hits her, I massage her clit through the waves of ecstasy smiling to myself when she grips the sheets tightly, arching her back off the bed.

"Ryker!" she cries. "I am yours!"

Those three words hit me square in the chest. It brings out the Wolf in me. I close her legs and straddle her, looming over her, pressing my hands into the bed on either side of her head.

I see the fleeting fear in her eyes as her thoughts go to places I don't want them going. I keep my body away from hers. I don't touch her with any part of me as I hover over her.

"Say that again," I whisper to her.

"Yours," she whispers back. "I am yours, Ryker."

I close my eyes and savor the words as they wash over me. I ease up the pressure and sit back, opening my eyes again.

"I am yours, Bree," I murmur and open her legs again. This time I grab her thighs and drag her towards me.

"Ryker," she says, shaking her head as I kneel and grab my cock in my hand.

"Do you trust me, Bree?"

She hesitates, but I don't take offense. She has no idea what I'm about to do to her and she knows I could overpower her in a second.

"Do you trust me?" I ask again.

She nods stiffly and forces herself to relax.

"I will never hurt you, Bree," I say quietly and lean into her. She tenses up again, shaking her head wildly.

My eyes bore into hers as I press the tip of my cock against her clit. She gasps when I start to circle the head over her most sensitive spot. She opens her legs wider.

"Do you trust me?" I ask again. I need the words.

"Yes," she breathes. "I trust you."

I exhale and exert more pressure on her clit with the tip of my dick. She cries out, arching her back again, showing off her perfect tits with their rock-hard nipples.

"Twist your nipples," I pant gruffly. "Let me see it."

There is no pause now. She reaches up and takes her nipples between her fingers, twisting them gently as my cock rotates against her clit, harder, faster. I'm sweating with the effort of holding onto my cum. I'm not ready to end this yet. I need her to explode with pleasure. She writhes on the bed, moaning, a sweat forming on her own brow.

"Ryker," she pants. "Please."

"Please what?" I rasp.

"More," she begs me, twisting harder on her nipples.

"Fuck," I mutter and stop circling her clit, only to rub the head furiously against her now.

"Ryker!" she cries and shudders on the bed as the orgasm hits her. A flood of juice slicks her pussy, and I can't resist scooting back a bit and swiping my tongue over her entrance.

"Jesus, Bree," I pant and sit up again, her cum coating my tongue and lips.

I start to jerk off now, fisting my cock roughly, nearly hurting myself in my need for release. "Fuck," I pant, "Fuck...uhn..."

It hits me hard. Harder than any other orgasm ever has. My balls tighten, my dick stiffens even more in my hand as I shoot my load in a thick stream of cum. I lean over her so it can splat on to her tits, onto her chin, all over my stomach until the last of it drips onto her pussy. I've marked her completely. She is mine and no one can take her from me.

"Ah," she cries out and does something that not only stiffens my cock again immediately, but also melts my dark heart, thawing it out with the heat and passion she shows me.

She runs her hands down her body, smearing the cum all over her, rubbing it into her skin, outlining the swell of her tits with it, covering her nipples in my seed. Coating her stomach, she sits up and wipes it all down her inner thighs and then she swipes up the drops on her pussy and licks her finger clean, her eyes never leaving mine.

"Yours," she says with more confidence than I have ever heard in her tone.

I fall like a fucking idiot.

Chapter 31

Bree

I wake up in the pre-dawn hours and sit upright, wondering where I am. It takes me a second to remember that I'm with Ryker in his cabin, in his *bed*.
Naked...and covered in his cum.

I smile to myself.

Womanly power? Oh yeah, I felt that in spades last night.

I look over my shoulder at the sleeping Alpha and my heart skips a beat. He showed me things I have only ever dreamed about and his respect for my boundaries staggered me. Yes, I had a momentary lapse in that faith when I thought he was going to take me fully, but he didn't. I put my trust in him and he kept his word.

Maria asked me to tell him what was in my heart, and I wasn't sure, but I know now. I'm falling for him in a way that is turning my world upside down. I still don't understand it, but we fit.

Truly and completely.

I know without a doubt that I will give my virginity to

him, and I also know that he will take it as the precious thing that it is to me and not abuse the privilege. He has an honor that is growing, and he is proving to me and the rest of the Pack what an amazing man and Wolf he is. He has taken this sudden regime change and made it his own. I've heard the Wolves talking. They all thought he would be completely useless and run this Pack into the ground.

Hell, *I* thought that.

However, he has proven us all wrong in the few short weeks since he took over. Dealing with the loss of his father must've been hard anyway but taking his place as Alpha must've been even more difficult.

I reach out and stroke his face with the back of my hand, watching his features relax before his eyes fly open.

"Hi," I say softly.

"Everything okay?" he asks, blinking and sitting up before he scans the cabin quickly looking for signs of danger.

"Everything is fine. Go back to sleep," I say and climb off the bed. "I should go. Hunter is waiting for me."

"Fuck him, he'll be fine," Ryker growls and grabs my wrist, pulling me back onto the bed.

I giggle. "It's rude. I told him I wouldn't be long."

"And I told him not to wait up," Ryker says with that sexy smirk that makes my heart beat faster.

"You're an ass," I remark. "You had no idea I would stay the night."

"No, but I'd hoped," he says, waggling his eyebrows at me comically. "Seeing as we are up, want to have some more fun?" he adds salaciously.

"Actually, yes," I say to his surprise. "But outside. I want to Shift and run with you."

His face drops into a fierce frown. "No, Bree. I don't want you out there."

"I'll be with you; how much safer can I be?" I ask quietly, cupping his cheek and stroking his ego at the same time.

He knows it. He's not stupid. He narrows his eyes at me and draws me onto his lap. I can feel his semi-hard cock under my pussy. My clit twitches, causing me to wiggle over him.

He inhales deeply. "Do more of that," he murmurs.

"No," I say. "I want to Shift and run. It's been a couple of days. I'm going crazy."

I see him take that in. He knows I need to do this. Not Shifting is dangerous for a Wolf and he knows that the compound has been put on guard, causing a lot of us to stay indoors and only venture out for necessary reasons. I've been too nervous to Shift. The anxiety has affected me in more ways than one. I feel more relaxed now than I have in days, and I know what I need.

"You stay right next to me. You do not under any circumstances run off, do you hear me?" he growls.

"Yes, sir," I comment wryly.

He chuckles. "Mmm, say that again."

I cup his face and lean closer, brushing my lips against his. "Yes, sir," I murmur.

He lifts me off his lap and climbs off the bed. "You first," he says.

I suddenly go shy. I've never had someone watch me Shift before.

"Please," he whispers. "I need to see you transform."

I bite my lip and look down, the feeling washing over me, dropping me to my hands and knees. I stretch my back out and growl low and feral as my bones crack and reform, causing a pain that is quickly replaced with pleasure when I've completed my Shift.

Ryker drops to his knees next to me and reaches out to

stroke my head and kiss my nose. "You are beautiful. And so small," he adds with a chuckle.

I snap at his fingers, baring my teeth.

He is still laughing as he Shifts into the magnificent gray and white Alpha, nearly twice my size.

I definitely don't need to be worried about roaming the woods with him next to me.

He bounds over to the partially open window and shoves it open further with his nose before he leaps out. I follow to see him waiting for me on the porch.

Together we head off into the woods and true to my word, I stay right next to him the entire time, even when I hear a rogue rabbit that catches my attention, I don't divert off the course he has set.

I know exactly where he is taking me. To the clearing where he saved me from the idiots and where he followed me when I had a panic attack the day after. He picks up his pace and I keep up, just barely. He is definitely trying to keep his stride slower to match mine, so I don't fall behind. I feel a bit inferior before I push it aside. I am not inferior just because he is bigger, stronger and faster than me. He is an Alpha. I'm just a normal Wolf, that is slightly on the smaller side, I know that. But I accepted it a long time ago and I know that he doesn't think any less of me because of it. Maybe at first, I did. I was ashamed to be next to him in Wolf form, but not now as we run through the woods towards a place that is special to us. I know he will protect me and I'm fine with that. Yes, I like to be able to take care of myself but the relief I feel when I think about his strong, reassuring presence next to me doesn't annoy me.

Entering the clearing, he pads across to the big boulder in the middle and I follow him. He turns in a circle and flops down. I curl up in front of him, enjoying the warmth of his body next to mine and his tail swishing over me protectively.

My wolf instinct wants to get up and prowl around, but I'm too content to move right now. I feel myself falling asleep again next to him, a sure sign that I'm comfortable and relaxed.

I wake up with a start, knowing straight away that Ryker isn't next to me anymore. Panic hits me and I stand up, sniffing wildly.

I see Ryker on the edge of the clearing. He looks over as he hears me stir and Shifts back to his human form before he strides over and kneels in front of me.

"It's time to go, Bree. It's not safe out here."

I tilt my head, asking him to elaborate.

He hesitates but then sighs. "We were being watched. Two, maybe three Wolves were here. We need to leave."

My heart thumps but his strong hand on my head reassures me. "They're gone now, and I won't let anything happen to you."

I lick his hand and watch as he Shifts again to his Wolf form, and we head off back to the compound. My nerves are pinging, which has his hackles up. He's not irritated by it; he is reacting to me.

Must get her back inside where it's safe.

I stop as I hear this thought that wasn't mine in my head.

"What?" I ask in my head.

He stops as well and looks at me.

"Did you hear me?"

"Yes. Can you hear me?" I ask tentatively.

"Yes," he replies.

"Weird," I respond. I have never been able to hear another Wolf's thoughts or have them hear mine. This is bizarre.

His intense gaze on me makes me uncomfortable. *"We need to keep going,"* he says eventually.

I bob my head and pick up my pace. I want to be back in my cabin now.

Soon, my home is in sight as it gets light and I waste no time in leaping through the open window. First thing I see is Hunter asleep in the chair I left him in.

He jumps up, ready to pounce but stops when he sees me and Ryker, who followed me in this time.

Ryker has already Shifted and is muttering to Hunter. I pad into the bathroom and nose the door closed before I Shift back to my human form and grab the thick toweling robe off the back of the door and slip it on. I tie it tightly and head back to the men.

"You don't move out of this cabin," Ryker says to me in a tone that I dislike, only because it's an order. I know he's got his Alpha head on, so I try not to let it show on my face that I disapprove.

I must fail in that though because his features soften slightly and he comes over, gloriously naked making my hands itch to touch him. He draws me to him in a tight embrace. "Please, Bree, don't fight me on this," he murmurs in my ear.

"I'll stay for now, but I've got knitting club at your mom's later," I inform him.

"What time?" he asks with a frown.

"After lunch."

"I'll escort you over and pick you up later," he says distractedly. He glances at Hunter with a grimace before he looks back at me. "Please consider moving in with me until this is over," he mutters quietly. "I need to know you are safe."

My first instinct to shut him down is curbed by the sheer concern on his face. I sigh and say, "I'll think about it." I already know the answer will be no, but it pleases him that I said I'd consider his request.

"Then we go tomorrow," I state. "Send word to Jackson to be ready."

Hunter nods and leaves me alone. Every bone in my body is screaming at me to go and sit outside Bree's cabin to make sure she remains unharmed, but not only will she kick my ass over it, the rest of the Pack needs me as well. This has just stepped up a notch. I'm sure whoever is behind this is about to make their move and better it be away from here when they come at me. I shove a few items in a holdall too distracted to really think about it. I need coffee but I can't risk making any in here.

I quickly head to my mom's cabin, knocking swiftly and waiting while she opens it. "Ryker," she says in surprise. "I wasn't expecting you."

Her concern that she didn't know I was coming hits me. Usually, she has the sense or whatever it is.

"Coffee?" I ask.

"Come in," she says, moving out of the way for me to enter. "Everything okay?"

I shake my head as I pour out a massive mug. I quickly tell her everything.

She is worried but remains calm. "Whoever this is wants the Pack, which means they need you out of the way," she muses. "With you off Pack lands, they will feel they have more of an opportunity to take you out, but it does leave the compound vulnerable."

"I know," I say with a sigh. "Jake is coming with me, but Hunter is staying here. The guards are patrolling twenty-four seven. We've had no incidents on the land since we've tripled the guards, which shows that we were stalked in the woods."

"I don't know if Bree is better off staying with me while you're gone," Mom says.

I couldn't love her more. "You will have to be the one to

ask her because she has flat out refused my offers," I say, throwing her a grateful smile.

"Leave it with me," she says, patting my hand. "She is a good girl and good for you. You need her in your life, and you have to keep her there, Ry. Have you told her yet?"

I shake my head, feeling guilty. "I want to, but every time I try, I just picture her panicking and running."

"That's not a good enough reason," she says sternly. "You cannot keep this from her. She has a right to know what she is in the middle of."

"I know," I mutter. "I'll tell her when I get back."

She growls at me, but I'm not changing my mind. I'm not telling her that we are Fated Mates and then just fucking off for who knows how long. What if I tell her and then I get killed? She will mourn me more if she knows and accepts the bond. I can't put her through that. It's lame reasoning. My brain tells me that, but I refuse to acknowledge a different course of action.

"This will end in disaster, Ryker," she warns me.

"It won't. Just keep quiet until I get back and then I'll tell her. Ask her to stay here when she comes over later. I need to know she isn't alone." It's an order, and she knows it. She purses her lips at me but stays quiet, only nodding her head in response.

I drain the rest of the coffee and head out to patrol. I have a dozen other things that I should be doing before I leave, but this takes precedence.

When the time comes to escort Bree to my mom's, I knock lightly on the door. I'm glad to see she closed the window and when she calls out for me to identify myself, I feel a bit better that she is taking precautions.

"Bree, it's Ryker," I say through the door.

I hear the bolt slide across and then she opens the door. "Hey," she says.

"Can we talk quick?" I ask.

She nods warily at my curt tone and beckons me inside.

"I'm leaving on the Recruit tomorrow," I get straight out. "Hunter is staying here along with all the guards. Jake is coming with me. I need you to be alert and be safe."

"Tomorrow?" she asks, her face falling. "That's early."

"I know, but I think whoever was watching us earlier will follow me. I want them away from you," I state.

"Oh," she says and looks away. "Will you be okay out there? Aren't you safer here?"

"You will be safer if I'm gone," I say, trying to be rational. Now that I'm with her, I don't want to leave her. Ever.

"Oh," she says again. "Okay."

I can tell she isn't convinced, but she doesn't argue with me. She has reverted to her shy, quiet self, probably because of all the stress from this morning.

She picks up her knitting bag and shoves past me. I grab her arm, stopping her in her tracks. "Bree, please. This is the right move."

"If you say so," she mutters.

"Come over tonight?"

She nods, but it's stiff and awkward.

I sigh and let her go, leading the way to my mom's cabin in silence.

Before she enters, she pauses and turns back to me. "You asked me last night to trust you and I do. With that and this. If you think this is right, then I support you. I'll miss you."

I close the distance between us, scooping her up into my arms. "I'll miss you more than you'll know," I whisper before I kiss her deeply.

She returns it and then wiggles out of my arms. "I get the feeling your mom is watching us," she says with a giggle.

"Probably," I agree with a sigh. "I'll come back in a couple of hours and then we'll spend some time together before I leave."

She nods and enters the cabin.

I hope my mom can convince Bree to stay with her while I'm away. I'll feel a lot better about leaving. As it is my heart feels like lead and my stomach is in knots.

I turn from the cabin and head back over the grounds, checking in on everyone and making sure everyone knows to be on alert over the next few days.

Chapter 33

Bree

My time at Maria's is subdued. She knows that I don't want to talk, so she doesn't push me. She is a lovely woman who makes me comfortable even though things are rocky in my mind right now. Ryker leaving so suddenly, leaving *me* is hard to digest. I know he has to go on the Recruit, but I wasn't expecting it so soon after we got together. I don't think I'm ready to be without him yet, not to mention he is leaving me here...alone.

"Bree, honey, can I have a word?" Maria asks when I'm packing up to leave.

"Uhm, sure," I mutter, wishing we had left it at goodbye.

She takes me by the elbow and steers me into a corner of the cabin. "I know Ryker is leaving tomorrow. I wondered if you wanted to stay here with me while he's gone. I'm lonely since Jefferson...died...and I would love the company," she says.

I blink, taking in her request. Why me? Why not one of her daughters?

"Uhm," I say again that feeling of comfort being ripped away slightly. I struggle to pull it back. Something doesn't feel right here. Maria is one of the strongest women I know. There is no way she would ask *me* of all people to invade her home to keep her company while her son, who doesn't even live with her, is away.

I grit my teeth. "Did Ryker put you up to this?" I ask bluntly.

She grins. "No, but I didn't think I could pull the wool over your eyes for very long. You got me. This was my idea, but my ruse makes it no less important. I don't want you on your own. Neither does Ryker, but this was my idea. Stay with me. We could have some fun girly nights."

I roll my eyes. This family. They are incorrigible. But it's nice how protective they are. "Sure." I relent fairly easily now that the cover-up is out of the way. In a way, it will be nice not to be alone during this uncertain time.

Maria smiles smugly. "Good girl. Now go and spend some time with Ry before he leaves."

"Yes, Ma'am," I murmur and turn with a small smile.

Before I open the door, I know Ryker is waiting for me on the other side. I open it and go to him straight away, pulling him to me and tilting my head up for a kiss. I ignore the catcalls of the other women as we kiss on the porch, enjoying it almost. It's about time everyone around here saw me for something other than the resident virgin.

Ryker takes full advantage of my come on, not caring either by the looks of it. He chuckles against my mouth and grips my chin tightly. "What's brought this on?" he asks with a sly smile.

I giggle and snuggle into him, feeling whole in his arms. I shrug. "I'm going to miss you while you're gone. Might as well make the most of tonight."

"Oh?" he asks in a tone etched with darkness and hope at the same time.

"Sorry, not that," I inform him. "How about we save that for when you get back. Give you something to think about."

"Fuck, Bree. You are a temptress," he murmurs. "You know that's all I'll be thinking about now."

"No, it won't. You have a job to do, and you will do it well because that is who you are. I know that now," I say, squeezing his hand. "You are a good man and a good Alpha. This Pack is lucky to have you."

"Jesus, sappy much?" he mumbles but I can see he is pleased with my comments. "Come. Hunter has prepared us his infamous spaghetti and meatballs and will get shitty if he finds out we're late and it's gone cold."

I snort in amusement. "He is a good friend to you."

"He is more than that," Ryker says seriously. "He is my brother."

We walk in silence until we reach his cabin where the smell of the food makes my stomach rumble. I haven't eaten all day because of nerves and anxiety and then learning that Ryker was leaving, I even refused Maria's homemade cookies, which are usually irresistible to me.

"I'm only going to ask this once more and then I'll drop it," I start. "Are you sure leaving is the right thing to do?"

He sighs. "I have to keep you and this Pack safe. Whoever is after me, will follow, I'm sure of it."

I nod, knowing already that he was going to say that. "I'll be staying with your mom while you're gone," I say and then add, "But I'm sure you already knew that."

"I knew she was going to ask. It was her idea, by the way..."

"I know," I say, taking his hand.

"I'm glad you said yes," he adds and pulls a chair out for me to sit.

The next several hours comprise food, conversation and sexy deep kisses before he takes me to his bed where he wraps his arms around me, and we lie quietly until we both fall asleep.

It is perfect.

※

I wake up to the sun just peeking through the windows. I look over my shoulder at Ryker. He is awake and smiles at me.

"Hey," I say, rubbing my eyes.

"Hi," he says and rolls over, bringing me with him so that I'm sitting on his lap. "I like waking up with you."

"Mm, same," I agree and lean over to kiss him.

"I'm falling hard for you, Bree," he says seriously. "It's deep and real and has nothing to do with the Alpha bond, I know it in my gut..." He trails off, his eyes clouding over.

"Alpha bond?" I ask curiously. What is he talking about?

"Nothing," he says and sits up, removing me from his lap and standing up.

"Not nothing," I press, whatever it is, he is acting like he didn't mean to say it. Has he been hiding something from me? I kneel on the bed. "Ryker," I say. "What do you mean by the Alpha bond?"

He runs his hand through his hair, letting out an exasperated sigh. "It's nothing, Bree. Forget it."

"Oh no," I say, my temper rising. I climb off the bed. "You said it and now you're trying to cover something up. What is the Alpha bond?" I mean it kind of speaks for itself now that I stop and think about it. "Do you have a bond to me...as my Alpha?" I ask in confusion as I try to figure it all out.

"Just forget it," he growls at me and paces over to the windows.

"Ryker. Are you saying that what we have is something deeper? Are you saying that these feelings I have aren't real but part of some bond because you are my Alpha?" I'm starting to panic. Everything I thought I knew is crumbling away. I'm not here because of him and me, I'm here because of *him*. There is a world of difference and he kept it from me.

"I can't speak for your feelings," he grits out. "Mine are real."

"But what about mine?" I shriek at him. "You knew this all along and you didn't say *anything*?"

He spins to me, reacting angrily to my tone. I don't care. He had no right to hide this from me.

"We are Fated Mates, Bree. You and I are destined to be together. The bond only kicked in when I became Alpha. It took me a few days to know something was different because *we* are so different, but that's what this is. It's Fate. I didn't want to tell you because I knew you would react this way and probably run. Are you going to run, Bree?"

"What?" I spit out. Is he seriously putting all of this on me? How dare he. "You didn't give me a chance to figure any of this out. You've just dumped this on me and now I don't know if what I feel for you is real or this bond! How could you manipulate me that way?" The hurt in my heart is almost killing me. I knew he would hurt me. I should've stayed strong and stayed away.

"Bree, wait," he says as I pick up my shoes and shove past him.

"No," I say, holding up my hand. "No, I need to think about this."

"For how long?" he asks darkly.

"I don't know, Ryker. I need to process this. I need to figure out if this is all just because of this bond." Tears spring to my eyes and I turn from him. "I'll see you when you get back," I mutter and run as fast as I can out of the cabin, back to my own, bursting through the door and finally letting the tears fall. I slam the door closed and throw my shoes to the floor, flinging myself on the bed. This is the ultimate betrayal. He kept this important information from me and made a complete fool out of me. If he really cared about me, he wouldn't have done that. This entire relationship is built on a lie, and it stabs me in the heart over and over again because I really thought I was falling in love with him.

Chapter 34

Bree

I don't know how long I lie on the bed, sobbing, soaking the pillowcase. I've tried to see this from Ryker's point of view, but I can't. It keeps coming back to the fact that he lied to me and that lie has made me think my feelings might not be true. I could've given myself to him fully and completely based on a lie and *that* is what hurts the most. He didn't respect me enough to tell me.

A knock at the door interrupts my weeping. "Go away," I mumble.

"Bree, it's Maria," she calls through the door. "Can I come in?"

"No," I mutter but my manners get me off the bed and, staggering to the door, I drag it open.

Her surprised look at my disheveled appearance doesn't help matters and just makes me cry harder.

"Oh, Bree, honey. What's the matter?" she asks, pulling me into her arms. "Is it Ryker leaving?" she adds.

The sound of his name hitches my breath, making it even worse. "He-he lied to me," I blurt out.

"Oh?" Maria says, pushing me gently back so she can look me in the face. "What about?"

I roughly pull away from her. I can't talk to her about this. She is his mother. She will take his side. "Nothing," I mutter.

"Bree, you need to talk. I'm here to listen. Please tell me what happened."

I want to. I want the whole sordid story to come out, but I don't want her looking at me any differently. I couldn't bear it.

But it's too late.

The words tumble from my lips, and I tell her everything from how I thought I was feeling to his slip up and then his explanation of why I feel this way.

It doesn't make me feel any better, if anything, it makes me feel worse.

"I see," she says carefully. "And you don't know now if what you're feeling is real or not?"

I shake my head, brushing my tears away. "It's not just that. I was going to...going to..." I can't even say the words to her.

"Going to what?" she presses.

"I was going to give him my virginity when he got back," I mutter, turning away.

"Oh," she says knowingly. "You think that if you'd done that without him telling you about the bond it would be a betrayal. You're right," she adds to my surprise. "It would've been. We will never know if he would have told you, but I like to think my son isn't as big an asshole as that. He cares for you, Bree, really cares for you. I have never seen him like this before and it just isn't the bond. What he feels is real."

"How am I supposed to tell the difference?" I ask, taking

that in, not dismissing it outright because it hurts too much to think that way.

"It's hard, I know," she says, and the penny drops.

Of course she knows. She was an Alpha's mate. I groan and feel ridiculous. Did she act this way? Probably not.

"I know because I went through the same thing when Jefferson told me about the bond. But it took me all of five minutes to figure out that I loved him, anyway. He, like Ryker, kept it from me for a while. I don't condone it, but I understand *why* they, he, feels the need to hide it. It isn't malicious, it's because he is scared of losing you. He was scared you would run, and he was right, wasn't he? You ran." There's no accusation, just fact.

"I did," I say, ashamed of my actions. "Did you?" I ask hopefully.

"Yes," she says with a smile. "But I knew it was meant to be and not because the Fates deemed it so. We fit together. I knew it from the start."

"I'm not that sure," I admit quietly. "We are so different. It made little sense to me why we were suddenly involved so deeply. It does *now*, but how does that help me?"

"Different is good, sweetie. You keep him on his toes because he doesn't know how to be with someone like you."

"Someone like me," I state coldly. "You mean a shy virgin?"

"I do and I don't mean it in a negative way, at all. You are doing what is right for you, your body and your heart. You are to be applauded, not scorned. Ryker isn't used to that. He has always chosen the easy relationships because he never really cared enough. With you, he cares. A lot. I can see it when he talks about you, looks at you. You have captured his heart."

"Why couldn't he tell me all of this?" I whine.

"Probably because he is a man, and an Alpha Wolf on top of that. It's amazing that he has even given you what he has."

Well, I can't argue with that. He has fallen to his knees for me. That is definitely not Alpha Wolf behavior.

"What is the first thing you feel when you think about him?"

"That I care about him," I reply instantly. "I just don't know if it's real or not."

"Oh, it's real. If you don't need to think about it, it's real," she says. "How did you leave things?"

"Terribly," I moan, dropping my face into my hands.

"He is leaving in a few minutes. Go to him and tell him how you feel. But there is something that he won't have told you about the rejection process. I don't want to add to your pressure but if you reject him, or he rejects you it will be bad." She purses her lips.

"Rejection process?" I ask tentatively. It doesn't sound good.

"If you choose not to be with him, it will affect you, Bree. I know that doesn't help you make this decision right now, but you need to know. You need to be very careful how you handle this."

"What do you mean?" I ask, dread welling up in me. This is going from bad to worse.

"Just don't be hasty with your words. Tell him what you're feeling right now. That's all you need to do. You can discuss it properly when he returns."

I nod slowly. Fuck. There just isn't another word for it.

"Go, quickly," she urges me.

"Okay," I say, knowing that Alpha bond or not, rejection process or not, I need to see him before he goes. He deserves that much from me.

I race past her barefoot, heading towards his cabin. I slow when I see him a bit further along, the minivan already fired up and ready to go. Kane climbs on board with another couple of Wolves. I see Jake hovering on the other side, eyes on Ryker and…I gulp.

Valerie.

I come to a complete halt when almost in slow motion, I watch as she cups his cheek and raises up on her tiptoes to give him a quick kiss before she slides into the back of the minivan.

My heart stops beating for just a second before it starts to pound in anger.

Ryker's face darkens as he slides the door shut and then he turns and climbs into the driver's seat, slamming the door closed.

He didn't even see me.

Instead of being sad about me running away from him before, he packed up his whore and is about to drive off with her on the road where he can fuck her until his dick bursts and forget all about me and my *lack* of fucking him.

He replaced me without a second thought.

The tears fall freely again but I brush them aside. He is a complete asshole. He has no right to hurt me this way. Not once but twice.

My gut twists inside me, the sweat forms on my forehead before my head spins making me nauseous.

Or have I been completely naïve about this all along?

Has he still been hooking up with her all of this time and that's why he was so easy going about me withholding sex from him?

The thought makes me feel sick.

Of course he has.

Why would he wait for me when he has *her*, legs wide open and ready for him?

"No, no, no," I whisper. "Ryker…"

I turn, clutching my stomach to stop myself from throwing up all over my bare feet.

I run in the opposite direction back towards my cabin, but when I see Valerie's on my way back, I pause. I look over my shoulder but don't see anyone. Making a rash decision that will probably come back to bite me on the backside, I make my way determinedly to her front door and shove it open. The answers I seek are in here. He wouldn't take her back to his cabin. He would come *here*. I just need to find the proof.

Chapter 35

Ryker

I grip the steering wheel grimly, feeling more lost than I ever have. Bree running out on me before was the most painful thing I have ever experienced. I wanted so badly to go after her, but I just probably would have made it worse. She needs to deal with this on her own and I have to hope and pray that she doesn't reject me.

"What?" I growl at Jake but keep my eyes on the bumpy track as we head out of the compound.

Out of the corner of my eye, I see him glance over his shoulder before he looks back at me. "Val? Thought things were getting hot and heavy with Bree," he says quietly.

"It's not what you think," I growl. "Her niece is sick, and she's her only family. She's catching a ride to Thorpesworth because it's on the way. That's all."

Silence.

I know why.

"She's grateful for the ride, otherwise she'd have had to walk. It saves her a couple of days. Let it go," I snarl.

"I see," he says and drops it.

After a pause, he says, "So Bree, huh? Didn't figure you two as a pairing."

"It's a long story and probably one with an abrupt ending. She is pissed, and it's probably over."

"That's two probablys," he says. "What makes you think it is *probably* over?"

"Nuthin'" I mutter.

"Come on, Ry. Tell Jakey what you did," he snorts.

"What makes you think *I* did something?" I snap.

"Please," he says with a laugh. "I know you better than you know yourself."

"Fuck off."

"Touchy," he drawls.

I hunch my shoulders more if that's possible and ignore him for as long as I can. That's about half an hour. We've hit the main road, and it's about thirty miles until we can drop Valerie off. I don't want her in the van. I don't want her lips to have touched me. She leaned in before I knew what she was doing.

All of this is wrong. So wrong. I should have Bree with me. We left things so broken, I don't know if they can be fixed. I fucked up, I know I did, but she has to know that I didn't mean to hurt her. I definitely did not mean to manipulate her. That she thinks this, stabs me in the guts. I want to turn around and head back but what would I say to her now? I need time to figure out my next move and so does she.

"Thanks for the ride, sugar," Valerie purrs, trying to kiss me again, but this time, I push her away.

"It's fine," I snap and without waiting for another word from anyone, I stamp on the gas and shoot away from the curb, lucky that I didn't drive over her feet. Her very presence rankled me but now that she is gone, I relax a little bit.

"Ouch," Jake says, surfacing from his phone for the first time in ages. "Maybe you need to call Hunter and ask to speak to Bree." He waggles his phone in front of me enticingly.

"No," I grit out. "Hunter has other things to focus on than my disastrous love life." I shove the phone out of my face.

Fact is, I don't want to speak to Bree. Not yet. I haven't got my head on straight enough. I will just end up fucking it up even more. Besides, it has to be a face-to-face conversation. Unless *she* called *me,* then I wouldn't hesitate.

"No signal now, anyway," Jake comments and stashes his phone in his jacket pocket.

Great. Now the option is completely off the table.

"Your face says you need to talk about it," Jake says after a beat.

"I kept something from her, and she is furious with me. There. Happy?"

"What did you keep from her?"

"That she is my Fated Mate," I mumble.

"Your what-now?" Jake asks.

I sigh and launch into the story, not surprising him really.

"Figured there'd be something like that," he says, nodding his head.

"Oh, did you now?" I growl.

"I mean, yeah. Makes sense, you know?"

"Whatever," I mutter, white knuckling the steering wheel even more. It's about to snap under the pressure. "What time are we meeting Jackson and his crew?" I change the subject.

Jake checks his watch. "In an hour at Westview. We'll be there in plenty of time."

I nod and carry on cursing myself for letting it slip about

the bond. It was the absolute wrong time to say it. I only hope she can forgive me and give me what I need from her, which is her love. True and real.

Fuck.

I'm living in a dreamworld.

I'm fucked.

Chapter 36

Bree

My hands are shaking.
I'm back in my cabin after finding out more than I ever wanted to in Valerie's home. She is wild. Her underwear is practically non-existent, and those that I did find were all lacy thongs and nippleless bras. It made me shudder. I tried not to pry, but I wanted to know. Her nightstand is full of dildos of every size and shape, but it was in the bottom drawer of the dresser, under her ripped jeans, where I found the worst of the worst. Photos of her and Ryker. Well, not of her and Ryker together in any of them, but photos of Ryker, naked and highly aroused, clearly amused to be snapped that way and pictures of *her* chained up like a neglected dog, whipped and abused but definitely enjoying it. Photos of bits smushed together, engaged in intercourse, both front and back.

I feel sick knowing that Ryker's dick has been inside that woman. I knew it before, obviously, but *seeing* it with my own two eyes, captured for eternity for everyone to see, is not only vomit-inducing but humiliating beyond belief. Everyone must think I am such a fool, being so doe-eyed over the new Alpha and thinking he cared about me, when all the time he was still hooking up with Valerie and doing God only knows what to her.

"I hate you," I mutter, letting out an ugly sob. "It's not fair. I'm a good person. I don't deserve to be treated this way."

I moan in distress, my insides churning. I double over, feeling the waves of nausea hit me over and over again. I make it to the toilet just in time to throw up, clutching at the bowl in desperation for it to end, my hair falling in my face.

"You're an idiot," I groan. "A fucking idiot, Bree. He lied to you about the Alpha bond, made an absolute fool of you and you let him."

I wipe my mouth on some toilet paper and flush, slumping down against the bathroom wall and placing my hot forehead against the cool tile. It takes me another minute to crawl over to the basin. I run the cold tap, swishing my hands around the water and wiping my mouth again, patting my sweaty face down, trying to cool down.

I know that after speaking to Maria, I could look past the Alpha bond if he was willing to explain to me exactly why he lied to me, but the Valerie thing is non negotiable. I can't be with a man who is so willing to dismiss me because I won't give him sex. I didn't think he was like that, not anymore anyway. He had convinced me he was willing to wait for me. He *promised*. But the evidence points to him cheating on me with her. I know the photos are from a while ago. Common sense tells me that, but the t-shirt I found the photos wrapped up in is his. One that he wore only a few days ago when he was with *me*.

My head spins and I lean over the toilet again to vomit up

the last of the contents of my stomach, which wasn't a lot to start with.

"You're a bastard," I mutter. "You are a bastard, and I don't want to…"

Even in my fevered state that has come on so suddenly, I stop. Maria said to be careful with my words.

But why should I? Why should I be the one to sit here like a—a *dickhead* while he is probably riding Valerie like the slutty Wolf she is.

I don't want to be careful with my words. I want to say them out loud. I want to break ties with Ryker and his whorish ways, never to look back. I want to hide myself in my cabin until the humiliation passes and the Pack finds something else to talk about. Or maybe I'll just run away and join another Pack. Maybe I can make amends with Casey and go where she went.

I shake my head, my eyes closed against the movement. Now I know my brain is fried. Casey is the worst. She is as bad as Ryker. I am better off without either of them in my life.

I draw in a deep breath and haul myself to my feet with the help of the basin. I look at my reflection in the mirror and cringe. I am a mess. My eyes are puffy and red from crying, my nose is running, my hair is plastered to my head. I don't know why I feel so terrible, so *sick,* but I don't care. I stare into my swollen eyes and exhale. "I am better off without you in my life, Ryker

"I reject you."

There is a short pause before I hear an agonized wail. I clap my hands to my ears before I realize it's coming from me. I drop to the floor, twitching controllably, the noise level increasing until my throat is raw with screaming.

And then everything goes quiet.

Chapter 37

Ryker

I'm on my third beer and whisky chaser.

Big mistake.

I want to kick someone's ass, which is never a good thing.

We connected with Jackson about an hour ago but decided to lie low for the rest of today, check out the local Wolves, see if there was any interest before we go in hardcore. This dingy bar attached to the even dingier motel is full of both humans and Wolves, as rough as each other.

"Think you should go sleep it off," Jake says to me as I drain the last of the bottle.

I give him the stink-eye. It's not even dark out yet.

"'Nother," I slur, holding up my empty bottle to the man behind the bar.

"Nope," Jake says. "I'm cutting him off."

"Fuck you," I grit out. "You don't own me."

"No, but I have your back and you are way drunker than I've seen you. Go sleep it off."

It's a fucking order, and it makes the Alpha in me jump to attention. I stand up and round on him, fists clenched. "Wanna say that again?" I growl.

"Don't be a dick, Ry," he warns me.

I'm about to relent as all the fight goes out of me and all I want to do is curl up and sleep for a week, when a pain in my heart hits me so hard, I slump against the bar, clutching my chest.

"Ry?" Jake says, voice full of concern.

"Bree," I choke out.

No, no, no.

Bree, don't do this.

I can feel what she has done. It's too late.

She has rejected me.

Without even trying to clear the air between us, she has rejected me.

I stumble, going blind momentarily.

Knocking into a huge guy on my other side, I growl when my sight clears. I see him turn around; his face etched with anger. Not a human, definitely a Wolf.

"Fuck you," he snarls at me.

I suck in a deep breath and without even thinking about the consequences, I bunch my hand into a fist and draw back, punching him in his ugly motherfucking face. "Fuck *you*," I retort, not having much brainpower for more of a comeback. Bree has ripped my insides out and now all I can focus on is kicking the shit out of this dickhead and enjoying every second of it.

I slam my foot into his knee, making him drop. He is massive, but I'm an Alpha. There is no way he is winning this fight, even with me sunk under three beers and whiskys and having just been hit with a formal rejection from my Fated Mate.

He doesn't stand a chance.

I knee him in the face, busting his nose, gripping the collar of his denim jacket before Jake grabs hold of me.

"Ryker," he barks at me. "What the fuck?"

I shake him off and punch the asshole in front of me again, and again, bloodying my knuckles along with his face. The darkness inside me has risen and I'm out for as much blood as I can spill. I want to beat him into the ground...I want to kill him.

Rage is all around me.

The entire bar has now kicked off into a brawl. I can smell the anger and frustrations; the beer and whisky, and it has gotten my hackles up.

I'm rushed by three of the asshole's buddies, but they can't get me off my feet, even though they try.

Punched.

Kicked.

A broken bottle held to my throat.

"Do it," I hiss, feeling the rejection swamp me in utter desolation. "Just do it."

"Fuck's sake," Jake snarls and wrestles me away from the Wolves that have surrounded me. He shoves me forcefully outside and towards the van.

"Pull yourself together, asshole," he growls.

I slump against the van.

"What has gotten into you?" he hisses.

"Bree rejected me," I moan, hearing the pussy-whipped tone but not even caring at this point.

I wipe my bloody nose on my arm, smearing blood all up it, before I rub my face with my hand.

"I felt it. I can *feel* it. She has rejected me. She doesn't want me," I mutter.

"Fuck," Jake breathes out. "Shit. Ry..."

"Don't say anything," I interrupt, holding my hand up. "I just want to Shift and get away from here."

"Good idea," he says, patting me on the back.

Movement over his shoulder catches my eye. I see two female Wolves, one a curvy redhead that is eyeing me up like a bowlful of candy.

I avert my eyes. I'm not interested. Even in my sorry ass state. I turn my back and strip off, Shifting quickly and darting off before Jake can say another word to me. Seconds later, I hear rustling behind me and see a smaller, reddish Wolf following me. I know it's the redhead, but I ignore her. I don't want company. I just want to wallow in my pathetic life for one night before I have to get my head back on straight. Bree rejecting me is for the best. We don't fit. That much has always been clear. I need to mourn her loss and then move on.

I tell myself it's that simple, but the pain in my heart informs me that it is going to only get worse before it gets better.

Chapter 38

Bree

A banging in my head rouses me. I'm on the bathroom floor, drooling uncontrollably.

"Bree? Bree, honey, you in here?" Maria's voice filters through the door.

"Guurrr," I mutter, wiping my mouth.

My vision is blurred, my head feels like a stake has been driven through it and my heart...I can't even begin to explain the agony coursing through me.

"Bree!" Maria exclaims, bursting into the bathroom and apparently seeing me curled up. "What happened?"

She drops to her knees and lifts my head onto her lap. Moaning, I stifle the urge to throw up all over her jeans.

"Dammit," she mutters and then her voice fades out again.

I wake up with my head on a soft surface. I chance opening my eyes and groan. I turn onto my side and pull my knees up to my chest. I'm on my bed, which is a damn sight more comfortable than the floor, but I still feel like death on a stick.

"Bree," Maria says, coming over. "How're you feeling?"

I shake my head slightly. My tongue is stuck to the roof of my mouth.

She lifts my head and presses a bottle of water to my lips. I gulp it back, unsticking my tongue and quenching my fiery thirst.

"Easy," she says, taking it away before I'm ready.

I moan my complaint.

"What happened?" she asks.

Tears spring to my eyes and I shake my head again, causing the nausea that was being held at bay to rise up again.

"Did you speak to Ryker?" she asks quietly.

"N-no," I croak out, not meeting her eyes.

My vision has cleared a little bit, but goes fuzzy again in a wave of queasiness, so I close them again.

"What did you do?" she asks after a pause.

It's not an accusation. Maria isn't like that. She is merely trying to get to the bottom of what is wrong with me. I wish I knew.

"I saw him drive off with Val after kissing her," I mumble, wishing with every cell in my body that it wasn't true.

"What?" she snaps.

I flinch from her tone.

"Sorry, honey," she mutters, stroking my head. "Can you tell me more? There has to be an explanation for this."

On a staggered breath, I tell her everything about going into Valerie's cabin and finding the t-shirt and photos of them together, leaving out the naked bits because it's his mom, after all.

"I see," she says, drumming her fingers on the bed. "Did

you...Bree, I have to ask, when you saw all of this, did you... reject...him?"

"Yes," I whisper, ashamed of my actions. It was rash, I know that now. I meant it when I said it, but I was hurting. Now, I know that I shouldn't have said it. I don't mean it. Well, I don't think I do. Yes, what he has done is awful and humiliating, but shouldn't I give him the benefit of the doubt before jumping to such a drastic conclusion.

"Oh, sweetie," she says with a sigh. "That's why you feel like this. You are going through the rejection process. He will be feeling it as well."

"I'm sorry," I mumble. "I want to take it back."

She strokes my hair in silence. It's comforting and I start to drop off.

"The rejection process is harsh, Bree. It is potentially fatal to you. I tried to warn you, but my words weren't enough. I should've taken the time to explain it properly. You are in danger. We need to fix this," she says desperately.

"How?" I croak.

"Just get some rest, sweetie. I'll fix this, I promise you," she mutters, but she doesn't sound convincing even to my hopeful ears.

It doesn't take me long to fall asleep again and when I wake up, it's fully dark out. Maria has fallen asleep on the sofa. I smile, grateful she stayed with me. I feel a tiny bit better than I did earlier. Enough to be able to see and to haul my body out of the bed. I'm dressed only in a tee and my underwear. I drag on a pair of shorts and stumble to the kitchenette, gasping for water. I run the taps, splashing water on my face and pouring a glass of water that I gulp back quickly.

My head swims again. I place a hand on my forehead. I

need air. It's stifling in here. I'm sweating and red-hot to the touch.

Without a second thought, I stumble to the front door and pull it open, tripping onto the porch and down the steps.

Water.

It's all I can think about.

The lake. I need to get to the lake and submerge my feverish body into the cool water. There isn't a single part of me that doesn't want this. I *need* it.

Staggering to the back of the cabin, I make my way unsteadily into the dark woods. Somewhere deep down a warning triggers in my foggy brain, but I ignore it.

Water.

The lake.

Nothing else matters.

The muggy summer air does nothing to clear my head. If anything, it confuses me further.

What am I doing out here?

Where am I going?

Why am I feeling this way?

Ryker?

The thought of his name slams into my heart and brings back all the pain that had numbed into a ball deep in the pit of my stomach.

I lurch, choking out a sob.

Ryker and Valerie. Together.

I rejected him, but I didn't want to. I wanted to speak to him, figure this out. Try to see if it's all a misunderstanding.

The tiny voice in my head that screams at me at how naïve I'm being spurs me on to start running towards the lake. I crash blindly into trees as tears stream down my face. I bruise my arms, my bare feet are cut on stones, but I keep going until I reach the shore, needing to cool off.

I wade into the water. I'm not a strong swimmer, but that doesn't even factor into my decision to get as deep as I can.

I'm up to my waist when my feet slide on a slippery rock, plunging me under the cold water. I come up spluttering, feeling a strong hand wrap around my arm, hauling me up above the surface.

"Ryker?" I gasp.

"Not exactly," a voice I don't recognize says to me, the tinge of arrogance noticeable.

My heart thumps. The panic reflex sets in, and I start to struggle, but I'm no match for the Wolf that has hold of me. He is huge, all muscles and height.

"Let me go!" I bleat, struggling uselessly in his grasp.

"Oh no, little Wolf," he says with a cruel laugh. "You have fallen into my lap quite unexpectedly. This encounter is quite fortuitous and there is no way you are getting away from me."

His hand tightens around my arm before he lifts me off my feet, cradling me against his hard chest.

"Put me down," I cry out, scratching his face as viciously as I can, squirming to get away from him.

But I'm so weak, it's useless.

He has hold of me and I'm not going anywhere.

"I can see why he likes you," the strange Wolf whispers to me when I'm too tired to struggle anymore. "You're a bit of a firecracker, aren't you, little Wolf?"

"Who are you?" I mumble, all my fighting having made my head go fuzzy again, my vision blurry.

"You'll find out soon enough. Now that my patience in waiting for you to be alone and vulnerable has paid off, my timetable has been pushed up and I have plans to make. How stupid of Ryker to leave his Mate to wander the woods alone. I figured he'd care more than that. Oh well, his loss...my definite gain."

What is he talking about?

My eyes close because I'm unable to keep them open a second longer. My terror at being abducted has frozen me, even though I'm in no fit state to move, let alone fight for my life.

"Ryker," I mumble as the Wolf wades back to the shore and bundles me into a nearby boat, snapping a zip tie around my wrists, binding me. "Ryker. Help me…"

Chapter 39

Ryker

My eyes snap open.

Something has woken me.

Someone calling my name.

It's pre-dawn and I'm freezing. I'm naked, in human form, in the trees, my head banging.

I groan and rub my eyes, moving my stiff body and lifting my head off the cold, damp ground.

The scent of blood hits my nose and I look down at myself, sitting up right immediately. It's not coming from me, but close by.

Turning my head towards the coppery smell, I balk and scramble back, eyes wide and fixated on the mauled corpse of the curvy redhead slumped up against a nearby tree

"What the fuck?" I mutter and get to my feet. I'm a little bit unsteady, which is strange. Yes, I'd been tipsy before the Shift but that should've been taken care of. This feels harsher, more hardcore than being a bit drunk.

Drugged?

I have a funny taste in my dry mouth, but that could just be the hangover. I look over my shoulder to make sure I'm alone. I don't sense anyone else. Even in human form, I'd know if someone was close by. It's quiet and still, no signs of birds or wildlife.

So, who called out for me?

I approach the dead woman cautiously.

Definitely dead, so it wasn't her.

She appears to have been mauled by a wild animal, a *Wolf*. She has deep claw marks all over her body, her guts are spilling out and her throat has been ripped out.

"Jesus," I say, closing my eyes briefly in the hope that when I open them again, she isn't there.

But she is.

And she reeks of me.

Did I do this?

I don't remember. I don't remember anything after I Shifted and ran off after the bar fight…after Bree rejected me.

The woman is naked and covered in my scent. Did I screw her before I killed her? Or just one or the other? None of this makes sense.

My head spins and I crouch down, my hands on my chin as I try to figure this shit out.

I wouldn't screw her. Would I?

Bree hurt me more than I ever thought possible, but I still didn't want any other woman to drown my sorrows in dick first.

I cautiously sniff at myself but come up with nothing. That is even more curious.

"Fuck," I groan and fall to all fours. I Shift quickly and turn around, running straight back to the dive motel. I need Jake. If anyone can help me figure this out, he can.

Reaching the car park, I pad past the van and stop.

Jake is there, leaning up against it, stuffing a bacon muffin into his face. "You want?" he asks, holding out a brown paper bag to me.

My mouth waters and I Shift, instantly reaching for the backpack he hands me. I pull out the clothes from inside and hurriedly get dressed.

"You need to come with me," I say quietly.

At my serious tone, he straightens up. "What's up?"

"Just come with me," I repeat and turn, heading back into the trees.

Jake falls into step beside me. "How're you feeling today?"

"Like shit and it's even worse than before."

"Why?" he asks suspiciously. "What did you do?"

"I don't know," I whisper, feeling a sense of dread overwhelm me. What if I did this? I wish I could remember. I need to remember.

In silence, I take Jake to the place where I woke up. "What the fuck?" I ask in confusion, looking around. The dead woman is gone. "This is the place, I swear it."

"What place? Ryker, what is going on? Speak to me, man," Jake says, grabbing my arm to stop me mid turn.

I grimace. "I woke up here in human form. There was a woman..."

"For fuck's sake, Ry," Jake says in an exasperated tone.

"No, it wasn't like that," I snap. "She was...is...*dead*." I hiss out the last word. "Mauled by a Wolf. Me, maybe? I don't know. Fuck. She was here, I know it."

"Okay, I believe you," Jake says, taking me seriously with a fierce frown. "But where is she now?"

"Good fucking question," I growl.

"I have to ask, buddy. Did you do it?" Jake asks in a business-like tone that I don't give him crap for. Of course he needs to ask. I was in a bad way, still am if the truth be told.

"I don't know," I answer truthfully. "I don't remember."

"Anything?" Jake presses.

I shake my head. "I don't know if I screwed her. I don't know if I killed her."

Jake's eyes narrow. "Screwed? That was an option?"

"Well, she was naked and covered in my scent. How the fuck should I know?"

"Jesus," Jake mutters and comes closer, sniffing at me. "You don't smell like anyone else," he points out.

"I know," I grit out. "What the fuck is going on?"

"Set up?" Jake asks. "I mean why, who, something to do with your father's murder?"

"All good questions that I need the fucking answers to," I practically yell. I'm not angry with him, just frustrated at this situation and now that I've come to a bit and reality has set back in, the rejection from my Fated Mate settles over me again, making its agonizing presence known.

"Let's get back to the van. I think you need to get back to the Pack," Jake says slowly. "I'll call Hunter, he can pick you up."

"No," I state. I can't go back to the Pack, to *Bree*, not yet.

"You're going," Jake says. "You need to be as far away from here as you can get and, dude, you need to speak to Bree. Try to sort this mess out."

I shake my head. "I don't want to see her," I mumble. "It hurts too much."

"I can't say that I understand how much with the Alpha bond, but I've been dumped before, Ry. I do know the pain of that. You need closure from her, one way or the other."

He's probably right. I do need to get away from here. If I killed that woman, that *Wolf*...Fuck, I can't even think about that. I'm an Alpha, but it doesn't make me above the law.

"Jesus," I mutter and drop to my knees, feeling weak and exhausted all of a sudden.

"Ryker," Jake says, steadily. He grips me under my elbow and hauls me to my feet. "Let's get back to the van."

I nod slowly, my head feeling as heavy as lead. My heart explodes over and over again as I feel the rejection process stabbing at me repeatedly. "Why did she do this?" I mumble.

"That is something you have to ask her," Jake says matter-of-factly, leading me out of the small clearing and back into the thick trees.

I catch his worried glance in my direction. I must look like an absolute mess.

He bundles me into the passenger seat of the van and slams the door, climbing into the driver's side. He pulls out the sat phone and calls Hunter, who picks up on the first ring.

I tune out Jake's instruction to meet halfway, but frown when I see him pause in his movements and clear his throat. He slides out of the van and shuts the door, walking away as he gestures wildly while talking quietly into the phone.

"What's up?" I ask, hearing the dead tone in my voice and so does he, when he climbs back into the van and hangs up. He flings the phone onto the back seat.

"Nothing," he states coldly. "He's going to meet us at Wicksville. We need to go."

I nod numbly. The longer I sit here, the worse I feel. I can't move. Is this how Bree is feeling as well? Or does she feel worse?

A small, dark part of me hopes she feels worse.

Then the part of me that cares about her is swamped with guilt about wishing that. It only adds to my morose mood, which further aggravates the rejection process. I'm on a slow, downward spiral and the only one who can save me, doesn't want me.

I have no idea how to even begin to survive the next second, the next minute, the next *hour* without her.

Chapter 40

Bree

Breathing in deeply, I open my eyes. Keeping them closed for extended periods makes it easier to see clearly when I do open them for a short while. I'm in a small shed, with a window and a door. The sun is streaming in through the window, letting me know I'm facing East. My wrists are still tied behind my back, uncomfortably tight. My shoulders are aching. The air smells damp and slightly moldy. Probably coming from the dirt ground that I'm sitting on.

I try not to panic. That won't help anyone.

I was blindfolded shortly after getting on the boat. I *think* we came to the left of the lake, but it's hard to tell because my kidnapper drove around in a large circle first, which disoriented me.

The rejection process is still hitting me in waves, and I push back one of those swells now before I lose the water that is the only thing currently left in my stomach.

Speaking of my stomach, it rumbles, reminding me that despite the fear and sickness, I'm starving and thirsty.

I close my eyes again slowly, trying to keep my breathing regular. I can't Shift. I tried that already. I think there must be silver somewhere in the zip tie that is preventing me. But my anxiety probably also isn't helping.

"Ryker," I whisper. "Please, if you can hear me, I'm sorry. Please help me."

I've been trying this on and off since I was taken. He either can't hear me, or he doesn't care. Probably both. All I know is that I was taken *because* of Ryker, but I don't know why or by whom. My connection to the Alpha of the Silvercrest Pack is what has landed me here. Unfortunately, the fact that I rejected him has pissed off the strange Wolf, and that's why I ended up in this shed, shoved in, sprawling on my backside, in the early hours of this morning. He wanted me connected and bound, it seems. I'm still useful though, and that's why I firmly believe I'm still alive. If I wasn't, he would've killed me. He has to be the one who killed Jefferson. Not knowing why doesn't help me. Maybe if I had a clue, I could use it. I'm not the smartest Wolf in the Pack, but I'm not the dumbest either. Especially when it comes to survival.

My eyes fly open again when I hear the shed door open.

I gasp and shrink back when I see who saunters in, a vicious smirk on his face. The fear bounces off me, which makes him inhale deeply. That is doubled, no tripled, when two other men join him and close the door quietly behind them.

It's the three young Wolves who tormented me that day at that lake.

"Well, look who it is," the bolder of the three says, laughing cruelly at his friends. "And look, she is all tied up." His gaze lands on me and hardens. "Do you know what you did to us, slut?" he asks. "You had us beaten so badly, and for what? All we wanted to do was have some fun."

I shake my head. "Please, don't hurt me," I stammer. "I didn't mean for you to get in trouble."

"Oh, she didn't *mean* it," he jeers. "That makes it all right then, doesn't it?"

"I'm sorry," I croak out, fear constricting my throat. I shrink back as he approaches, pulling my knees up to my chest.

"I'm not going to hurt you," he says, crouching down. "Well, not much, anyway," he adds with an evil smirk. He leans forward, shoving my knees away from my chest and grabs the collar of my t-shirt. I strain my head to the side, knowing what he is going to do seconds before he does it. He rips it down the middle, exposing my breasts to him.

"Please," I beg him. "Please, I'm sorry."

"Sexy little thing, aren't you," he murmurs, pushing my hair out of my face before he reaches into my bra roughly and pulls my breasts out over the cups. He pinches my nipples, making me whimper.

He stands up again and unzips his pants.

My mouth goes dry, and the bile rises in my throat. I press my lips together tightly, but he doesn't force his dick in my mouth, to my relief. Instead, he starts to jerk off, his eyes on my breasts. "Patrick said we couldn't touch you, but I can still humiliate you, little slut. I can still cover you in my cum for your Alpha to find you when he tracks you down."

Patrick.

I don't recognize the name, but I think I'm starting to figure this out. I close my eyes but open them again quickly when one of the other men, steps forward and yanks on my hair. "Open your eyes. I want to see the degradation in them when all three of us mark you with our cum."

Clenching my jaw, I keep my eyes open but on a spot over the top of the man's head. He speeds up. I think he is ready for his release.

I brace myself but I can't help the flinch when his cum hits my skin in warm little puddles, covering my nipples and dripping down in between my breasts. I gulp back the urge to vomit when he aims his dick at my face and the last of his cum sprays out over my chin and lips. I want to wipe it away, but I don't move a muscle.

The first man laughs and puts his dick away, zipping his pants back up before the next man takes over, jerking off in front of me. I grit my teeth and exhale in relief when the door opens and *Patrick* stalks in, fury on his face.

"Get out!" he roars at the three men. "She is mine, you pathetic assholes."

"We didn't touch her," the first one complains.

"You've ruined her," Patrick sulks, taking in my appearance with a disgusted look. He tuts at me as if it's my fault and bends down to grab my elbow, hauling me to my feet. I stumble as my legs have gone dead and my head starts to spin again. I need to close my eyes to get my vision to steady out again, but I can't as Patrick roughly shunts me forward and out of the shed before taking hold of my arm again to practically drag me across the compound. Yeah, I knew it. He is an Alpha of a new Pack. Somehow, my tormentors defected from the Ridge Pack and ended up here as part of this new Pack.

Patrick throws me into his cabin. It's tiny compared to Ryker's. More and more slots into place. He wants the Silvercrest Pack, and he thinks murdering Jefferson and getting to Ryker through me is going to get him that somehow.

"Ryker won't come for me," I inform him as he thrusts me forward and lifts me onto his bed. "He doesn't care about me."

"Oh, that's where you're wrong, little Wolf," he growls. "He will come even after what you did."

He stalks over to the sink and wets a cloth. He marches

back to me and wipes me clean, hesitating when he gets to my breasts. He licks his lips but doesn't follow through with whatever perverted thought goes through his head. He pops my breasts back into my bra and closes my ripped tee, tying it off in a knot to keep it together.

"The rejection process you started hasn't finished yet," he says. "Use whatever means you still have hanging on by a thread to tell him you've been taken. I want him here thinking he has found you before I kill you in front of him."

I don't for one second take that as an empty threat.

"I-I can't," I whisper. "I can't reach him."

He grabs my hair, yanking my head back to stare into my eyes. His face is a hard mask. "Try, little Wolf or you are no good to me."

I run my tongue over my teeth and gulp back some air. I nod, making him think I can do this. I know I can't. I've tried but whatever fledging connection we had, is well and truly severed.

I'm as good as dead.

Chapter 41

Ryker

I'm handed off by a grim-faced Jake to an even grimmer faced Hunter. I feel like a child that needs supervision. Although it's not all wrong. I'm incapable of much thought apart from how ragged my emotions are right now. I sit in the pickup with Hunter behind the wheel in silence. A weird silence.

A silence that I've never encountered with Hunter before.

"What aren't you telling me?" I ask eventually, drawing on every ounce of strength in me to have a proper conversation.

"Nothing," he says darkly. "Everything is fine."

I raise an eyebrow at him. Now his behavior is too suspicious and for the moment, it shoves away the desolation that has wrapped itself around my soul.

"Don't lie to me," I growl.

"I'm not," he says, avoiding my eyes.

"Like hell," I snap.

He hunches over, gripping the steering wheel tighter.

"Do you want me to kick your ass?" I ask. "Because trust

me when I say I need to kick *someone's* ass and you are the closest person to me right now."

"Just leave it alone," he grouses.

"Yeah, like that's going to work," I snort. "Out with it, Hunter."

"I don't want to tell you," he says quietly. "Not yet."

My twisted guts, twist a little bit more. The blood drains from my face. "What is it?" I ask, deadly quiet.

He sighs and sits back, rubbing his hand over his face quickly. "Don't freak out, we are still half an hour away from the compound..."

I reach out and grab his shirt, bunching it up in my fist. "What happened? Is it Bree?" Panic rises and I want to throw up at the thought of something bad happening to her. As much as I want to hate her for what she's done, I can't.

"She's missing, Ry," he murmurs. "We don't know what's happened to her or where she's gone. She was in her cabin and now she's...not."

"Missing?" I roar, letting him go before I punch him in the face. "How could you let this happen? You were supposed to be watching her!" Fury doesn't even cover it.

"I know," he says. "Maria was with her earlier, she was in a bad way, she can't have gotten far..."

"Jesus!" I exclaim and strike out at the dash, needing to hit something. "Stop the car."

"Ryker, be reasonable. You can't Shift and run the rest of the way home."

"Says who?" I snarl.

"Me. Stay where you are, we will be back soon and then we can carry on searching for her."

"You mean the search has stopped?" I ask in disbelief.

"No," Hunter says calmly to my storm. "I mean you and I can search for her."

"How long?" I ask after a beat. I'm about to lose it but I know I have to keep my head.

"A few hours."

"And no one thought to tell me until now?"

"Look, Ry. We know that she rejected you. We know how you're feeling about that right now. We didn't want to add to that. We thought she'd probably just wandered off to be alone for a bit and would be back by now."

"What makes you think she hasn't just done that?" I ask.

"It's too much of a coincidence with everything else that's been going on," he grits out.

I can't disagree. But I can't let it affect me. If I needed anything to pull me out of my funk and to stop me thinking about the dead woman in the woods, Bree going missing is it. I have to stay calm or I'm no good to her.

I curse loudly when I recall hearing someone calling to me when I was passed out next to the woman.

"Fuck!" I roar, slamming the dash again. "She tried to get to me. I wasn't there for her when she needed me!"

"What?" Hunter asks in confusion at my outburst.

"I heard her calling for me. She's in danger and I wasn't there for her. This was a mistake. All a big mistake. Fuck, Bree. I'm sorry," I end on a whisper. I glare out of the side window. "I'll find you, I promise you, if you can hear me now, I'll find you."

Silence.

With each passing minute, the rejection is getting stronger. That probably means she is getting weaker. She is vulnerable and alone and probably scared out of her mind.

I hate myself for leaving her. I loathe myself for lying to her about the Alpha bond and above all, I'm furious with myself for letting her walk away from me.

I don't deserve her. I never have. I'm weak with too many

vices, and she deserves someone strong and steady who will fight for her.

The minutes tick away and finally after bouncing over the dirt road to the compound, Hunter pulls up outside my cabin. I'm out before he has even cut the engine, racing towards Bree's cabin. If anyone can pick up her trail, it has to be me. I know her scent as well as I know my own.

"Ryker!" Mom calls out when she sees me. "Thank God you're back. You have to find her."

"I will," I say determinedly.

"No!" she exclaims, grabbing my arm. "You don't understand, she is in a really bad way. The rejection is killing her. She is weak and she can't think straight. She won't know how to protect herself out there, please, Ryker…"

Her desperation hits me so hard; I feel tears spring to my eyes.

I pat her hand. "I'll find her. Just let me go so that I can pick up her scent, okay?" I say quietly.

She nods and lets me go, wiping away her tears.

I turn from her and enter the cabin, grabbing a balled-up t-shirt that I find in her laundry hamper. I sniff it, breathing in deeply, reminding myself of her sweet smell and then I drop it and run. I pick up her scent almost immediately heading out into the woods. There are a dozen other Wolf scents that have headed this way. Common sense tells me they've tried to track her, but *I* haven't tried.

I pass through the clearing and end up on the shore of the lake where the trail abruptly ends, stopping my heart along with it.

Where the fuck did she go?

Chapter 42

Ryker

Inhaling deeply, I close my eyes. I turn my head to the right and then left and then turn around. All I can pick up is the scent trail that I followed here. There isn't a return path so whatever happened to her, she didn't go back into the woods, she went into the water.

"Find anything?" Hunter's voice interrupts me.

"Yes," I state and stalk past him. "Go back and get the key for my dad's boat."

"Oh?" Hunter asks, striding after me as I make my way down the lake to the dock.

"Why are you still here?" I ask him, thumping onto the jetty. "Go get the key."

"Ryker, wait. You can't search this entire lake all on your own. It's massive, you'll be out here for days."

"And?" I snap. "Bree is missing. Her trails stopped at the shore, she didn't go back, she didn't go right or left, so that means she went out there!" I point to the middle of the lake. "She told me she isn't a good swimmer. Hunter, if she went out there not feeling her best, anything could have happened to her!"

"I get that, man, but you have to think about this for a minute, formulate a plan..."

"Fuck a plan, I need to get out there!" I roar at him. "I fucking love her, Hunter. If she's in trouble, I need to get to her."

Hunter blinks and then a sad smile crosses his face. "I hear you," he says. "I'll be back and ask to borrow another boat. We'll split up."

I nod quickly and bend to throw the tarp off my dad's old motorboat.

"Ryker! Ryker! You need to come quick!"

I look up with a frown. "What is it?" I ask the young male who is racing towards us.

"There's news, you need to come now..."

I don't even ask for more details, I just launch myself off the jetty and start running, crashing through the woods and making it back to the compound with Hunter hot on my heels.

"Here!" Mom calls out and points to the woodshed on the other side of her cabin.

"Is she in there?" I ask, bursting in and disappointment hitting me hard. Bree is not in the woodshed, safe and sound, but some young asshole with wild curly, black hair, tied to a chair with a face that tells me how pissed off he is to be in this situation.

"Ryker?" he asks, squinting at me as the light hits his eyes in the gloom of the windowless shed.

"Who are you?" I bark out, marching towards him.

"William," he says. "I know where your missing Wolf is," he adds.

I lunge for him, grabbing his shirt in both of my fists, hauling him to his feet with the chair still attached to his ass.

"Where is she?" I growl. My eyes have Shifted to my Wolf's. That has never happened to me before, although I saw it once or twice on my dad when he was furious with me. The Wolf in my grip practically shits himself, stammering and stuttering.

"Let him go, Ry," Hunter says calmly. "Let the man speak."

I fling him back to the ground. He rocks on the chair and falls backwards. Hunter catches him, shooting me an irritated look. He rights the Wolf and says, "Where is she?"

"There is a new Pack about ten miles from here, down the West side of the lake. The Alpha has her. He is a fucking... psycho!" he spits out to my surprise.

"Is she alive, unharmed?" I ask, my heart pounding in my chest.

"She is fine. A prisoner for now, but untouched. Patrick won't allow it," is the reply.

"Patrick?" I ask scowling. "Never heard of him."

"Like I said, we're new, about three months old. He recruited me from out of state with promises that I know now were lies. He is an arrogant asshole and dangerous. He will fucking kill me if he knew I was here," he adds.

"How do I know that you're telling me the truth?" I ask.

"You don't, I guess, but I swear it, your little Wolf is with him. Black hair, blue eyes, small build, yeah?"

I nod stiffly. "Bree," I murmur.

"This could be a trap," Hunter points out. "This Patrick might have sent him to come and get you." His eyes bore into the stranger's, who glares back at him.

"You are right to be cautious of that dickhead, but I'm coming to you in good faith," William states. "I want out of that Pack, or at the very least, Patrick removed from being Alpha. He isn't fit. He gives good Wolves a bad name."

His disgust appears to be genuine, but can I risk Bree's

life on it? Can I go off on this potentially wild goose chase only to find her nowhere near the area?

I make a decision to trust him, at least to the point where he will lead me to Bree. Whatever I find when I get there remains to be seen. "You will take me to her," I state.

William nods. "I will take you, but you have to promise to get rid of Patrick," he counters.

"Oh, don't you worry your little head about that," I say darkly. If he has Bree, I will fucking kill him.

"Then let's go," William says determinedly.

"Wait," Hunter says. "Ryker, a word?"

I huff out a breath but go outside with Hunter. I know he is being the über cautious Beta and I have to respect what he has to say before I ignore it all and go after Bree.

"This could be a trap," Hunter says again.

"I don't care…"

"I know," Hunter says. "I'm coming with, and I don't care what you say, we are going in heavy."

"Fair enough," I reply and stalk off towards my mom's cabin.

"Is it true?" she asks me, wringing her hands. "Does he know where Bree is?"

"Yes," I state and push past her to enter the cabin.

I make my way to the locker on the far side and break the lock on it with the strength of the Alpha Wolf simmering right under the surface.

"Ryker," Mom says quietly.

"Don't talk me out of this," I say, reaching into the cabinet and hauling out my dad's hunting rifle. "That asshole is as good as dead."

"I'm not going to talk you out of anything," she says steadily.

The steel in her tone makes me turn around, mid reach for the bullets.

She is holding out a wooden box with an intricately carved top. She opens it to reveal the empty red velvet lining and then slams it closed and throws it on the table. "If he was the one responsible for your father's death, I want his heart in that box. Can you do that for me?" She points to the box.

"Done," I say, scooping it up and shoving it under my arm before I gather up the bullets for the rifle and head on out without another word. I have absolutely no doubt that this is the murderer we have been looking for. A new Pack on the block with a megalomaniac in charge is grounds to assume he is after claiming mine.

He can try but I will show him who he has picked a fight with, and he is seriously going to regret this, even more so for bringing Bree into it.

I march over to the pickup where Hunter and William are waiting. William is still bound and growling at Hunter when he shoves him into the back seat. I take the driver's seat and stash the box under it, the rifle propped up next to me.

I can sense Hunter's approval, but he doesn't comment.

"What does he plan to do with Bree?" I ask the question that has been plaguing me since he told me she was there.

"He won't hurt her. At least not until the rejection is out of her system. He plans to force a pairing with her, make her his Mate," William says.

I close my eyes, my breath hitching. "Oh, does he now?" I growl quietly.

"He has threatened to kill her, but he won't," William adds. "He wants her."

I feel sick at that. She will be so scared and it's all my fault. This entire situation is my fault.

"There's something else," William pipes up as we set off.

"Oh?" Hunter snarls, turning around menacingly.

"Patrick recruited three Betas. I use that term very loosely. They are as fucked up as he is. They defected from the Ridge Pack. I think there's bad blood between them and Bree. They've been tormenting her and telling everyone who will listen."

"Tormenting her how?" I ask murderously quietly.

Silence.

"How?" I thunder, slamming my fist on the steering wheel.

"Look, I didn't hang around to listen to the details, okay," he says in a quiet tone that is completely real with disgust. "I respect women, those dicks and Patrick are just...beyond."

"Fuck," I mutter. "Fuck! I left her all alone. This is all my fucking fault."

"Don't go there," Hunter says. "Fall apart later. Focus on getting her back first."

I know he's right. I have to get her back. Nothing else matters. Absolutely nothing at all. Not even my revenge. If I have to leave Patrick alive to get Bree out of there safely, then so be it.

The rest of the winding drive passes in silence, until William says quietly, "You'll have to stop here. We'll go the rest of the way on foot."

I nod and pull over, hoping that my judgment isn't skewed and that trusting this Wolf won't come back to bite me on the ass.

Chapter 43

Ryker

We traipse through the woods, William stumbling along behind us.

"Untie him, would you?" I growl at Hunter, when William trips up, crashing into me for the third time.

"You sure?" he asks.

I nod and stop, turning to William. "You do *anything* that hurts Bree even remotely, it'll be *your* heart in that box alongside Patrick's, got it?" I snarl, pointing to the backpack that Hunter stuffed the box into. It is also brimming with weapons. When he said, 'heavy', he pretty much meant it.

"Got it," William says, eyeing up the backpack warily.

Hunter pulls a knife out and cuts the tie binding William's wrists behind his back.

"Thanks," he mutters, rubbing them and then pointing over my shoulder. "About half a mile that way and we will come out near Patrick's cabin. He chose a strategic place for the compound, between the woods, the lake and the mountains. It's a bitch of a place to get to."

I nod grimly and turn to head in the direction that he indicated, trying to keep Bree at the back of my mind so I can concentrate on the task at hand, which is getting to the compound.

"Can you fight?" I ask William.

"I can," he states. "And I will to get this Alpha overthrown and those Betas out of power."

I don't reply. I have no need to. His reasons for doing this are his own. I don't give a shit. All I care about is getting to Bree, getting her safe and then facing the Wolf who murdered my father and set about a course of action that will lead to his own demise.

"As soon as we know where Bree is," I say to Hunter, "get her back to the pickup and leave. Don't worry about me, I'll find my own way back. Okay?"

"Got it," Hunter says and then stops, a hand on my arm as we hear a crack behind us.

I turn, aim the rifle in the direction of the rustle, and then make a frustrated noise when I see my sister tracking us.

"Stevie," I hiss. "What the fuck are you doing?"

She hoists the shotgun onto her hip and gives me a sassy smile. "Helping," she hisses back.

"Go. Home," I state and turn my back on her, dismissing her.

"Not a fucking chance," she snarls at me. "Mom filled me in. I want that fucker's head on a spike."

"Heart in a box," Hunter says, holding up the backpack.

They exchange a look that excludes the rest of us, and I roll my eyes. Now isn't the time for this.

"Stevie, you will just get in the way. How did you even get here?" I snap.

"Phillipa gave me a ride. Don't tell me you didn't see us?" she snorts with mirth.

I glare at Hunter, who shrugs.

He knew and didn't tell me. Asshole.

"She is *so* fucking excited about all of this drama for her books..." Stevie laughs, but then bites her lip. "Look, she left, so if you want me to walk all the way back to the compound on my own, then that's on you, brother. If not, then let me help."

"Fine," I mutter and turn around, knowing that there isn't a chance in hell she is getting involved in this. I will have to figure out how to get her to stand down. Just another problem to add to the steaming pile of shit.

We walk along in silence for the half mile that William told us of and then stop just inside the tree line. I can see a cabin a short distance away, guarded by those three fuckers that clearly weren't beaten hard enough the first time they fucked with my girl. I'm going to enjoy this way more than I should.

"Ready?" I ask.

"Ready," comes the reply.

"Stevie, stay here. That's an order," I add, knowing she can't refuse her Alpha.

"Fuck you," she hisses in my ear. "You're not sidelining me. I'm just as good a shot as you."

Well, that's true. Dad made sure she was. I may dislike guns, but it doesn't mean I don't know how to use one and with a skill that made my impossible-to-please father proud. Probably why I shun them now. Out of spite.

I mentally shake my head at myself knowing how ridiculous that sounds.

"I will take a piece out of these assholes without hesitation," she says seriously.

"Physical fight? Can you handle it?" I ask.

"You know I can," she states arrogantly. "Need I remind you of the Lucy Kramer incident?"

I snort despite the tense situation. "No, you kicked her

ass good and proper. Fine," I relent. "But you get hurt or put Bree in jeopardy, I will never forgive you."

"Oh, how will I live with myself?" she asks sarcastically before she smiles and squeezes my shoulder. "I can take care of myself. You do you."

I grimace and gesture with my head to William to go first.

He nods grimly and primes himself for the fight ahead. He stalks out of the trees and over the few hundred meters over to the cabin.

Hunter and I follow with Stevie behind us and then all hell breaks loose.

William wasn't kidding when he said he wanted to take those Betas down. He wastes no time in diving into a challenge that by the looks of it, he will win all on his own. I throw Stevie my rifle, which she catches deftly, swapping it out for her shotgun. Hunter chucks the backpack down at her feet with an instruction to have our backs.

Then, we both lunge forward.

I grab hold of the nearest little prick to me, punching him in the face which satisfies me more than I thought it would, especially when I hear the crunch of his nose breaking. "Where is Patrick?" I bellow in his face.

"Fuck you!" he shouts back holding his nose. "You broke my fucking nose!"

"I will break every bone in your body if you've hurt Bree," I snarl. "Where the fuck is your Alpha?"

"Oh, I'm right here," an arrogant voice calls out from the direction of the cabin. "Nice of you to join us, Ryker."

I kick the ankles out from under the so-called Beta, leaving Hunter and William to deal with the other two and whoever else decides to defend their worthless piece of shit Alpha. Making a decision, I gesture that Stevie follow me as I stride over to the cabin, hands clenched.

"Come in," Patrick says, surprising me with his hospitality.

"There's someone here that I'm just dying to kill while you watch." He turns and in a flash of speed, he is inside the cabin with me right behind him, but I have no choice but to stop, hands up. He has a knife to Bree's throat and while William's words echo in my head as Stevie joins me, gun levelled at Patrick, I can't risk Bree's life on the say-so of a stranger.

I have to assume he is willing to kill her.

And as much faith as I have in my sister's aim, Patrick is just too close to Bree to take out.

He knows it.

I know it.

Bree knows it.

When Patrick digs the knife into her throat, drawing blood, I place my hand slowly on the barrel of the gun and lower it, even as Stevie growls at me.

He has me right where he wants me for the moment.

Chapter 44

Bree

I can feel the trickle of blood down my neck. Seeing Ryker has sent my head into a tailspin. I didn't expect him to come. But maybe this isn't about me. Maybe it's about his dad and his Pack and I'm just collateral damage.

I watch, the terror coursing through me, as he lowers the barrel of Stevie's gun.

The blade digging into my neck eases up slightly, but I don't relax. I fully believe that Patrick will slit my throat without a second thought. He is completely unhinged. I don't know why he is so deranged, so it's got something to do with Jefferson, Ryker and the Silvercrest Pack.

"Let her go," Ryker says calmly. "She doesn't have anything to do with this."

"Actually, she does. I wasn't sure at first but when you stayed behind to make sure she was safe instead of chasing after me, I knew she was special to you. Only a Fated Mate would do that."

"She's rejected me," Ryker says.

I cringe. Maria said he would feel it, but to hear him say it out loud and avoid my gaze makes me feel even worse if that's possible.

"She has," Patrick says with a laugh. "Even better for me. Now, I can mate with her without the complication of your bond in the way."

"Touch her and you will find out that rejection or not, she isn't yours in any way."

Patrick sneers and lifts the knife from my throat completely to walk away. I don't know if he realizes what he just did, but Stevie does. She raises the gun again and cocks it.

Patrick laughs and holds his arms out to the sides. "Go for it. Something tells me Ryker will stop you because he wants to kill me himself. Am I right?"

"Personally, I don't give a shit how you die or who kills you, as long as you exit this world in the next few minutes, I'm game for whatever happens."

I lick my lips.

This is the Alpha in Ryker that I haven't seen before. None of us have. He is calm, collected, hard, focused and... cold. His eyes are dead, his face an impassive mask. I gulp knowing that this is going to be a messy end and I'm stuck right in the middle of it.

"Stevie," Ryker says before Patrick can respond. He is spluttering and making it appear he doesn't care, but I can see that his body is primed. So is Ryker's. His muscles are bunched up, his fists loose at his sides. "Get Bree and get out of here," he adds, never taking his eyes off Patrick.

Stevie nods and still holding the gun with one hand, which is remarkably steady considering how much the thing must weigh, she pulls a knife out of the back of her jeans and walks over to me, shoving Patrick out of the way with the barrel, a sneer on her face that shows how much she wants to pull the trigger.

But she doesn't.

She is waiting for Ryker.

Her Alpha.

Our Alpha.

It truly drives home his new role to me and what I've done by rejecting him. My vision goes blurry again and my legs and arms go numb.

My wrists are jarred when Stevie cuts me loose, taking a quick moment to rub each wrist quickly to get circulation flowing again. "Come," she murmurs to me.

"No," Patrick says suddenly. "You aren't walking out of here with her."

"Wanna bet?" Stevie asks, hauling me to my feet.

I stumble and will myself to stand up straight, using every ounce of strength that is left inside me, which is very little.

Ryker edges closer to us as Stevie shoves me gently towards the door. I trip up and curse myself for being so weak, especially now. I need to find some fortitude or I'm going to mess this up for all of us.

Patrick growls and throws the knife suddenly. It whizzes past my ear and slams into the door, vibrating at the force with which it was thrown.

Stevie and I pause and then hear the click of a gun being cocked behind us.

"I said, you aren't leaving here with her," Patrick says.

"Why do you want her so bad?" Ryker asks. "She is weak and doesn't have what it takes to mate with an Alpha."

I gasp, his words hitting my heart and burying deep inside to infect me even more than the rejection is.

Stevie's hand snakes around my upper arm and she shakes her head slightly. I can barely see her, but the movement is obvious. She is asking me to trust Ryker.

"Well, that's true," Patrick says with a laugh. "She is a bit pathetic, *but* she is yours, supposedly, so I want her, just like I want your Pack and I'll be taking both before the day is out."

"Over my dead body," Ryker growls. "You are delusional if you think I'm going to let some stranger run over me to take my Pack away. You clearly have no fucking idea who you are messing with."

"Oh, I do know. I know a helluva lot more than you think I do, *brother*," Patrick says.

The silence is deafening.

Stevie's gasp and her loosened grip tells me that she also heard what I did. I thought I'd imagined it.

Brother.

Did he mean that literally or as a familiar term?

I turn my head towards Ryker. He is frozen still probably wondering the same thing.

No one moves.

No one says a word.

Chapter 45

Ryker

Brother.

I take that in for a second and then react with a small laugh that irritates the shit out of the delusional fuck in front of me. He raises his handgun higher.

"You don't believe me?" he asks, the desperation in his tone makes me laugh harder.

"Oh, no, I believe you," I comment and turn to Stevie. She is in shock but at my hard gaze, she snaps to attention and lets out a thin laugh that could've been better but will do.

I have absolutely no doubt that he speaks the truth. He may be mentally fucked, but he wouldn't go to all this trouble unless he had facts. I *know* he doesn't belong to our mother, that much is blindingly obvious, so an affair? He appears to be older than me though so a prior fling that Jefferson engaged in before he...it all falls into place.

Before he became Alpha.

"So dear old dad had you and abandoned you and now you think you have a right to *my* Pack?" I ask, my tone more incredulous than the shock I actually feel. The more he thinks he has me on the back foot, the better.

"That is *my* Pack, brother," he grits out. "*I* am the firstborn." He points his gun at his chest briefly before remembering that he is holding Stevie and Bree hostage with it. Stevie noticed though and edged her and Bree closer to the door and the knife still buried into the wood.

I snicker behind my hand. "Firstborn to Jefferson, *not* the Alpha of the Silvercrest Pack, *brother*," I sneer at him. "Sorry, you lose."

"Like hell!" he roars at me. "I'm owed and I'm taking what is rightfully mine!"

"You know nothing about Pack rites. Only an Alpha's firstborn son can become Alpha. That's me, asshole. I was Chosen. Chosen by birth. Chosen by blood. Chosen. You, on the other hand, are a mistake that our father made, a dirty little secret that he shipped out of the Pack, or wait...probably more like *Grandfather* did to protect his son and legacy. Man, what a story, but an Alpha of the Silvercrest Pack it *does not* make you."

"Fuck you," Patrick sneers at me. "You don't know the first thing about it."

"Think I do. Pretty much just spelled it out for you," I retort. I'm no fool when it comes to this shit. I know everything about Alphas and how they come to pass. I've searched for loopholes, anything that would get me out of the responsibility. There aren't any except abandoning the Pack and thus shunning yourself or being challenged and losing.

"I bet Dad didn't want anything to do with you and that fucked you off. Believe me when I say, you probably got the better end of the stick," I say, just to piss him off.

"He *abandoned* me!" Patrick shrieks. "Me and my mother. Left us all alone without a second thought. He deserved to die! He deserved...to die." His rant comes to an abrupt end, and the gun drops a few inches.

"Go," I say to Stevie, and she doesn't hesitate. She shunts Bree towards the door, opening it quickly and launching them both through it before Patrick can react.

When I look back at him, he has recovered his attitude, but now I have Hunter at my back, levelling two guns at his head and he knows he is outmatched. If he shoots and kills me, Hunter will fill him with lead before he can take his next breath. If he fires at Hunter, I will have his guts in my mouth as a tasty treat before he can move. I've been prepared for a split-second Shift from the moment I entered this cabin. If he hasn't prepared for the same, then he is a bigger fool than he is making out, which right now, is pretty big. He just admitted to killing my dad, he kidnapped my Fated Mate, done God only knows what to that poor woman in the woods to mess with me and has thrown my life into turmoil.

He is going down, and I promised my mother something of his.

"I can't let you live," I inform him.

"I have prepared for this fight; you won't beat me. I will be Alpha of the Silvercrest Pack the second I kill you."

"Is that an official challenge?" Hunter barks out.

"Yes," Patrick says and flings his gun on the bed.

I don't even wait for his next move. In a burst of fur, claws and fangs, I Shift and with my Alpha speed and strength, launch myself at Patrick, who is a bit slower to Shift than I was. He is smaller, slower and completely *un*prepared for the attack that I am merciless in administering.

Snapping my jaws tight around his throat, I slam him to the floor, pinning him with my superior weight and strength. He flails, his claws catching me, but I don't notice the damage.

I am completely focused on finishing this fight before it even begins.

It's only when his claws gouge the underside of my belly that I flinch and he takes advantage of my loosened grip, getting free. We snarl at each other, teeth bared, but there isn't a chance in hell he can beat me. Blood is dripping from the puncture wounds in his throat, and he is unsteady on his feet. He growls like a rabid Wolf, but I can see how much pain he is in.

I hunker down and then lunge, knocking him off his feet, my teeth sinking back into his neck. I can taste the feral blood on my tongue, I can smell his fear. He knows he is about to take his last breath, but he doesn't stop fighting, scrabbling for a foothold but he misjudged how powerful a *real* Alpha is. Any Wolf can start a Pack and call themselves an Alpha. When it's your legacy, when it's in your blood the way it is with me, it's a whole different ball game. One that he has learned too late.

I increase the pressure of my grip, growling low in my throat and then issue the final blow, snapping his neck and ripping his throat out when I pull back.

I watch as he Shifts back to his human form and then I Shift as well. Hunter throws me some spare clothes from the backpack, seeing as I've just lost mine—again.

"Fuck," he comments. "You don't fuck about, do you? Remind me never to challenge you in a fight."

"Fuck off," I growl but roll my eyes at him, so he knows I'm not about to do the same to him.

He snickers and throws the box and his hunting knife to me. "You owe your mom something."

"Do you think she knew about him?" I ask, staring at the knife.

"Doubtful," Hunter says. "This was definitely a big cover-up."

"Yeah. Shady fucker. The perfect Jefferson, not so perfect, after all," I mutter.

"No one is perfect," Hunter says. "Everyone makes mistakes."

"Yeah," I murmur. "Where are Bree and Stevie?"

"Waiting in the pickup."

"Are they safe?" I ask, rounding on him.

"Stevie will shoot anything that comes near them," Hunter assures me.

I nod grimly. "Leave," I say. "Take them back to the compound. I'll make my own way back."

"You sure?" he asks warily. "I mean, the three so-called Betas have been subdued and no one else has stepped forward to defend their Alpha, but they could be waiting for precisely this."

"I'll be fine," I say. "I need you to take the girls and get them back home."

He nods and chucks the backpack at me before he turns to leave without another word.

I think he knew I needed to do this next step on my own.

I've killed before, but always in Wolf form. The darkness in my youth was too strong for me to control. It got easier when I found my way to sate it with rough sex and domination. Mutilating a body in human form is going to take a bit more stomach and having a witness will just make it worse.

I toss the knife in the air and catch it by the hilt, then I drive it into Patrick's chest expecting to feel something.

I don't.

I feel absolutely nothing as I slowly carve his heart out of his chest and place it in the box my mother gave me. I drop the lid and place the box inside the backpack. Mechanically, I pick up the bag and sling it over my shoulder, wiping the blade of the knife on my jeans, staining them but barely noticing.

Without a look back, I exit the cabin and close the door.

I wasn't expecting an audience to greet me. I go on the offensive, priming myself for more fighting but William steps forward, hands up so I can see he doesn't mean any harm.

"He gone?" he asks carefully.

"Yep," I reply. "Give him the burial of an Alpha and then you have some decisions to make."

"Pah, he doesn't deserve it," William sneers.

"Still, he was your Alpha," I point out.

"You give him too much," William says.

I shrug. What do I care? Bree is safe, my Pack is safe. I can go back to eating my own food and figuring out how to do this Alpha shit without complications.

I thump down the steps of the porch, but William stops me. "These Wolves...none of them are Alpha material, they need help," he implores me.

"You don't want it?" I ask.

"Me?" he asks, surprised. "Err, no, hard pass. I'm a follower, not a leader."

I nod and make a decision. I turn to the crowd. "My Pack is currently on Recruit. If you feel like you might be a good fit, come to the Silvercrest Pack tomorrow and we'll see what we can do. The Silver Peak Pack is also recruiting if you'd prefer to go there. You don't need to stay here."

The relief that floods through them is palpable in the air.

William grins at me. "I'll see *you* tomorrow," he states and turns on his heel to walk away.

"Wait," I call out. He stops and turns. "You got a car I can borrow?"

He snorts. "I'll drive you," he says.

I give him a half-smile. "Thanks. I wasn't looking forward to walking home."

He leads me to a beat-up truck, and we climb in. He flicks the sun visor down and grabs the key, starting it up. It chokes to life, and he maneuvers us onto a narrow dirt track, the brush scraping the sides as we bounce down it. I can see why he made us stop further back for the surprise attack.

"What you gonna do with those three dickheads?" I ask casually.

"I'll be bringing them to the Silvercrest Pack tomorrow to face sentencing," he says just as casually.

I nod. "Good call," I reply.

We fall into an easy silence for a few minutes before he speaks again. "That girl loves you, don't accept the rejection."

Grimacing at him, I ask, "Yeah, how do you know?"

"All she cared about was you when she and your sister left the cabin. If she didn't care, she wouldn't have been in such a state."

"Humph," I mutter rudely. "She should've thought about that before rejecting me."

I feel his eyes on me briefly, but he says no more. Neither of us do, each lost in our own thoughts.

Chapter 46

Ryker

After saying goodbye to William, I run into Hunter, hovering around, anxiously awaiting my return by the looks of it. He rushes me, but then cools his jets when he sees I'm fine.

"You good?" he asks.

I chuckle. "Fine. You get back okay?"

He nods. "Listen, there's something I want to talk to you about..."

I nod and hand him the backpack, making him hold it out while I remove the box and then I zip it up and give him back responsibility for his weapons. "Go on," I say gruffly. I think I know what this is about, and I'll listen and then do what I'm going to do about Bree, whatever the fuck that is. I don't know yet. I need a minute of peace and quiet to figure stuff out.

"Uhm," he starts, suddenly nervous.

I frown. Okay, I called this all wrong. This isn't about Bree at all. Which can only mean it's about Stevie.

I could just tell him again that I approve but watching him stammer and fluster his way past the first words of his planned speech is amusing, and I need the distraction.

"I—I, uhm, you know that I would never…there's something there though and…shit…she, *Stevie*, is a remarkable woman. I would never do anything to hurt her, or you if you don't want us together…I guess I'm asking…"

"Oh, for fuck's sake, man. How many times do I have to say it? I approve, okay. Go for it." I slap him on the shoulder. "You have my blessing or whatever the fuck you're after here."

His cheeks go bright red, and he looks down. "Thanks," he mutters. "I don't know what will happen, but I'm ready to go to her and find out."

"About fucking time," I mutter. "Do you, Hunter. Casey was a complete bitch, and you deserve so much better than that. Go find happiness."

"Same goes for you," he says gruffly.

"Well, I'll settle for appeasing my mother's need for vengeance on the asshole who killed her husband, which by the way, how the hell did he even do that?" I wish I'd taken the time to ask before I killed his wayward son.

Hunter sighs. "I've been thinking about this. About a week before your dad first got sick, he told me he was heading into town on an errand. I asked him to give me the details, even to go with him, but he refused, saying he'd only be a couple of hours and he 'didn't need no fucking chaperone'. Who was I to argue?" He snorts at the memory but sobers up again. "Maybe he went to see Patrick? I dunno, it's speculation…" He shrugs.

"Yeah, I suppose we will never know for sure, but it's something, I guess." I sigh and leave him to make my way to my mom's cabin. She opens the door immediately and then disappears inside to let me in.

The first thing that hits me is that Bree is there. On my mom's bed, with Stevie holding a cold washcloth to her face.

"What is *she* doing here?" I ask, not meaning to sound harsh, but this is family shit. She doesn't belong.

"Ryker!" Mom barks at me. "Bree is in a bad way. She needs help."

I glare at her and then at the Wolf who rejected me. My heart twangs with guilt before the old barriers that she tore down go up to protect myself. She doesn't want me, so what can I do?

"Here," I say and place the box carefully on the table.

Mom licks her lips and opens it. She breathes in deeply and nods when she sees the contents. "I knew you wouldn't let me down," she murmurs.

"Do you know who he was?" I ask.

"Stevie filled me in."

"And?" I press when she doesn't say anything else.

"I didn't know about him, if that's what you're asking. Jeff never mentioned having another son. I'm guessing he decided to keep it a secret to protect your legacy, Ry. I know you think he hated you but everything he did, he did it for you."

"Yeah," I mutter. "I need to shower, change and drink coffee that *I* made and wasn't delivered to me. I'll catch you later." I turn and walk away.

"Wait, Ryker! You need to fix this," she says urgently, following me to the door.

"Fix what?" I ask, playing dumb.

"The rejection between you and Bree, you idiot. Can't you see how much pain she is in?"

I cast my glance to her on the bed and then look away. "I can't right now. I need to get my head on straight. It's been a day, a fucking month, from hell. Just let me do this my way."

She looks upset but has no choice but to nod and let me go.

After a burning hot shower, which made my body feel better but clouded my mind even more, I step out of the bathroom and stop dead, glad that I had the foresight to sling a towel around my waist.

"What do you want?" I ask with a huff, glaring at Stevie, sitting on my sofa, legs and arms crossed.

"We need to talk, asshole," she grits out. "Put some clothes on, man. I don't need to see what you've got going on down there." She averts her eyes and I roll mine.

I remove the towel and pull on a pair of sweats and a tight tee. "Happy?" I ask sarcastically.

"Ugh, it's better," she says, raking her gaze over me. "You're too bulky. I don't get what they all see in you," she adds loftily.

I snort. Trust my sassy sister to get her digs in where she can. "Prefer the more slender form, do you? Like Hunter, maybe? Hmm?" I dig back.

She blushes like her cheeks suddenly set on fire and bites her lip. "This is about Bree," she says to deflect.

"Stevie, don't," I snap. "I don't need you weighing in on this as well. Mom and Hunter and even fucking William have had their say and I've let them. You, no. Just no. Leave it."

"No, I won't leave it. That poor girl is in agony. No way am I going to sit back and watch her die over *you*."

"She isn't going to die," I grit out, my heart thumping at the thought of it. "It's all a bit dramatic on Mom's part."

"She is weak and in a bad way. I wouldn't like to rule it out, Ry," she says quietly.

I sit heavily on the bed and drop my head into my hands. "I don't know what to do," I admit eventually.

"Talk to her," Stevie says straight away. "I know why she did this. Her reasons are...well, I'll let her explain."

I look up at that, a furious frown on my face. "What do you mean?"

"Just go and speak to her. Drop those damn barriers that you've had up your whole life and let her in, Ryker. You need her. You need love in your life, and she can give it to you."

"It isn't just about that. I'm worried about the darkness inside me, the Wolf, it needs more than I think she can give me," I say quietly.

"How do you know? Have you even let her try? I have a darkness too, you know. I may not be his son, but an Alpha was still my father as well. Don't you think I struggle?"

"It's not the same..."

"So what? It's similar but I don't use it as an excuse not to love."

"Don't you?" I ask nastily. "When was the last time you had a real relationship instead of pining after Hunter?"

"You're being an asshole and that's fine. Say what you must to me to make yourself feel better, but you know I'm right. Bree is your Fated Mate. You belong together. If she couldn't give you *everything* that you need, the Fates would've chosen someone else. You just need to give her a chance."

"She doesn't want me," I say, knowing it came out all sulky and childish

"She does. She is just confused and hurt. Talk. To. Her."

"Dammit, you are infuriating," I snap.

"So the fuck are you," she snaps back.

"Fine!" I yell, standing up, "I'm going!"

"Good!" she bellows, also standing up. "Don't let the door hit your stubborn ass on the way out!"

I growl at her and march to the door, yanking it open. I step through and slam it but then realize that I've left without my shoes.

With a curse upon my sister's head, I open the door again,

to see her standing there with my boots in her hand, a cocked hip and a sassy smile.

"I should banish you," I snarl, snatching them from her.

"You wish," she sneers. "Sorry, brother, but you need me to be your common sense."

"Pah," I mutter and turn, stalking off and sitting down on the porch steps to put my shoes on.

It takes me a full minute to pick myself up again. By this time, Stevie has joined me.

"You don't need to be afraid," she says quietly, wrapping her arms around me. "You've got this."

I want to roar that I'm not afraid, but the truth is, I am. If I let Bree back in and she hurts me again, I'm not sure I will be able to handle it.

But there is only one way to find out which way this will go.

I have to speak with her and find out once and for all, what the fuck is going with us.

Chapter 47

Ryker

I quietly shove open the door to my mom's cabin and peer inside. Bree is still in here, my mom taking care of her. I walk inside, my mouth dry. I don't even know where to start with this. Conversations of this nature have never taken place with me before for a damn good reason.

I'm seriously uncomfortable with emotion and this is chock full of it.

Mom looks up and gives me a firm nod before she stands up and leaves us alone, taking her knitting with her.

"Hey," I say, hearing the awkward note in my tone.

She gives me a wan smile. "Hi," she mutters, avoiding my eyes.

I hover for a moment, feeling like I should have a hat in my hand or something. I eventually sit on the bed and regard her closely. "We need to talk," I state the obvious with a cringe at how lame that is.

"Yeah," she replies but doesn't say anything.

Okay, I guess it's up to me to start. Great. I was really hoping she would take the lead and I could just follow along like a little Wolf cub.

Great big Alpha, totally whipped by this tiny creature.

I stifle my groan and lick my lips.

"Bree," I state at the same time that she says, "Ryker."

"Me first," I blurt out, making her smile.

I'd already made the decision to speak, so now I just want to get it out.

"I'm not sure what has happened here," I say truthfully. "I know I hurt you by being less than honest about the Alpha bond. It was something that I should have mentioned right from the start, but I was so afraid that you wouldn't get it, that you would assume anything that I felt, or you felt would be down to that and not real. I didn't want you to run and think too hard about it so that you convinced yourself that what was developing between us wasn't real. I regret taking that decision away from you. It was stupid, selfish and cowardly and if I could take it back, I would. I shouldn't have let you leave the other day without explaining all of this. I'm —I'm sorry, Bree. I know I was wrong but you rejecting me over this has really hurt me. I don't know what to do about it, or where we stand now..."

I trail off feeling that whatever I say now will just sound like a defensive excuse.

She bites her lower lip and attempts a smile. "Thank you for saying all of that, but you should have let me go first," she says, struggling to sit up.

I help her, feeling how weak and fragile she is. I feel like my grip on her arm is going to break it and it makes me sad and sick that I did this to her.

"I didn't reject you over the Alpha bond thing," she says, confusing me.

I frown at her and shuffle back slightly, creating a distance between us that she sees and feels sad about herself.

She sighs and pushes her tangled hair out of her face. She is pale and gaunt. I want to help her, but I just don't know how.

"After I ran out of your cabin, yes I was hurt and confused and—and *mad*," she says, giving me the stink-eye, "but it wasn't enough for me to reject you. I had no intention of doing that. I spoke to Maria, and she convinced me to find you before you left so that we could at least try to clear the air before you went away. That's when I saw you with...Valerie."

Her eyes bore into mine, searching them, looking for something.

I, on the other hand, want to drop to my knees and explain that she has nothing to worry about.

"I saw her kiss you and then you drove off with her!" she spits out, fire in her eyes, but it dies quickly as she gets exhausted. "I'm sorry," she mumbles. "Stevie told me that it was nothing...it still stabs at my heart to see you two together. I thought you had replaced me because I ran away. Then, even worse, I thought that you had never stopped seeing her while we were trying to make this work."

"What?" I spit out, angry and frustrated that she could feel that way. "I told you..."

"I know," she says, holding her hand up briefly before it drops to the bed. "I *know*. But I was sore and when I saw you kissing, it really got to me. I broke into her cabin, and I saw the photos of the two of you and your t-shirt and...my head spun. I felt sick and my paranoia got the better of me. I said the words, but I didn't mean them. Well, I meant them in the heat of the moment, but then I regretted saying it. I'm sorry, Ryker. I know that I did this to me, to you, to *us*. I don't know how to be in a relationship because I have never been in one. I work on instinct and that instinct is to protect myself."

"Yeah, I know exactly how you feel," I say, risking taking her hand.

She lets me.

"You have absolutely nothing to worry about with Val. She needed a ride to visit her sick niece, and the kiss was nothing and all her. She leaned in...I was lost in my thoughts about you...it happened before I knew what was going on."

A small part of my brain yells at me to tell her about the woman in the woods. I don't want to, but I've learned that keeping secrets is the way to destroying everything. I have to give her a chance to process it and understand.

"I get that now," she says.

I want to weep with relief and sadness that I'm about to ruin it all with my next words.

"But there is something else, something that will hurt you..."

Her eyes go hard but she nods, anyway. "Tell me," she says. "No more secrets."

I gulp and launch into my tale of the bar fight, the feeling of desolation and isolation I felt when I felt her reject me. I explain about waking up next to the woman and not knowing, *still* not knowing, what I did. I try to shift some of the blame to Patrick and his psychosis, but I make sure she knows that I'm not using that as an excuse.

"Oh," she says, flustered, her eyes scrunching up.

"Please, Bree, I'm sure that I didn't do anything, but I know that it doesn't sound good," I blurt out when the silence grows painfully awkward.

"I believe you," she says after another hefty pause. "Whatever it is, it was Patrick, it has to be. Probably to drive you back to the Pack. You leaving messed up his plans."

I couldn't love this woman more right now if I tried. Trouble is, I can't say the words. Not yet. Not until I know things are okay between us.

"You are such a special woman, Bree," I say instead, gripping her hand. "I will be the luckiest Wolf alive if you tell me we will try to fix this."

She nods. "I want to fix it, Ryker, but I don't know how..."

"I do!" Mom's voice shouts through the open window.

Bree and I exchange a mortified glance, her cheeks going as red as tomatoes.

"Fuck's sake," I mutter, rubbing my hand over my face. I should've known better and checked all the windows and doors before we started this conversation.

"And?" I yell back. "You might as well come in now, eavesdropper."

Mom sticks her head through the open window, pushing the voile aside, a mad grin on her face. "This can be fixed with a bit of work. The Fates need to know you are serious. You need to spend time together, repair the damage that the rejection has caused. You will know when the Fates have accepted that you are serious about fixing this, but I can't tell you how or when that will be."

I look back at Bree. "Is this what you really want?" I ask quietly.

"Yes," she replies instantly. "I want to fix this."

I nod and lean over to scoop her up into my arms. I stand up, cradling her against my chest. "Then we can't do that here," I inform her with a laugh.

"Definitely not," she says, giggling back.

"You are coming back to my cabin, and you aren't leaving until the Fates are satisfied," I say sternly. Not only to repair our bond, but so I know she is safe and unharmed.

I think she knows that, but she nods anyway. "Well, I

don't want to piss them off any more than I already have," she murmurs, snuggling into me, setting my heart on fire.

Knowing in my soul that things will work out for us, I stalk out of the cabin and make my way back to mine, my arms tight around Bree. I never want to let her go now that I have her back.

Chapter 48

Bree

Ryker settles me into his bed, tucking me up and making sure I'm comfortable with more than enough pillows and blankets. I giggle as he adds another but I'm freezing despite the muggy heat that is still plaguing us. The season will turn soon, and I can't wait. I'm definitely a fall girl. Watching the leaves change color and fall, the distinct smell in the air as it turns crisp and pulling out my warm sweaters to snuggle into.

I sigh, trying to feel happiness but it is clouded. It's there though, lurking under the heavy blanket of the rejection. I just need to find the courage and strength to push it aside. I need to tell Ryker exactly how I feel about him and *show* him. It makes my mouth go dry and spikes my anxiety at the thought, but I know that we cannot move forward unless I do this. He is wary. I can see it in his eyes. I broke his trust by rejecting him and there isn't a single chance in hell he will open up first. Everything he said in Maria's cabin is all I'm going to get unless I speak up first.

I need to do this.

Not only to feel better but because we both need to hear it.

"Stop fussing," I murmur, grabbing his hand. "Lie with me."

He smiles down at me, brushing a stray lock of hair off my forehead. "Are you comfortable?" he asks.

"More than," I assure him and tug on his hand.

He kicks off his boots and climbs on the bed with me, tentatively wrapping his arms around me.

I feel more content now that we are touching, connecting, but it's still so off, almost cold. I place my hand on his chest and grab that last ounce of bravery that is dangling down, probably put there by the Fates because hell if I know where else it has come from. That in itself gives me hope that we can fix this. They want it. They're demanding it.

"I'm sorry," I start, licking my lips. "I broke your trust and I never wanted to do that. Do you forgive me?"

He freezes and then looks down at me with a frown. "I should apologize to you," he says slowly.

"You can after you listen to what I'm saying," I say lightly, even though my heart is pounding. "I know that I care deeply about you, Ryker. I wouldn't have reacted to seeing you and Valerie kissing if I didn't and if it wasn't real."

He makes a noise of protest, but I tap his chest to shush him. "Valerie kissing you, is that better?" I ask, with more than a bit of sass but it's not malicious.

"Humph," he grunts.

"Point is…" I say sternly to get this back on track, "If I didn't care, I wouldn't have rejected you. Does that make sense?"

He sighs. "Yes, it makes sense."

"Good," I say, feeling slightly stronger all of a sudden. It spurs me on to keep going. "But 'care' doesn't really cover it, Ryker. I am so in love with you, I ache when you aren't touching me. I need you next to me to feel whole and alive. I want to be with you in every possible way. I love you." I reach up to stroke his face when he turns it towards me, shock registering on his ruggedly handsome features.

It takes him a few moments to gather himself. I give him the time, not pressuring him into anything. If he doesn't feel the same, I will have to accept it.

"Bree," he says hoarsely, pulling me on top of him when he rolls onto his back. "I adore you. You are everything to me and not just because of the bond. You have captured my heart and torn down my barriers in a way that no one has ever been able to. One look from you is enough to set my soul on fire and I know that I would die to protect you. I love you, Bree. Probably more than I will ever be able to tell you or show you, but I will spend the rest of my days trying because it's what you deserve. Can you ever forgive me for being a controlling dickhead?"

I snort in amusement and nod quickly. When the feeling of pure happiness drops over me, I see it hit him at the same time. The Fates are accepting what we are saying but it isn't enough to convince them completely. I can still feel a nagging part of me deep inside that isn't satisfied, that is still hurting and weak. I have to show him and them that I'm all in.

I hesitantly lean forward and brush my lips against his.

He lets out a soft groan, grabbing my hips gently.

"I'm ready," I murmur against his mouth.

"Are you sure?" he murmurs back.

I nod, staring into his serious gray eyes and loving him more than I ever thought I was capable of. I trace my fingertips over the curve of his lips and nod. "Surer than I have ever been," I reply.

He sits up suddenly, his hand slipping under my baggy tee and pulling it over my head to expose my bare breasts to him. I push away the horror of the humiliating scene in the shed, vowing never to tell him about that. He will commit murder and I don't want that on my conscience. It's not so much a secret as protecting him from himself. It happened and it's over. Luckily, Stevie shoved me in the shower when we arrived back at Maria's, probably because she knew Ryker would hit the roof if he smelled another male all over me.

Ryker latches onto my nipple and sucks gently, pinching the other one with more pressure than I find comfortable, but only for a few seconds. When he twists slowly, I shiver in delight.

"Mm," he moans into my mouth and turns us over so that I'm underneath him. "I need you, Bree. Are you absolutely sure?"

I place my hand over his mouth with a giggle. "Absolutely sure. I need you."

"If I hurt you, tell me," he mutters and moves his mouth back to my breasts, licking and sucking until my skin feels so sensitive to his touch. He moves away slightly, trailing his fingers down in between my breasts and over my stomach until he reaches my panty line. My cheeks go hot when he breathes in deeply, his nose right between my legs. Hooking his fingers into the sides of my panties, he drags them down and kisses my mound. I lift my backside up so that he can get the panties off me completely. He pulls them off and drops them on the floor, parting my legs even more so he can get fully in between them. I stiffen when his tongue laps at me, but when his thumb circles my clit, I relax instantly. His tongue moves further down, flicking out at my entrance. I freeze, my blood running hotter than it ever has when he inserts his tongue inside me. The invasion is startling but not unpleasant. I scrunch my eyes shut and concentrate on feeling instead of thinking.

"Ooh, yes," I cry out as the combination of his tongue inside me and his thumb on my clit sends a rocket of desire shooting through me that surpasses anything else I have ever felt before.

"You taste so good," he mutters gruffly.

"Ah," I gasp when he slides a finger inside me.

It stretches me, triggering my instincts to close my legs.

"Am I hurting you?" he asks quietly.

I shake my head, my thighs clamped together.

"Then let me play with you. The wetter you are, the easier it will be when I enter you," he whispers.

I. Am. Mortified!

I want to crawl away from him and under the bed.

Covering my face with my hands, I let him thrust his finger gently inside me before he pulls out and rubs my clit, only to repeat the process.

I have to admit that it feels good. The rhythm of it, the tease on my clit. I want more. I lift my hips, encouraging him.

He chuckles. "Do you like that, tiny Wolf?"

I nod and remove my hands from my face. "Yes," I croak out.

"I'm going to add another finger, but don't clench, okay?"

I nod again, unable to find my tongue.

He teases my clit a few more times before he slides two fingers inside me. I gasp as the pressure increases but I know that I'm lubricating his fingers with my arousal from his teasing.

"Just do it!" I blurt out suddenly, unable to bear the anticipation. "Please just do it this time and next time, we can go slower, or whatever."

He stops thrusting, a smirk on his face. "Eager, aren't you?" he chuckles.

"Don't take this the wrong way, Ryker, but I want it over with. Please, just do it," I say earnestly.

His face goes serious. "I see," he says and crawls over me. "I hear you, Bree, but are you sure?"

"Yes," I reply with grim determination. "I have absolutely no expectations about this. I know it's going to hurt and I doubt I will orgasm, so I want it over with so next time I can enjoy it. Okay?" I bite my lower lip.

"Okay," he says to my relief. I can see the hesitation on his face though, so I smile and nod, giving him the go ahead.

He quickly removes his clothes and grabs his enormous cock. I force myself to relax. He circles my clit with the tip a few times to try and relax me before he positions himself at my entrance. I brace myself, closing my eyes.

With one quick thrust, he is inside me. I gasp at the burn and the strange feeling of having him there.

"You okay?" he murmurs.

I nod, once again unable to speak.

He nods back and pulls his hips back slightly before thrusting again. "Do you want me to stop?"

"No, finish," I implore him. I would die of embarrassment if I left him unfulfilled.

"Jesus, Bree," he rasps. "This isn't about me."

"It is this time," I say fiercely. "Please, just carry on."

He presses his hands on either side of my head and lifts himself up. He stares into my eyes with an expression that I can't quite read but he does as I ask. He thrusts, having sex with me so he can fulfil himself while I just lie here like an absolute idiot with no idea what to do, how to act or how to feel.

"I can't do this," he mutters eventually, pulling out. "I need you to enjoy it."

The nervous laugh that bubbles up earns me a fierce frown and a growl. "Sorry," I choke out. "I'm not laughing at you! Nerves...I do this...I'm sorry...gah!" I cover my face with my hands again, but he pulls them away and kisses me firmly on the lips.

"You are such an enthralling creature, tiny Wolf. I do love you, but this isn't working for me."

"Me either," I admit. "What do you suggest?"

"Let me play with you while I do it," he says, sitting back on his heels and pulling me closer to him by my hips.

I nod my consent and force myself to chill the hell out when he places his fingers on my clit again. He teases me to the point of a climax, and just as I'm about to explode into a million fireworks of ecstasy, he rams his cock into me, thrusting deep as I fall apart underneath him.

"Yes, Ryker!" I cry out, getting into it now. "Yes!"

"Oh, you feel so good," he rumbles and thrusts once more, before he grunts and comes inside me with a loud noise of satisfaction that he couldn't fake even on a good day.

I'm pleased with that.

Panting, he asks, "How was that?"

"Absolutely perfect," I reply with a happy smile and feel the rejection fade even more now that our love is manifesting in a perfectly physical way that I could only have dreamed of.

Chapter 49

Ryker

It's getting late.

Real late.

Bree and I can't seem to keep our hands off each other, though, and even though we have tried to go to sleep, we keep ending up back in each other's arms. I never want to let her go. Being inside her is a revelation, one that I did not know was possible.

She has sated the darkness of the Alpha Wolf.

I don't know how.

From a very young age, I knew it lurked inside me. I could feel it trying to diminish any light I had. I turned into a brooding, moody teenager. But when I discovered that rough sex and domination could sate the Wolf inside, I used it as a regular tonic to feel something other than the depraved man that I had become.

Momentary relief, at best.

The darkness always returned. The depravity always needed more.

Now, being with Bree, I can feel a shred of light shining in my dark heart and it makes me happier than I ever thought I could be.

"No more," I murmur to her, eventually. "You must be sore."

She giggles. "Little bit, but I love you and I want to show you that."

"You have," I say, brushing her hair out of her face and rolling her over so that she is flat on the bed. "Now sleep." I kiss her nose, watching her eyes close.

She is exhausted and I love her deeply for wanting to carry on, trying to keep up with me, but she has no need.

I am satisfied.

One hundred percent.

The Fates have given me that reprieve by giving me *her*.

"Thank you," I murmur and then climb out of bed to get some water. I leave a glass on the nightstand for Bree. I have no doubt she will wake up soon, as thirsty as I am.

I down mine in a few gulps and then climb back into bed with her wrapping my arms around her and closing my eyes. Usually sleep brings torment and little rest, but tonight, I know that is going to be different.

Slumber drags me under and within minutes, I'm fast asleep.

※

I wake to the sun shining through the open windows, the smell of coffee drifting on the air, a tantalizing aroma that forces me to open my eyes.

I see Bree in the kitchenette, wearing one of my black tees. Her hair is tumbling around her shoulders as she bustles about, looking perfectly at home.

"Morning," I say quietly.

She turns to me, her smile bright. "You're awake! Just in time. The coffee's ready." She pours me a big mug and brings it to me, the too-big tee grazing her thighs. I take it from her, eyes narrowed.

"What?" she asks.

"I don't think the Fates are satisfied," I comment before taking a gulp of hot coffee.

She smirks. "No? I don't think so either."

"I think you should move in here with me so we can appease them completely." I wait for her protest, but it doesn't come.

"I agree. I'll go and get some of my things. Make me room, somewhere?"

Raising an eyebrow at her, I bite my lower lip. "Yeah?" I ask.

She nods. "Yes," she says and turns towards the door.

"Uhm, where do you think you are going?" I ask with a frown at her bare feet and sexy attire.

"To my cabin," she says, "to get some things."

"Not dressed like that you aren't," I state, getting out of bed and stalking towards her. "You will have every male Wolf drooling on your feet if you step out of this cabin looking like a sex goddess."

She lets out a loud guffaw, clapping her hand over her mouth to stop herself from laughing further.

I growl at her, but it only ignites the fire in her eyes.

"Sex goddess?" she asks slyly.

"Oh, you know what you look like, skin all glowing, hair tangled, my cum sticking to your inner thighs," I tease her.

"Mm," she purrs, which stirs my cock into action.

I place my mug on the table and stalk towards her, my dick stiff and ready to take her.

"Does that mean you'll go and collect some of my things and *I'll* make some room for them?" she asks.

"You fucking bet, I will," I say hoarsely. "No woman of mine wanders around the compound looking like she is after a good time."

"What if I am though?" she teases.

"Then get over here and let me show you one," I counter.

"Fuck me, Ryker," she says suddenly, startling me with the crudeness of her words.

I tilt my head. What is she asking of me here?

"I want to be fucked," she murmurs. "I want the passion to overtake you. I want you to take what you need from me. I need to feel what it's like."

"I don't want to hurt you," I mutter, desperately wanting what she is offering.

"You won't," she says quietly. "Fuck me, Ryker. Fuck me hard and fast..."

Before she has finished speaking, I slam her up against the front door, lifting her up by her hips and sliding her onto my cock in one swift motion that has her crying out.

"You want to be fucked, tiny Wolf?" I ask darkly.

"Yes," she pants, wetting my dick almost instantly as her arousal goes off the charts. "Fuck me."

I don't need asking again.

I thrust high and deep inside her wet pussy, gripping her hips tightly, bruising her, but she doesn't complain. Instead, she moans with delight as the long, even strokes of my cock ride her hard and fast, just as she asked.

"Yes!" she screams, creaming all over my dick. "Yes! More! More!"

I pant, rasping for every breath as I slam into her over and over again. My balls are aching for release, but I keep going until she shudders in my arms, crying out my name for all to hear as her climax thunders over her, allowing me to finally burst my banks, flooding her with my seed until I feel like I've drained every last drop out of my ball sack.

"I love you," I murmur. "Fuck, I love you so much."

"I love you too," she whispers. "That was…"

"Not how I wanted your second day as a non-virgin to go," I interrupt her sternly.

"Not for you to say," she chides me, kissing the tattooed wolf over my heart. "If I want the man I love to fuck me, then that's my decision."

"Stop saying 'fuck'" I grouse. "It gets me all riled up. Your mouth plus dirty words are too much for me."

"Fuck, fuck, fuck, fuck, fuck," she says with a laugh. "Now go get my stuff before I do. I want our life together to start right here, right now."

"Yes, Ma'am," I drawl with a roll of my eyes. "Bossy little Wolf, aren't you?"

"Big bad Alpha worried?" she teases.

I snort. "Pah, hardly," I respond. "But maybe you need a little reminder of who is in charge here," I add, a shade darker than the joking tone I used before.

"I'm not afraid of you," she murmurs.

"I don't want you to be," I reply, pulling on some sweats. "I want you at my mercy."

"Oh, you already have me there," she says with a sassy smile before she saunters into the bathroom and closes the door.

I chuckle, shaking my head as I get the rest of my clothes on. She is a firecracker. She will keep me on my toes, that's for sure, and I can't wait to see what the future holds for us.

Chapter 50

Bree

Smiling, I go about peeing and flushing. Then I wash my hands. I splash some cold water on my face and contemplate going in the shower. But it's probably easier to wait for Ryker to return with my stuff. I hope he remembers to bring toiletries and towels as well as clothes and shoes. I bite my lip. Maybe I should've gone after all. He isn't going to know what to bring me.

I hear the door open and close and, with a smile, leave the bathroom.

"That was quick," I say, but then I freeze.

It's not Ryker. It's Valerie.

"I'm going to tell you this once, bitch," she snarls at me. "Ryker is *mine*, so I suggest you get your slutty self out of this cabin before he gets back."

"Or what?" I ask, stupidly but slightly stunned that she has the audacity to come in here uninvited and try to kick *me* out.

"Or I will beat your skinny ass into the ground and trust me when I say, you won't be getting up any time soon."

"I see," I say, licking my lips slowly, trying to think. "Because Ryker is *yours*?"

"That's right," Valerie says with a smug smile, thinking she is getting to me.

All she has done though is piss me off. I've had enough of being pushed around, tormented, *kidnapped*, and generally treated like a weakling.

"Actually, *bitch*," I retort, hoping that she doesn't smash my face into bits because no way am I winning a fist fight with her. "Ryker is *mine*."

Her eyes flash dangerously, and she pulls a silver knife out of the back pocket of her skintight jeans.

"Is that right," she asks darkly.

"Yes, that's right," I say, sticking my chin up. "He is my Fated Mate, so there is no way you can get in between us. I know you tried already and look how that went."

She glowers at me, furious that she isn't getting her own way.

"*You* have no idea how to satisfy an Alpha Wolf," she growls, coming closer, lifting the blade higher. "You are nothing but a virgin conquest that he can brag about screwing and then ditch the second he gets bored with you."

I grit my teeth against the insecurity that swells up.

Don't listen to her.

Ryker loves you.

"Wrong," I say, hearing the slight quiver in my voice. "I will give him everything he needs. You have to work for it, submit to him, and degrade yourself to feed his darkness. I don't need to do that. I shine *into* his darkness. I know I do. I can see it when he sleeps."

Valerie's face goes thunderous. It doesn't take a genius to

figure out she has never slept with him. Screwed him, yes, but he has never let his guard down enough to *sleep* with her.

"You little bitch!" she shrieks at me and lunges forward.

I'm not quick enough. I couldn't, *didn't*, anticipate the action.

The knife slides into my gut, burning white-hot as I gasp in shock and pain.

Blood trickles out of my mouth, the coppery taste making me feel sick.

"That's right," Valerie snarls, shoving the blade even further into me.

I choke and drop to my knees when Valerie pulls the knife back out and holds it to my throat.

"He screwed that fucking red-headed slut on the road, and I mutilated her. Tore her throat out with my bare teeth, and now I'm going to do the same to you."

"No-no time," I choke out, *feeling* Ryker's presence on the other side of the door. His fear, his anxiety…he knows.

He bursts into the cabin, taking in first me, and then Valerie.

"Shit!" she mutters and darts into the bathroom to probably escape through the window.

"Go," I mutter weakly as he drops to his knees, cradling me against him.

"Bree!" he roars, putting his hand to my wound, trying to staunch the flow. "Don't you fucking dare die on me! Not now, not like this…"

I close my eyes and feel his tears drop onto my face. "L-love y-you," I stammer.

"No!" he yells, but it sounds like it's really far away now.

I want the oblivion that is beckoning me. I want the pain to go away. It hurts too much. Everything hurts and I'm thirsty.

I want to tell Ryker to get Valerie and make her pay for cutting short our happiness, but I don't have the strength.

I just want to sleep.

"Bree! No! Wake up!" Ryker yells at me. "Please don't leave me."

"I'm sorry," I mutter. "Not strong enough."

"You are," he grits out, shaking me, hurting me.

I groan in protest.

"Stay with me," he says, handling me gently now.

"No, I mean..."

"Shh," he murmurs. "I'm going to get help. Please, Bree, don't leave me."

He picks me up, jostling me painfully. He places me on the bed and then he is gone, shouting for Maria.

Clarity swarms over me for a few seconds. I'm not strong enough to be with him. I'm constantly targeted and picked on because I'm so weak and everyone knows it. He will have to spend the rest of our lives protecting me. He needs a woman who can take care of themselves and that he doesn't have to worry about.

That woman isn't me.

"You picked wrong," I mumble to the Fates, hoping that they hear me. "I'm no good for him. Take me and give him someone worthy..."

The blackness that has been threatening to consume me finally takes me and I sigh in relief as the pain recedes and I go numb.

Chapter 51

Ryker

Bursting through the front door, I shout for my mom. I skid to a stop when I see her closer than expected, brandishing a plank of wood at Valerie, whose foot is stuck in a bear trap placed outside my bathroom window.

I don't even ask.

"You stay the fuck away from my son and his Mate!" Mom screams at the howling woman and swings the plank, whacking Val over the head with it, rendering her unconscious.

"It'll hold her for a while," Mom says, throwing the plank down and stalking towards me.

"Bree!" I say desperately.

"I know," she says simply. "Phillipa is on her way already."

I turn as the Wolf known to be an excellent healer strides over, a bag in her hand.

"In there," I say, not questioning *any* of this. I don't care how my mom knew; I just need Bree to be okay.

We troop back inside and Mom's small whimper when she

smells the blood and sees Bree lying on the bed, does nothing to squash my own fucking worry.

I move over to stand next to Phillipa, taking Bree's hand as I slump to the bed.

"Move," Phillipa mutters to me as she places gauze over the hole in Bree's side.

"I'm not going anywhere," I grit out.

"If you want me to work on your girl…move," she states, giving me a shove.

"Ry," Mom says, pleading. "Let her work."

"If anything happens to her…"

"It won't," Mom says. "She is strong."

"Silver," Phillipa says before I step away. "She won't be able to Shift yet." The worry etched on her face scares the crap out of me.

If we can't get Bree to Shift to her Wolf form, she won't heal up anytime soon. I just needed someone to help her get her strength up enough to be able to do it.

"I'm going to have to cauterize," she mutters to herself.

I feel sick.

Mom takes my arms and moves me over to the other side of the cabin.

"She will be fine. I saw all of this…" She gestures around the shitshow that has dropped over my life.

I give her a curious glance, despite my fear.

"The sight. It comes and goes now that your father is gone," she says quietly, taking my arm. "But I knew something was going to happen."

"That's how you trapped Val?" I ask, knowing it has to be true. Why else would a bear trap be outside my bathroom window?

"That woman is a *viper*," she spits out. "I knew she was going to cause trouble the moment you became Alpha. She is a…"

"I don't care," I snap. "I just need Bree to be okay."

Mom nods and turns to the door, just as Hunter and Jake appear on the other side.

"Ryker," Hunter says. "You need to…"

He pauses, taking in a deep breath and then looking over to the bed. "Shit," he mumbles.

"Whatever it is, has to wait," I choke out, turning back to Bree just in time to see Phillipa heating a blade over a lighter.

"Fuck," I mumble and turn away again to compose myself long enough to step up. I stalk over to Bree and take her hand. She is completely out of it. I hope she won't feel anything.

My stomach churns when Phillipa places the hot blade to Bree's wound, making her groan.

"No," I say, slapping Phillipa's hand away. "Stop."

"If I don't do this, she will lose too much blood. She is already too weak," Phillipa says, shoving my hand out of the way so she can carry on.

The smell of burning flesh hits my nose and I retch but tighten my hold on Bree's hand.

It's over a few seconds later. I feel like I've been run over with an 18-wheeler that then reversed over me, only to drive over me again.

"Fuck," I mutter, wiping the sweat off my forehead, before I take the damp cloth Mom hands me to pat at Bree's. She is as white as the cotton pillowcase her head is resting on, scaring me more than I have ever been in my entire life.

"I can't lose her," I mumble.

"You won't," Mom says grimly, but then turns back to Hunter and Jake. "What is it?"

"The cops are here," Hunter says quietly. "They're looking for Valerie. What do we tell them?"

"You fucking give that murdering bitch to them," Mom shrieks, gesturing to the side of the cabin.

"What?" Jake asks, shaking his head. "Back up a bit. What the hell is going on here."

"She stabbed Bree!" Mom yells, marching over to the door. "She's out there!"

"Uhm," Hunter mutters, confusion on his face. "They're here because of a murder that happened the other night outside Wicksville," he says, eyes narrowed. "They have an eyewitness who described Val and led them *here*. This is serious, Ry. Human cops getting involved in Pack business is..."

"Yeah," I interrupt him. He doesn't need to spell it out for me. "But we make an exception for that bitch," I add, the rage clouding my thoughts.

"Here," Mom says, slapping something into my hand before she stalks out of the cabin.

I look at the small vial in my hand. "Liquid Silver," I murmur and, with a glance back at Bree, I head after my mother. "What is this for?" I demand.

"Her," she says, bending down to release the bear trap around Valerie's ankle. "It will stop her Shifting for a few months while it works its way through her system. I'm sure Jake knows someone he can bribe to keep giving it to her while she serves her time. Pack law isn't an option here, Ryker. She's going away. End of. She is nothing but trouble. Always has been." The look of utter disgust she throws the unconscious Wolf is telling.

"Fuck," I spit out. "Fuck!" I punch the cabin wall once, twice, bloodying my knuckles. Handing her over to the police is unheard of in our world...but I don't see how we have another choice. Bree means *everything* to me. If she dies because of this bitch at my feet, there isn't a saving grace for Val. I will kill her and have that on my conscience for eternity while I mourn the loss of my Fated Mate.

I draw in a deep breath and bend down. I uncork the vial and dump the contents into Valerie's mouth. She moans and writhes as the Silver burns its way through her system, her eyelids fluttering.

"Jake?" Mom's voice cuts through my thoughts.

"I know a guy," he says grimly. "This will be sorted before she needs another dose."

"Good," Mom says and strides back into the cabin.

"Shit," I say, shaking my head. I can't go back in there. I can't go back in there to see if Bree is dead.

"Yeah," Jake states. "Go back to your girl," he says. "We've got this."

I nod slowly. I don't have the capacity to deal with any of this. Drawing my next breath is enough of a chore.

I plod back inside the cabin, imminent death hanging in the air. "Is she...?" I ask with a gulp.

"She's not losing any more blood," Phillipa says. "Give her this..." she shoves a bottle of something at me, "...in about an hour. It should help get her strong enough to Shift."

I nod, taking the bottle.

She grabs my arm and says seriously, "I don't need to tell you how important it is that she Shifts as soon as she is able."

Nodding again, I mutter my thanks to her and then drop back onto the bed with Bree. Her color is still too pale, but she doesn't look as ghostly as she did a few moments ago.

"Please, Bree, hang in there. I need you," I mutter, bringing her hand to my lips to kiss.

"Need you too," she mumbles back, her eyelids fluttering.

"Shh," I whisper. "Save your strength," I add, stroking her face, glad that she is lucid, but not wanting to get my hopes up just yet. She is still in a bad way and now only time will tell.

Hours later, after giving her the vial of tonic, and as darkness falls, I feel Bree stir on the bed next to me. I sit up and stare into her face, willing her eyes to open.

When they do, they are dull and bloodshot.

"Hey," I croak out.

"Hey," she rasps back. "Water?"

I leap up and grab the glass on the nightstand, pressing it to her lips. She gulps back a mouthful and then I take it away, to her annoyance. "Easy," I murmur. "You've been through a lot."

"Did you get her?" she asks.

"Mom did," I snort.

Her eyes light up at that. "Go, Maria," she mumbles. "But, Ryker, there's more. She…"

"We know," I say. "She's gone now. You don't have to worry about her ever again."

"Gone?" she asks warily.

"Long story. I'll tell you another time," I say with a sigh.

She nods, accepting that, and closing her eyes again.

"And don't worry about the three men who tormented you," I add, feeling the need to tell her this now. "William, an ally who helped us rescue you, has brought them here for sentencing. *But* Hunter and I thought it best to send them straight on back to Winston. They defected from the Ridge Pack, and he is out for blood. *I* will undoubtedly kill them, but Winston is out for revenge. They will suffer, I promise you that."

She nods weakly, but I can see the relief on her face that it's being handled.

"You scared the shit out of me," I inform her then. "Please don't do that again."

"I seem to be doing a lot of that lately," she says sadly. "Maybe you are better off without me."

Tears pool in her eyes, which she scrunches up even tighter.

"Don't ever say that again," I say gruffly. "You are mine, Bree and I will die to protect you. I don't care if that is every week or ever again, do you hear me? We belong together and that is final."

"I love you," she says. "Any other male would've given up on me by now, probably."

"Never," I say forcefully, gripping her hand tightly.

Her lips curve into a smile and she opens her eyes again. "How bad is it?" she asks seriously.

"Bad. You need to Shift as soon as you can," I state, not sugar coating it.

She nods. "I'm too weak."

"I'll help you," I say. "Bree, I need you to get up and Shift."

She shakes her head. "I can't."

"You can," I argue. "And you will. That's an order."

She snorts. "Oh, big bad Alpha, throwing his weight around?"

"You know it," I state. "Now sit up."

She shakes her head. "I'm sorry, Ryker. I'm not as strong as you want me to be."

"You are and you will do this," I say, grabbing her upper arms and hauling her to a sitting position.

I feel sick when she pales and groans as the action tears at her wound. But I have to be the bad guy here or she won't do it.

"Ryker!" she gasps, tears falling out of her eyes at the pain. "Please..."

"Stand up and Shift," I say, climbing off the bed.

"No," she whimpers. "I can't."

"You can," I state.

"I take it back," she moans.

"What's that?"

"Don't love you. You are mean and a bully," she says, flopping back to the bed.

"Bree, get on your feet *now*," I say quietly.

"No," she says, digging her heels in, but she clearly has no idea how stubborn I can be.

"Don't you want to feel better?" I ask. "Don't you want the pain to go away?"

"Asshole," she mutters.

"Then get on your feet."

With her eyes closed, she sits up gingerly and swings her legs over the side of the bed. "Hate you," she grits out.

"No, you don't. You love me, and you are doing this so we can be happy and healthy together for as long as we both have left on this earth."

"You are such a dick."

"Never said I wasn't," I retort. "Marry me."

Her eyes fly open. "W—what?" she stammers.

"You heard me," I reply. "But that can only happen if you are alive to do it, so get on your feet and Shift, goddammit. I want you as my wife."

"Well, Jesus," she mutters. "How romantic. I do believe I've just been swept off my feet."

"Fucking get up!" I roar at her. "No more stalling!"

Her eyes flash, the dullness retreating as I shout at her. The fire is there. I just need it close enough to give her the strength to do what I'm begging her to do.

With a grimace aimed at me, she fists her tiny hands and shoves herself to her feet with the help of the bed. She wobbles, and the blood drains from her face. Every instinct I have is crying out for me to grab her and help her, but if I do that, she will take it as a sign that she can collapse back to the bed and that is not an option.

In an action that makes me wince, she reaches down to

the hem of the clean t-shirt that I struggled to get her into while she was unconscious, her eyes fixed on mine. She pulls it up and over her head, making only a slight whimper as it jars her body painfully.

I hold her furious gaze as she painfully lowers herself to her knees and drops forward, bracing herself on her hands. She screams with agony as she lets the Shift start. My stomach turns over and twists into a knot, the bile rising in my throat, tears stinging my eyes.

Be strong for her, Ryker. Don't be a fucking a pussy. She needs to do this.

It takes a few minutes of her crying out in agony for the Shift to be complete, ending with her howling woefully, panting and sweating.

I fall to my knees next to her, stroking her head. "Perfect," I mutter. "You are perfect, strong and a true queen, my love. I have never been prouder."

She snaps her jaw at me, just missing biting the end of my nose. I chuckle and kiss hers. Then she turns and is gone, shooting out of the open window, all healed up as expected. I waste no time in stripping off and following her. My strength and speed as Alpha have me catching up with her in seconds. I slow my pace and let her lead. She has a clear idea of where she wants to go, and I'm pretty sure I know where we will end up.

Turns out, I'm right.

We burst into the clearing near the lake minutes later and slow down, breathing in the clean mountain air heavily but alive and feeling it with every second we are together. Bree Shifts first, kneeling in front of me naked and glorious.

"Okay, I still love you," she says with a giggle. "Shift and take me, right here, right now."

In a second, I am in my human form, taking her in my arms. "You are a warrior," I murmur. "*My* warrior."

"Worthy?" she asks shyly.

"More than. If anything, I should be asking you if I am," I respond seriously.

"Don't be a dick. You are Alpha. The Chosen one."

I kiss her then, deeply and with a growing passion that my cock reacts to. She presses her body closer to mine.

"This has been a crazy fucking ride," she murmurs, pulling back slightly. "I'm so much younger than you. I'm not ready to go into heat and give you kids or any of that yet. Does it matter?"

"Obviously not," I reply honestly. "I told you I will wait, and that means for everything. Besides, I think you might be more ready than you think." I inhale deeply, closing my eyes against the scent that is hitting me in the heart as well as the gut.

"What?" she stammers. "What do you mean?"

"I think you're going into heat, Bree. Being with me must've brought it on. You are becoming more irresistible to me with each passing second." I brush her hair away from her face and lower her to the ground, covering her body with mine.

"Really?" she asks, scrunching up her nose.

"Well, I'm no expert, but, yeah, I think…"

She laughs and wraps her legs around me. "Made for each other."

"Definitely," I murmur and slide into her without any foreplay. I don't think she wants it, I sure as shit can't wait, anyway. I need to be inside her. I bury my cock balls deep inside her wet haven and sigh happily.

She rolls us over, her hands resting on my chest to balance herself as she moves her hips, a questioning look in her eyes.

I nod, giving her the affirmation that she is looking for that she is doing it right. Still so innocent in some ways but an absolute goddess in every other.

"Yes," she says suddenly.

"Yes, what?" I groan when she stops moving enticingly over me.

"Yes, I will marry you," she says with a shy giggle.

I snort. "Well, I should fucking hope so," I growl, grabbing her hips to get her to ride my dick again. "I want to wake up every day with you and fall asleep with you in my arms."

"Always," she says and speeds up, seeking her own fulfilment.

I let her use me, enjoying watching her unleash on me. I might have gone into this thinking the Fates were fucking with me, but they were right.

We are Fated.

We belong together.

Now and forever.

Epilogue

Ryker

Eighteen months later

"Well?" I ask, leaning in the open doorway and asking my wife what she thinks.

Bree looks up and smiles, placing the book on the table. "Once I got over the fact that *Brenda* is in fact *me*, and *Ryan* is *you*, then it's pretty good. Smutty!" she says, her cheeks going red.

"So I hear," I grumble. "Everyone on the compound is reading it."

"Philippa has a way with words. This series is pretty damn good."

"Only because *we're* in it," I say, pushing off from the doorway to go to her. "What's for dinner?"

"Lasagna," she replies, standing up to give me a kiss. "But you will have to eat alone tonight. The knitting club is meeting at your mom's, and they are all dying to see the Shift."

"Of course they are, nosy bitches," I grouse good naturedly.

She snorts. "Stop it. It's a big deal."

"I know," I reply with a smile of pride at my first-born son's first Shift. Jefferson is a year old and completed his first Shift to his Wolf form earlier this morning. He is the cutest thing I have ever seen, a miniature version of me but with his mother's sparkling blue eyes. "I'll miss you," I add, bending down to kiss her.

"I won't be long," she says.

"You will," I sigh. "Once you girls get going, it never ends."

"Nice," she comments sarcastically, rolling her pretty eyes at me.

It gets me going. Not that it takes much. I'm like a randy teenager around her. Nearing my thirty-fifth birthday hasn't slowed me down in the sack at all. Maybe her youthful vibrancy is keeping me going.

"Ryker," Hunter says, coming up behind me. "The guy is here about the septic tank repair."

I nod and kiss Bree again. "When you get back..."

She giggles, lowering her eyes. "You know that I'm ready," she mutters.

"I know," I reply. Truth is so am I. We agreed that we wanted a big family and once Jefferson turned one, we would try again during her next heat.

Today.

"Have fun later," I say, kissing her nose. "I love you."

"Love you more," she replies and lets me go with Hunter to see about the septic tank.

I have a sense of pride as I take in the compound, all the Pack, *my* Pack hard at work to keep things running.

I hope that my dad would be proud of me, but I guess I will never know. No Alpha will ever know.

Suddenly, I stop, a feeling of warmth dropping over me.

"You okay?" Hunter asks with a frown.

I smile at him. "Yeah," I reply. The spirit of the Alpha deep inside me, that was my dad's and his before him has flashed to life, letting me know that I'm doing a good job.

Chosen by birth.

Chosen by blood.

Chosen.

This is my legacy, and it's good to know that I'm doing it well. I will make sure that *my* son knows how loved and appreciated he is and that one day he will take my place as Alpha of this Pack and that I will be proud of him in every way.

The End

To read Hunter's story, stay tuned for the 2nd book in this series of standalone Wolf Shifter Romances. Hunted is available to pre order on: https://geni.us/SCP2

Join my Facebook Reader Group for more info on my latest books and backlist: Eve's Lair - A Paranormal Romance Reader Group

Discord Reader group receives exclusive updates: https://discord.gg/cDxFjukBCh

Join my newsletter for exclusive news, giveaways and competitions: http://eepurl.com/hx-mo5

About the Author

Eve is a USA Today Bestselling Author with a specialty for paranormal romance with strong female leads.

She lives in the UK, with her husband and four kids, so finding the time to write is short, but definitely sweet. Eve has a number of series, both completed and on the go and hopes to release some new and exciting projects in the next couple of years, so stay tuned!

Facebook: http://facebook.com/evenewtonforever

Twitter: https://twitter.com/AuthorEve

Website/Blog: https://evenewton.com/

Also by Eve Newton

https://evenewton.com/books-by-eve

The Forever Series:

Forever & The Power of One: Double Edition

Revelations

Choices

The Ties That Bind

Trials

Switch & The Other Switch

Secrets

Betrayal

Sacrifice

Conflict & Obsession: Double Edition

Wrath

Revenge

Changes & Forever After: Double Edition

Arathia

Constantine

The Husbands of Forever (Part 1)

The Dragon Realms Series:

The Dragon Heiress

Claiming the Throne

A Baby Dragon for Christmas & The Dragon Empress

The Dark Fae Kingdom Series:

The Dark Fae Princess

Dark Fae's Desires

Dark Fae's Secrets

Enchained Hearts Series:

Lives Entwined

Lives Entangled

Lives Endangered

The Bound Series:

Demon Bound

Demon Freed

Demon Returned

Demon Queen Series:

Hell's Belle

Pandora's Box

Belle's Hell

Anna's Heir

Annabelle's Apocalypse

Pandora's Legacy

Circle of Darkness:

Wild Hearts: Book One

Savage Love: Book Two

Tainted Blood: Book Three

Dark Hearts - A Prequel

Darkest Desires: Book Four